I0572792

PUCKING FATE

A SECOND CHANCE HOCKEY ROMANCE

SHOT AT LOVE
BOOK TWO

L.A. HART

COPYRIGHT

This book is a work of fiction. The characters, incidents, and dialogue were created from the authors' imagination and are not to be construed as real. Any resemblance to actual people or events is coincidental.

The authors acknowledge the copyrighted and trademarked status of various products within this work of fiction.

© 2025 L.A. Hart

All Rights Reserved.

This book or any portion thereof may not be reproduced or used in any manner whatsoever without the express written permission of the publisher except for the use of brief quotations in a book review.

Editor's Choice Publishing

P.O. Box 10024

Greensboro, NC 27404

Illustrated Cover Design by Gowtham Thangaraj
Discreet Cover Design by Jessica Mohring | Raven Ink Covers, www.
raveninkcovers.com

SYNOPSIS

How do you tame a puckboy?

Maya Lawrence knew that such a feat was impossible. That's why, when she got pregnant as a teenager and hockey star Christian Riley signed with the pros, she let him go.

Maya gave up on all her dreams to become a single mother. Her parents and Christian abandoned her when she needed them the most, leaving her to turn to her brother Preston to help raise her son Finley.

Christian Riley never blamed Maya for ending things and breaking his heart after how badly he treated her. In fact, while he never got over her, he didn't expect Maya to ever speak to him again. But when Christian's rival, Preston, finally breaks the news to him that he has a son, all bets are off.

The last thing Maya wants is the playboy from her past breaking her son's heart or hers again. That's why she makes Christian a deal. She'll give him the summer to spend with Finley as a "family friend" to show her that he's committed to being a father before letting him have a permanent place in their lives.

Proving to Maya that he can step up to be a father to Finley, and that his puckboy days are behind him, will be the toughest challenge Christian has ever faced.

Fate has finally given him a second chance to take a shot at love, so this time he better not puck around and miss.

Pucking Fate is perfect for fans of swoon-worthy athletes, sizzling chemistry, and second chances that come when you least expect them.

1

Maya Lawrence

"**M**om, please...please do something. Y-you can't let Daddy kick me out," I whisper. My throat feels like it's on fire as a cascade of tears run down both my cheeks.

"You heard your father, Maya – just marry the boy and make this right," she replies while wringing her hands, refusing to look at me from the edge of her seat on the sofa.

"Maya isn't going to marry Christian," Preston grumbles as he paces in front of the fireplace. "Her and that asshole ended things weeks ago, before she even found out she was pregnant." Then he turns to me with his eyes softening. "It's going to be okay. Dad's just...angry right now," Preston says. "He'll calm down in a few minutes and take it all back–"

Before he can finish his thought, our father storms back into the house carrying a stack of cardboard boxes piled so high I can't even see his face. The sudden bang of the boxes hitting the hardwood floor *right in front of me makes me jump. "Go start packing. I want you out of here tonight. Don't come back until you make this right."*

"I'm...I'm sorry, Daddy. I didn't mean for this to happen..." I say as I begin to sob. I knew my parents would be angry and disappointed, but I didn't think they would throw me out of the house like I'm trash.

"Your mother and I are going to Bible study, and when we get back tonight, you better be gone from here."

"You can't do this to her!" Preston shouts as he gets in his face, taller and more intimidating than even our father now.

"This is my house and my rules! She broke them, so now she has to deal with the consequences of living in sin. Your sister will not step a single toe in my house again until there's a ring on a finger!"

"That's bullshit!" my brother argues.

"You can take her in since this is your fault as much as it's hers and that careless boy's. It was your job to look out for her and you failed!" he shouts at my brother.

"This isn't Preston's fault. It's mine..." I sob.

"You're both a disgrace to this family," my father says. "Your brother can help you raise the bastard, because your mother and I don't want anything to do with it."

Maya

Nearly six years later...

I hate change.

Whoever said "change is good" lied. Change is never good, just inevitable.

I especially hate big changes like the one I feel coming this morning. My brother is already showered, dressed, and awake with a cup of coffee in his hand, his back braced against the kitchen counter. His brow is furrowed, as if he's thinking hard way too early this morning, one of the first days of his summer break that's supposed to be relaxing.

"Morning," I say in greeting as I pour a cup of coffee for myself. Between the two of us, we can go through a whole pot, which is why we prefer the old-fashioned method to the new single cup machines.

"Morning," he replies. His tense, six-foot-four frame doesn't move from his contemplative stance as I sit at the breakfast table.

"What's up, Preston?"

"So, I've got some news," he says gravely, as if preparing me for the worst. Which is confusing since my brother just won the freaking national hockey championship, everything he's ever worked toward his entire life.

"Okay. Give it to me," I tell him, since the suspense is killing me.

"I signed a contract this morning with the Greensboro Bobcats."

The mention of the Bobcats automatically makes me think of Christian.

"Oh wow. So, it's really happening? You're moving to North Carolina?" Moving to the same city as the man I still can't stop thinking about years later. And just thinking about the M-word nearly has me breaking out in hives thanks to old trauma.

"Yes, it's definitely happening."

I should've realized it was a done deal. Why wouldn't he want to move to be in the same city as his sweet girlfriend Elle?

"My offer still stands," he says. "I know you hate the idea of packing up and moving, but I want you and Finley to come with me to Greensboro. I'll find us a house big enough for the three of us."

I lift a single eyebrow. "I think you mean four."

"Huh? Oh, Elle." A slight smile lifts his lips at the mention of his girlfriend.

"Yes. Elle! Don't even pretend like you two won't be living together before the end of the year. Heck, I would put money on you two moving in together before the season starts!"

"That's not...I don't know." He shrugs his wide shoulders. "I hope so, but I'm not going to rush Elle into this when everything is so new." Turning to pour himself another cup of coffee, Preston goes on to say, "But that doesn't change the fact that I won't feel right in Greensboro if you and Finley aren't there with me."

In Greensboro...the city that worships Christian Riley, which means I would likely see his face on billboards and possibly run into him at the grocery store.

"I think we should stay here in Maryland." In this house, the only house Finley knows since he was an infant the last time we moved, and far away from a certain puckboy.

"Do you really think you can raise him here on your own?"

I scoff at my brother indignantly and cross my arms over my chest, leaning back in my chair. "Preston, you know I appreciate everything you've done to help me raise Finley, but he's my son. I don't need you to keep supporting us."

"Don't you, though?" When I glare at him, he holds up both of his palms in surrender. "I'm not trying to be an asshole; I'm just being realistic. You don't have a job. Hell, you've never worked a day in your life."

"I know I haven't, but I'll find a job this summer." It can't be that hard to find a job, right?

"Maya…" Preston says, his voice full of doubt.

"Just because I don't have a college degree or experience doing, well, anything other than distributing snacks at preschool, I'm sure I can find some sort of work."

"I'm not trying to be mean, but even if you do find a job, do you really think you'll make enough in an entry-level position to support you and Finley?"

Well, crap. Probably not. I don't even know what the minimum wage is, though I'm guessing it's less than fifteen dollars an hour after tax deductions, which would be around six hundred dollars a week.

"The house is paid for and I'm not selling it," Preston goes on to say. "I can help with the other bills, even if I'm not living here."

"I don't want you to do that."

"I have plenty of money, Maya. And I'll be making more than before, thanks to the new contract."

"I appreciate the offer, but it's time for me to fend for myself for once," I tell him. "You've been my crutch for too long as it is." I'll never forget the look on my brother's face when our father told him it was his fault that I got pregnant within my first few months of my freshman year of college, a burden Preston still wrongfully carries. "I'm so glad you helped give me the time to stay home with Finley all these years, but since he's starting kindergarten in the fall, I'll have the entire day to work before having to pick him up from school."

"You could apply for jobs in Greensboro just as easily…" Which would also require moving.

When I just stare unblinkingly at him, Preston sighs and takes a seat across from me at the kitchen table. "Fine. I hope it works out and that you can find work in this area, but if it doesn't, I'm here. Or I'll be there, and I can send money here. Dammit, I hate this!" he grumbles as he shoves his fingers through his dark hair. "I wish you and Finley would just come to Greensboro with me."

"I hate it too," I tell him with a smile. "Not because we're losing our financial stability, but because we're losing you. Finley is going to miss you so much. You're the closest thing he's had to a father his whole life."

"Right, so will you at least think about it? For Finley? You don't have to decide today."

"No, I wouldn't have to decide today, but I would have to decide before school starts this fall," I point out.

"Right," he agrees. Then, clearing his throat, Preston nervously rubs the back of his neck. I'm pretty sure I know what uncomfortable topic he's going to bring up before he even speaks. "Speaking of fathers…what are you going to do about Christian?"

I shrug with my arms still crossed in annoyance, since this is not a subject I like to discuss. A few weeks ago, Preston told Christian Riley that he's Finley's father after years of him being in the dark. Without warning me.

"What is there to do?" I ask him. "Christian knows he's Finley's father now. What that means going forward is ultimately up to him, I guess."

"It's not going to be easy," Preston remarks.

"You think I don't know that?" I huff. "I was finally beginning to close that chapter of my life and now he's right back in it..."

"I meant for Christian. It's not going to be easy for Christian to be a part of Finley's life when he doesn't even live in the same state!"

Shaking my head, I tell him, "That's not my fault."

"No, it's not. You have the right to live wherever you want with Finley. You're his mother. But what if Christian wants to take on the responsibility..."

"I'm not letting Finley stay with that playboy hundreds of miles away for a single night without me, if that's what you mean." Panic begins to rise, tightening my chest at the thought of losing any time with my son. "Wait. You don't think... would Christian take me to court for custody?"

With the millions the man earns playing professional hockey, how would I fight that? I know Preston would spend however much money it takes for me to get my own attorney, but I dread having to fight over my son. My son, who I have spent every single minute of every day with his entire life. I'm all Finley knows. Me and Preston. If Christian tried to take him, I'll never forgive him.

"Honestly, I don't know what Christian plans to do, Maya. Maybe he'll demand visitation or maybe you'll never hear from him again. Wouldn't it be better if you deal with him yourself, though? If you would just try to talk to him and ask him what he wants, you may avoid a world of trouble in the future."

"Well, that is a problem for another day. How about we tackle today's problem first?"

My protective brother perks up, as if suddenly on high alert for any and all lurking danger. "What problem?"

"You have to tell Finley your news before he hears it from one of his friends in the sports headlines."

"Oh, crap," Preston mutters.

2

Christian Riley

I'm not sure which is worse—losing the national hockey championships or finding out I'm a father who has missed the first four damn years of my son's life.

Never mind. The latter is definitely worse.

There's always next year to try to win the championships or the year after that. I have at least five more years in the pros to obtain that goal.

But being a father to Finley? I lost that chance. I wasn't there the day he was born, and I didn't get to see his first steps or hear his first words.

He grew up without me in his life and I'm not sure if Maya will ever give me a chance to be a part of it even now that I know the truth.

It's not like she's the one who finally told me we have a son together.

No, that was all Preston. I thought he showed up at my apartment a few weeks ago to beat me to death, not turn my world upside down. I'll never forget that moment when everything changed.

"You have a son."

"Huh?" I stare at Preston, unblinking after he says four little words that change...everything.

"His name is Finley. He's four and, of course, he loves hockey."

I jump to my feet. "What the hell are you talking about, Preston? I think I would know if I had a son."

I'm careful, always careful after the one time with Maya... Oh shit.

"Did you say...he's four? Like years? Like four years, the time since I've seen Maya plus about eight or nine months?"

"Yes."

I shake my head, my jaw clenched tight, pointing my index finger at Preston. "This isn't fucking funny, man. I'm tired of you fucking with my head, and now you're making more shit up!"

"I'm not making this up. My sister gave up everything to become a mother while you skated off into the night, going pro and then screwing every woman you met."

My head keeps shaking in denial. "No. You're lying! This is some trick to fuck with my head, so I'll lose the biggest game of my life tomorrow!"

"It's not your game to win or lose, jackass. It's the whole team."

Running my fingers through the front of my hair, I start to pace across the room, along the wall of windows that showcase the city below. "I saw...I saw Maya at game three with a little boy. I figured he was hers, that she had met someone else and they...you know..."

He looked so young, and we've been apart for so damn long.

"You didn't notice he looked four?"

"How was I supposed to know how old he was? I don't know shit about kids. I...I figured she ended the pregnancy in college as soon as possible, met someone, got married, and started a family with someone else! I didn't want any details."

"Right. You didn't want to know the truth."

"I would've wanted to know that I have a son!" I roar. "Are you fucking with me? Please, don't joke about this. Are you sure, like, a thousand percent certain that he's mine?"

Of course he's my son. It was stupid of me to doubt Maya for a second.

Ever since that day, I've felt like a complete idiot.

How did I not realize that Maya had decided to become a mother, that the little boy next to her at Preston's games was mine?

That's the other thing that's been nagging me after last week's loss.

Maya is never going to forgive me for walking away from her, even though she's the one who broke up with me. She's the one who refused to respond to my calls or text messages or even my goddamn handwritten letters. Love letters from a guy who barely graduated from high school because the only thing I've ever been good at is hockey.

I'm depressed and angry, lost in the memories of those few blissful weeks dating Maya in the minor leagues when there's a knock on my apartment door.

A knock, not a call from the front desk that's supposed to ask me if I want to accept visitors before sending people up here.

Trudging over to the door in my sweatpants and wrinkled tee, I look out the peep hole. The last person I expected to see yet again is Preston freaking Lawrence.

I unlock and open the door for him. "What do you want now? Have you come to brag about your championship win or tell me that I knocked up some other girl who didn't bother to tell me for five years?"

"You had a great season and played a damn good series. There's nothing for you to be upset about," Preston remarks.

"We fucking lost!" I shout at him, even though I don't blame him. Not really. His team was better. The Warhawks beat us fair and square in four games.

"I'm well aware that you lost. It's time to get over it and think about next season."

"Easy for you to say, since you got to kiss the girl and the championship cup."

"That is true," he remarks with a grin at the mention of Elle, my ex, before he strolls past me, right into my apartment as if I invited him to stay. "And I wanted to talk to you about my news."

"Your news about what? Elle picked you. I know that. Is she moving up to D.C. with you too or something? Thanks for the heads-up so I can start looking for someone else to cut my hair," I mutter as I slam the door closed and then go plop back down on the sofa.

Preston takes a seat in one of the matching swivel chairs, turning it toward me. "Seriously? You haven't heard?" When I don't respond, he says, "Elle isn't moving to D.C. She doesn't have to."

"I don't give a shit," I lie. I do give a shit. Not that I lost Elle to Preston, my former best friend, but that Preston gets to be with the woman he loves, knowing she loves him back.

"You really haven't watched any sports news or been on your phone this week?"

"Hell no. I don't want to hear all the criticisms about what we did wrong, what *I* did wrong in losing the championship."

"Wow. Well, if you'd been online, then you would've seen that the Bobcats have just signed a new defenseman."

"Good for us, I guess."

"Elle doesn't have to pack her bags because I'm moving to Greensboro."

"You're what?" I ask before it dawns on me, taking longer than it should since I'm not the sharpest skate on the ice. "*You* signed with the Bobcats?"

"I did."

"Damn."

"I thought you knew; Coach Bell said you gave them your approval."

"They asked me how I would feel about you getting picked up. I said it was fine, since I didn't think you would ever agree to come to Greensboro."

"I didn't think I would ever sign with any team you played for," Preston admits. "But it's time for us to bury the hatchet, don't you think? The truth is out. You know why I hated you for years."

"Yeah, I know. I knocked up your innocent sister and then had no idea she gave birth to my son four years ago." I try my best to push aside the anger at Maya for not telling me herself, for not telling me when she decided not to end the pregnancy. It's like pushing a thousand-pound elephant up a hill, but when I manage it, something else suddenly fills my chest — hope. "Wait. If you're moving down here, does that mean Maya and Finley are moving to Greensboro, too?" I ask Preston.

"No, they're not."

I deflate so fast it's a wonder I don't dissolve into the damn sofa cushions. "Why not?"

"Because Maya has got it in her head that she doesn't need me, that she can support herself and Finley on her own."

"Can she?"

Preston shakes his head. "I don't know. Maybe. It won't be easy, though. She doesn't have a degree or any work experience, so I'm not sure who would actually hire her. Whatever job she gets will be entry level, which means it won't pay shit."

"So, what is she going to do, then?"

"She'll probably be so stubborn that she won't ask me for help until bills are past due. At least the house is paid for…"

I don't like it. The idea of Maya struggling to make ends meet to raise my son or Preston stepping up to help them when they should be my responsibility.

"I can give her some money," I tell Preston. "For back child support, or whatever I owe her for the last four years of Finley's life. If she had just told me…"

"I know you would've done what you could for them if you had known. And I think you want to do the right thing now."

"The right thing? What's that exactly?"

"Being a father to your son."

"Of course I want that. I *am* his father!" I exclaim. "I'm not the one who decided it would be best to just meet him as a 'family friend.'"

The one time I was able to meet my son, Preston and Elle convinced me it would be better if we didn't tell Finley I'm his father. So, I pretended to be their friend when I wanted so badly to tell the amazing little boy the truth.

A boy who thinks I'm the fastest man on the ice and asked

me for my autograph the first time we met, making me feel like a goddamn superhero.

"What's the Bobcats training schedule look like for the summer?" Preston asks.

"Huh?" I reply in confusion, since he interrupted my thoughts of the first conversation I had with my son. A conversation I've relived a million times in my head.

"Is the off-season flexible enough for you to go up to D.C.? To spend time with Finley?"

"I don't know. If Maya would let me, then I would say to hell with what the Bobcats want and go anyway."

"Then do it. What's stopping you?" the jackass asks.

"Oh, I don't know, Preston. Maybe the fact that Maya doesn't want me around, that she probably never would've told me that Finley's my son!"

"Maya…I don't think she knows what she wants. She's freaked out worrying about you trying to get custody of Finley."

"Custody? Why would I do that? I don't know shit about how to be a father."

"Good. That's good. Then tell her that and ask her to let you come visit this summer. In fact, do whatever you have to do to convince her to let you spend time with Finley."

"Why are you encouraging this idea so hard?" I ask curiously. I would've assumed Preston would want me to stay away from his sister and nephew.

"Because I want Maya and Finley to come to Greensboro, and I think you're one of the reasons Maya is adamant about staying near D.C."

"Me?"

"Yes, you. You broke her heart and knocked her up. You

abandoned her when she needed you the most, just like our parents did."

"I...I didn't know that, about your parents. They really abandoned her?"

"They kicked her out of the house the day they found out she was pregnant. They told her they didn't want anything to do with her or her bast...baby if she kept 'living in sin.' That's when she moved in with me."

"Living in sin?" I repeat in confusion.

"They wanted you two to get married. My father declared that Maya couldn't step foot in his house again unless there was a ring on her finger."

"Oh," I mutter in understanding. "I would have married her."

Preston chuckles as he gets to his feet as if to leave, so I do the same. "Yeah, I find that claim very hard to believe, and I'm sure Maya would too."

"Find what hard to believe? I would've made her my wife. I would've done anything for her." The fucking diamond ring I bought when I signed with the Bobcats is still shoved somewhere in the back of my junk drawer.

"Anything except stick around when she needed you," he says. "And have you conveniently forgotten your reputation? Since you signed with the Bobcats, you've been nothing but a manwhore."

"Because the only woman I've ever loved broke my heart!"

Preston turns back to me with his brow creased. "You were in love with Maya? Wait. She's the one who ended it?"

"Yes! How did you not know that? Didn't you ask her what the hell happened between us?"

"No. I assumed you ended things with her after you got what you wanted."

Shaking my head, I tell him, "No! God, no. That's not...we only had a few dates before we ...before Maya told me she didn't want anything to do with me. When she wanted to meet up a few weeks later, I thought it was because she had changed her mind. I had no idea she was going to tell me she was pregnant! If she didn't want me, if she thought being with me was a mistake, then I-I just assumed she wouldn't want to have my baby either."

"Huh."

Since Preston doesn't sound like he believes me, I tell him, "That's the truth. Ask Maya. She dumped me, then refused to respond to my calls, texts, or letters." I withhold the part about her dumping me the morning after the first and only time we sort of had sex. That one terrible time, her first time, where I came faster than a speeding bullet, which was all it took to get her pregnant.

"Damn. If I had known that she dumped you, then I wouldn't have hurt you as badly as I did every time I saw your face. I thought you broke her heart."

"Well, now you know she broke mine. That is the truth."

"Well, what's done is done. Are you going to man up and try to be a father or keep sitting around here sulking in your own filth because you lost a couple of games?"

I had planned to sit around my apartment alone and sulk for at least a few more days or maybe weeks, but now....

"I'm going to D.C. Today. Right now," I tell Preston.

"Whoa," he says, holding up a palm. "I'm not sure if that's a good idea. You should call Maya before you just show up on the doorstep."

"I don't even have her fucking phone number!" I say, frustrated with his wishy-washy advice.

"Fine, I'll give you her number," Preston says as he pulls out his phone from his back pocket. Retrieving my own device from the charger, where I've been content to let it sit untouched for days, I enter in the digits he calls out.

"Thank you. I'll call her right now."

"Good luck," Preston says as he starts for the door. Over his shoulder as he opens it to show himself out, he says, "Don't fuck this up."

He's gone before I can ask him for advice on not fucking it up. I guess he's given me enough suggestions to get started.

The rest is going to be up to me to figure out.

3

Maya

The idea of picking up and moving Finley to Greensboro rattles around in my head like a loose puck on the ice.

It's been days since Preston brought it up so casually, as if he was only asking me to switch up my laundry detergent or try out a new coffee flavor. But this isn't a simple decision. It would be a huge change. And it sure as hell doesn't feel casual.

Just seeing the cardboard boxes around the house when Preston was packing gave me an anxiety attack. He moved out the day after he told me he had officially signed with the Bobcats, as if he was in a hurry to get to Elle.

Not that I blame him.

Still, his absence has put me in a foul mood. At this rate, I'll become as cranky as my loner brother was before Elle came into his life.

Preston's dating life was almost as non-existent as mine before he met the love of his life in a ploy to make her ex, Christian, jealous.

It's crazy how things work out sometimes.

I know I should be happy for them, but the house, Preston's house, is too quiet, too empty without his large presence in it.

There's also this doubt that keeps creeping up on me. Doubt that I may not be able to make it on my own without Preston's support.

Finley misses him just as much as I do. He's been moping around the house, refusing to go outside and play field hockey, his favorite summer activity, with his friends. Instead, he's just been sitting in his room stacking his Legos alone.

When I tried to play with him yesterday, he told me I wasn't building the bridge the right way, the way Uncle Preston built them, which is why they kept falling.

Seeing the sadness on my son's face, the first of its kind, is nearly enough to make me throw in the towel and start the daunting task of packing.

The thought of uprooting my life yet again, leaving behind everything we've built here in D.C. — just to follow my brother like a needy puppy dog seems insane. Well, to be near my brother and Christian.

My stomach knots just thinking about that handsome blond playboy.

The hockey star is a walking temptation, all rugged jawline, sharp hazel eyes, and a body sculpted from years on racing up and down the ice. The kind of body that makes girls swoon at his games, especially all the rabid puck bunnies.

Despite the short duration of our relationship years ago

before I got pregnant, I still feel sick thinking about Christian with anyone else.

And if he's part of Finley's life on a regular basis, I'll have no choice but to endure the endless revolving door of the beautiful women coming and going.

I've tried to tell myself that I don't want my son to have that kind of role model in his life, and god forbid, look up to a guy who carelessly sleeps with women and tosses them away.

Really, though, I'm…jealous of those women, even though Christian was only mine for a few weeks. Not long enough to even refer to him as mine since we barely dated after Preston urged me to say yes to going out with his best friend.

During the championship playoffs, more than one girl held up a sign asking Christian to marry her while others think he's a hockey god. I've seen clips of games where some girls even threw their bras and panties onto the ice!

Girls can be idiots sometimes. How do they not see the man for what he is—a carefree playboy who will sleep with them and rush to leave them seconds later?

I hate that I was once an idiot for Christian Riley, and somehow, I can't break free of his presence in my life, no matter how much I wish I could.

Now, thanks to my brother telling Christian he's Finley's father, I have no choice but to deal with him and all his… yumminess.

My cell phone rings, thankfully interrupting my idiotic sexy thoughts about the man I can't have as I recline on the sofa in the eerily silent house.

I don't recognize the number, but since it's a Greensboro area code, it could be Elle calling from her salon, so I decide to answer it. "Hello?"

There's nothing but silence.

"Helloooo?" I drawl. "Is anyone there?"

"Hey."

One word and my heart freezes solid mid-beat.

"It's Christian," he says, even though it's unnecessary. "Christian Riley," he adds, as if there is more than one Christian in my life. "Maya? Preston gave me your number."

"Oh." I cringe and facepalm myself for the brain-dead response. Then it occurs to me that he's in the same city as my brother now, playing on the same brutal hockey team, which could be why he's calling. "Is everything okay?"

"Yeah, yeah, everything is fine here," Christian says in a rush. "I was calling to see if I can come up to visit."

"Come up to visit?" I repeat slowly.

"I talked to Preston earlier today."

"Oh?" Again, I sound like a certified genius.

"And he said I should tell you that I'm not going to, like, try to take Finley from you or whatever."

"Or whatever?" I huff as my lungs decide to join in with my stopped heart.

"Yeah, I would never go to court and fight over custody of Finley or anything like that. I just want to see him as much as you'll let me."

"Okay. You want to come here for a visit? Here as in Bethesda, Maryland?" I ask, repeating his earlier question.

"Bethesda is near D.C., where your house is, right? I've been there once before..."

"Uh-huh."

"Then I'll drive up today or tomorrow if that's okay?"

"T-today or tomorrow? That's...really soon."

"Yeah, well, I only have a few weeks before training starts back up."

Rubbing my forehead, I try to process this unexpected conversation. "Right. Okay. I guess…I guess you could come visit tomorrow if you really want to drive all the way up here…"

"I do."

"As just a friend, right?" I ask for clarification.

"For now, but I hope we can talk more about that while I'm in town."

Part of me wants to shut down even the idea of telling Finley that Christian is his father, even though I know that's not fair to my son.

And the surprise visit will also be good for Finley, hopefully lifting his spirits since Preston's been gone.

"Okay," I agree and pray I don't regret it.

"Great, so should I, like, call you again tomorrow, you know, before I show up?"

"A call or text a few minutes before would be appreciated," I tell him since I'm already up and in panic cleaning mode, as if he's right outside the door.

"Then I'll see you tomorrow. Thanks, Maya," Christian says before ending the call. Well, I think he stays on the line for a few silent moments, as if he wants to say more, before ending it.

I start to go tell Finley to clean his room for a visitor tomorrow, but I stop myself. Part of me wonders if Christian will actually show up here or not, despite the assurance in his voice.

It's going to take some time before I'm able to trust a word the man says.

Ugh, I wish there was a way to prevent my little boy from getting caught up in all of this…drama. But Finley remains the bond between me and Christian, one I can't ever shake, no matter how much I may want to.

Since I'm a little pissed at my brother for giving Christian my number and not telling me, I decide to call him to let out some frustration.

"Hey, sis. I bet I know why you're calling," Preston says when he answers. Chuckling, he adds, "Christian doesn't waste any time, does he?"

"Why didn't you ask me first, or at least send me a text to warn me that he would be calling about setting up a visit?"

"I was going to call you when I got to Elle's," my brother says. "I should've called or texted when I got to my SUV, shouldn't I?"

"Yes, you should have!"

"Look, Maya, I'm sorry you were blindsided by the call, but trust me on this. Christian sincerely wants to spend time with Finley," Preston says.

"Trust you?" I scoff. "Trust you like when you said I should go out with him? *'Give him a chance, Maya. I think he's already half in love with you.'* Remember that time I trusted you?" It's a low blow to throw that in Preston's face, but I'm pissed at him for leaving and for continuing to make life-changing decisions behind my back. "Like he would rather spend time with a four-year-old instead of the hordes of beautiful women who throw themselves at him…" I feel my face warm with annoyance.

Preston's side of the phone is silent for a long moment. "You sound a little jealous there."

"Jealous? Please." I roll my eyes even though he can't see

me. "I'm not jealous. I'm realistic. A walking billboard for fornication is going to be my son's role model. What am I supposed to tell Finley when he asks what a puck bunny is and why his father is drowning in them, Preston?"

"Christian is finally growing up. I wouldn't dare say that or give your number to him to set up a visit if I wasn't convinced his heart is in the right place. Or if I thought he would screw up this chance. No matter what you think of the guy, he's still Finley's father."

Taking a deep breath, I close my eyes and tell my brother, "Trust *me*, I haven't forgotten that fact for a single second of my son's life."

The older Finley gets, the more he looks like his father instead of me or his Uncle Preston, which is annoying to say the least.

"I just… I don't know. What if Christian does screw this up? What if he breaks Finley's heart like he broke mine? I don't want Finley to go through all that."

"I don't either, but I'm not asking you to marry the man. Just give him a chance to spend time with his son. One last chance, for Finley's sake?"

"If this ends badly, I'm blaming you."

"Understood," Preston replies with a chuckle. "Good luck. And how exactly did he break your heart? Why didn't you ever tell me that you broke things off with him?"

"What?"

"Christian said that you broke his heart."

I scoff at the ridiculous notion.

"Was he lying? Did Christian break up with you?" Preston asks. "All this time, I thought he ghosted you or cheated on you."

"Well…okay, so technically I did tell him I didn't want to see him again, but that was after he acted like a complete jackass!"

"*Who's a jackass?*"

I turn around and find my four-year-old blinking up at me with big innocent brown eyes, waiting for me to answer his question.

"Nobody, honey. Someone, um, at the store, was acting like a…like a…"

"Jackass?" he supplies.

"Yes. But I shouldn't have called him that, should I?"

He shakes his head, looking at me in disapproval for using an insult that would put him in time out and lose his nightly video game privilege.

"Guess who's on the phone? Here's Uncle Preston," I say as I hand over my phone just to change the subject.

My son's eyes widen and a grin spreads across his face. "*UNCLE PRESTON!*" he screams into the device so loudly that my brother probably has some hearing loss.

A moment later they're talking about a hockey video game, much to my relief.

Whew.

I'm going to have to be more careful in the future. I shouldn't call my son's father names, especially not when he can hear me.

So, I vow right then and there that I'm going to try to give Christian Riley the benefit of the doubt going forward.

4

Maya

I'm not sure why I have to clean the entire house a second time while waiting for Christian to show up this afternoon. Maybe it's nerves or maybe it's a stupid, unconscious desire to make things look more perfect than they are.

Either way, by the time I hear the knock at the door, the kitchen is spotless and there's not a fleck of dirt on the carpet.

After the heartbreak of finding out I was pregnant, being disowned by my parents, and Christian leaving to join the pros without even a goodbye, I remember scrubbing Preston's apartment from top to bottom every day for two whole weeks after I moved in with him. House cleaning was all that I had to do while my brother was at practice. I guess it was my way of meditating, taking my mind off everything or a way to take back control in my spiraling life.

Today, though, I'm mostly just nervous for this face-to-face confrontation with Christian without Preston or Elle around to act as a buffer like the previous time.

Taking a deep breath, I finally open the door to find Christian standing there, looking way too hot for someone who holds all my good sense in the palm of his hand. Even wearing the casual Bobcats tee and jeans, his short blond hair sticking up every which way, he still somehow manages to look like he just stepped out of a GQ magazine.

And seeing him still draws all the air from my lungs.

"Hey," he says, his deep voice soft, his smile wobbly, like he's testing the waters. It finally occurs to me that despite his outward appearance, he's probably just as nervous about this visit as I am. Maybe even more so.

"Hey," I reply, stepping aside to let him in. As he walks past me, I catch a whiff of his cologne—woodsy and clean, and so him. My stomach does an unwelcome, eager flip at the familiar scent, and I tell it to settle down. Christian's gorgeousness has always made me feel like he's out of my league. Like we're not even playing the same sport. He's a superstar professional hockey player breaking scoring records, while I'm still stumbling around the empty field of my high school soccer team.

I still find it hard to believe that he once upon a time wanted to be with me. Wanted me enough that we made a son together.

A son who I would do anything for.

That's why I steel my spine before Finley realizes he's here to tell him, "We need to lay some ground rules."

"Ground rules?" he repeats. "Right. Sure. Anything you want."

"You're still just here visiting as a friend."

His sculpted, scruffy golden jaw twitches as he glances away toward the empty living room. "Fine, but how long am I only going to be a friend?"

"That depends," I reply. "*If* I decide it's time to tell Finley the truth, it will be after you prove that you're up for the job of being…more than a friend. I need…I need you to be a good role model for him and convince me that I can trust you to take care of him if you're alone with him for even a few minutes or possibly hours. But that's it. You won't get to take him to Greensboro overnight without me there."

Christian gives me a nod of understanding. "Okay. And I won't get an attorney and push for more…as long as you give me the entire summer to prove to you that you can trust me to be a good father to Finley."

"The entire summer?" I say in surprise at his unexpected terms of negotiation.

"You don't think it will take me that long to earn your trust and show you I can be a good role model?"

"Yes. No. I mean, I'm not sure." Flustered, I cross my arms over my chest and ask him, "How often are you planning to come up and visit?"

"As often as you'll let me. I could get a hotel room long-term so I can be here every day."

"*Every day*?!" I exclaim.

At my raised voice, Finley comes barreling toward us. "Holy crap! Christian Riley's in my house!" He launches himself at the playboy hockey player with a squeal of delight, as if the man he barely knows is now his favorite person in the world.

And I guess I'm a little jealous that while I was the one getting up three or four times a night to feed him as a baby, to worry about his every breath from the first one he took after a long, hard labor, I'm not a superstar athlete, just his boring, jobless, talentless mother.

Christian scoops Finley up effortlessly, his face breaking into a wide grin as he props him on his hip. "Hey, buddy. How have you been?"

"I'm good, but why are you here?" Finley asks, jumping right into this surprise visit headfirst, as if it's too good to be true.

"Your Uncle Preston and mom said I could spend time with you over this summer. What do you think? Are you up for hanging out with me?"

"Heck yes!"

I take a step back to watch the two of them together, my arms still crossed over my chest, feeling a strange mixture of warmth and unease.

This version of Christian makes it all so hard to stay wary of him—the one who acts so charming, sweet, and utterly devoted to Finley. It makes me question all the doubts and fears that kept me from telling Christian he's a father.

Maybe...maybe I was wrong to think he wouldn't care about Finley, wouldn't love him, just because he didn't love me.

Five years ago, I didn't think he was capable of loving anyone but himself.

That's why this version of him scares me the most. I was stupid to fall for it, to think he was mine when he so easily walked away when I needed his help to decide what to do.

And I know he's not really changed in the dating department, not after how he treated Elle...

But still, I want this warm, loving Christian to be real, for Finley's sake.

If I'm wrong, though, and he hurts my son in any way, I will kick his big, athletic ass.

"Mommy, can me and Christian play hockey in the backyard?" Finley asks me when Christian finally lowers him back to the ground.

He calls it hockey even though it's a modified field hockey version with sticks, a plastic ball, and two goals.

"That's fine with me, but you should ask Christian first."

My son, our son, tips his head back and blinks his big, brown eyes at his hero, making Christian laugh.

"Hell yes, we can play hockey," the playboy says with a grin before quickly eying me. "I mean, heck yes. Do you have two sticks?"

"My Uncle Preston has lots of hockey sticks! I use his instead of the other weird looking field hockey ones! He let me keep some when he moved out, but I still miss him."

Christian again looks to me, and I know I'm not going to like what he's about to say to Finley. "Then you and your mom should definitely come visit me in Greensboro…"

"That's where Uncle Preston moved!" Finley remarks excitedly.

"I know. He came to see me just yesterday. We're going to both play for the Bobcats this season."

Finley scowls at me as if angry at me for withholding this information. "Mommy, I don't have a Bobcats jersey with Uncle Preston's number on it! You don't either."

"I'm sure he'll give us one when the season starts," I tell him.

"Until then, you'll just have to wear mine, right?" Christian says with a smile that Finley returns with a nod. Glancing back at me, he adds, "I could hook you up with one, too, Maya. I've always wanted to see you in one of my jerseys."

"Finley, why don't you go find those hockey sticks?" I suggest, wanting to buy myself another moment to talk to his father. I have no doubt that if the playboy imagined me in his jersey, then that's *all* I'm wearing. Or maybe that's wishful thinking.

"I'll be right back!" Finley yells as he runs off to his room.

"New rules: Don't put ideas in his head about moving to Greensboro and forget about me wearing anything of yours," I warn him.

"I didn't say anything about moving," the jackass replies, still smiling like a smug fool. "I just said you should both come visit me in Greensboro."

"Same thing. He's upset enough as it is that Preston moved out."

Finally, Christian's perpetual smile slips. "Finley's lived with Preston his whole life, hasn't he?"

"Yes. The move…it's been a big change. One he's still really upset about."

"Then it's a good thing I'm here to take his mind off Preston moving, isn't it?" Again, he flashes me his panty-dropping smirk that I wish had never worked on me. Unfortunately, though, I can feel my comfortable cotton briefs inching down my hips even before the handsome bastard says, "I don't just want to see Finley this summer. I want to see you too."

He wants to see me too? I try not to read too much into that statement, but it's impossible.

Christian's tongue wets his lips in that awkward yet sexy

way he used to do when he wasn't sure what to say. "So, if I get a hotel room nearby, could I come over every day?"

"Every day?"

"Every day this summer."

"Let's start with every day for the rest of this week," I tell him. Oh crap. Did I just agree to an entire week of Christian Riley in my house? "We'll have to see how that goes before you try to move your arrogant ass into our house."

The man blinks at me, not because of the insult, but at my teasing comment. "Preston's room is empty, right?"

"Oh, hell no," I tell him.

"Mom! You said H-E-double hockey sticks," Finley huffs in admonishment when he returns, holding up the two sticks that just so happen to be in his hands, making me wince.

"You're right. I should've said heck, oh, heck no. Don't even think about it," I point my finger and lower my voice in warning at Christian. The man flashes me that patented grin that causes my denim shorts to drop an inch before I quickly tug them back into place.

Christian's eyes lower, as if just noticing my attire. His hazel eyes sweep over my bare legs for several long moments before moving up. They refuse to budge from my chest even after I clear my throat.

I know he was a boob guy back when we dated. Christian had begged to feel me up on our first date because he said he had dreamed of getting his hands on them. And I stupidly agreed since I had never felt sexier in my life than I did sitting on the tailgate of his old truck, listening to a ridiculously romantic playlist. God, I think the date box with the link to the songs is still stuffed in the top of my closet.

So much has changed since that night. I'm no longer an

innocent, gullible girl with a silly crush. Now I'm a single mother with a silly crush and boobs twice as big after having Finley. Which Christian seems enamored of.

His eyes finally lift to mine, not even a hint of embarrassment in them for getting caught gawking. In fact, his gaze reveals so much raw need that I must quickly look away.

"Go play before it gets too hot out," I tell them. "Dinner is at six. Hands need to be washed before the clock ticks over to the hour."

"You're not going to come watch us?" Christian asks, his slightly deeper voice teasing. I wonder if he remembers how I used to spend all my free afternoons watching my brother and Christian's hockey practices like a lovesick fool instead of studying, even before I knew Christian had any interest in me.

"I've got some cleaning to do, so maybe later."

Sitting and watching Christian run around our backyard is the last thing I need to be doing today. And I have to try to trust him. If he can't keep Finley uninjured in my backyard for two hours, then we've got serious problems.

"Be careful!" I still yell after them when they head outside through the kitchen door.

5

Christian

As I pull up to Maya's house for the second day, my fingers grip the steering wheel a little too tight. Despite how well the two hours yesterday afternoon went, it still feels like I'm preparing for the most important game of my life.

Except this time, it's more important than any game I've ever played before. It's about my son — about proving to Maya that I'm someone Finley can look up to, and that I'm worthy of her trust; that I won't selfishly run away when I screw up like the idiot boy she dated. I'm not even the same guy that dated Elle. That guy is pretty much dead and gone after I found out that I'm a father. That newsflash felt like having my head beaten in with a hockey stick.

It woke me up to how things could've been so different if I hadn't given up so soon on Maya when she ended things with me. I tried calling, texting, and writing to her for weeks before throwing in the towel. I had to try to move on because her rejection gutted me like nothing before.

Definitely worse than anything my father ever said to me. I grew up knowing he was disappointed in me and eventually accepted it when I decided to pursue a career in hockey. Still, nothing, not even dozens of women or any amount of time, could repair the wounds Maya inflicted.

I knock on the front door and take a deep breath while I wait for it to open. I tried to play it cool with Maya yesterday, but last night when I checked into my lonely hotel room after seeing her, being so close to her again, it felt like my heart and other parts of me would shrivel up and die if I couldn't touch her.

These past five years since I went pro, I've missed her like crazy. The distance and the distractions of puck bunnies helped me get through the worst of it whenever thoughts of her haunted me.

Now, though, I don't want to leave the house where her and my son sleep, and I don't have the slightest inkling to be with anyone else ever again. Not just because I want to set a good example for Finley. It's just how I've felt since the first day we met.

When Maya mentioned Preston's empty room, I would've done anything to stay here with her and Finley, even give up my autographed Wayne Gretzky King's jersey he wore the year they won the championship. It was years before I was even born, but I watched videos of him playing growing up.

But staying the night with Maya and Finley is a long shot right now. I have to play this right, to earn her trust back for

Finley's sake, rather than selfishly try to get her underneath me again.

God, just the thought of the one and only time we had almost-sex makes me want to put that shit off for as long as possible, no matter how much I crave another chance with her.

Nothing, though, is more important than earning her trust as a father to Finley and as a dependable man she can count on to be there for her.

When the front door finally swings open, there my dream girl is, looking like she's caught somewhere between relief and hesitation.

Maybe it's just wishful thinking, but I think Maya might still have feelings for me too. It's in the way she still looks at me like I'm hers, hers to command and obey, especially when she's laying down ground rules, trying to act tough and callous. It's probably all in my head since I think of her as mine—my home, my future, my everything. That's how it felt before I ever found out she was the mother of my son.

Yes, she kicked me to the curb after our one horrible night together years ago, but the connection between us was there way before the bad sex.

And I swear I would give anything for a do-over of that night, her first time that I greedily rushed her into and ruined.

Thinking about the other men the love of my life has been with since…no, I can't go down that road. I don't want to know who came after me, who made her toes curl the way I should have.

"Are you dating anyone?" I blurt out like an idiot rather than offering her a 'good morning.'

Maya folds her arms across her delicious looking breasts

and frowns with so much displeasure at the personal question that I want to take it back. She's not mine. I'm not hers. Not yet. "Not that it's any of your business, but no. I'm not dating anyone. At least at the moment…"

"Good."

Narrowing her brown eyes at me, Maya mutters, "You think that it's good that I'm alone? Well, now I need to go find a date."

"No, you don't. I mean, unless you want to. You're right. It's none of my business, but I'm glad there's no one else for you or Finley."

Her arms remain crossed tight across her cleavage like a shield. Cleavage that's way more enticing than it was years ago when I fantasized about falling asleep on the bare beauties. Her walls are still up, and I know she's trying to protect herself — and Finley, too. But I can't help hoping that there's still a part of her that wants to let me in.

"So," I start, keeping my voice casual, "any chance you'll be joining me and Finn for a little backyard hockey this morning?"

Maya raises a single eyebrow. "You think I don't have anything more important to do than watch you show off like a preening peacock? I'm already intimately familiar with your stick handling skills."

Her remark makes me chuckle. A tightness in my chest eases at the easy banter and my shaft lengthens in my cotton shorts because I'm suddenly assaulted with memories. Memories of winning games in a mostly empty arena and then celebrating with a Netflix night in Maya's dorm room. I remember her timidly asking me on our fifth date to show her how I liked to stroke myself. She wanted to imitate the moves with her small hand. "I used to love trying to impress you when you would come and watch our practices and games in the minor leagues," I tell her. "Back when I was so broke I could only afford fast food on our dates," I remind her. "I always wanted to play my best when you were there cheering for us. You were there for me before the money or the fame, unlike the puck bunnies who hang around the arena nowadays, flashing their tits at me like it'll convince me to buy them shit." Maya's eyes widen a second before I realize the words that came out of my mouth. "Fuck! I shouldn't have said tits or shit!" I apologize in a rush, then slap my palm over my big mouth to keep more filth from coming out of it. Around it, I say, "Sorry. About the t-word, s-word, and the f-bomb. I'll do better."

Rather than look furious at my slip, she glances over her shoulder to make sure Finley's not within hearing distance before she says quietly, "It's okay. I may have accidentally called you a jackass the other day and got caught."

My palm falls away from my mouth and my jaw drops open in disbelief. "You called me a jackass in front of my son?"

"No! Well, yes, but he didn't know I was talking about you," she replies with a grin. "I told him the jackass was someone at the grocery store. Don't worry. I wouldn't...I would never intentionally badmouth you in front of Finley regardless of what may have happened between us..."

Okay, that makes me feel better, the fact that she slips up now and then too and that she's not filling Finley's head to make him hate me the way she does, at least.

"I hope you will return the favor, even if you're married to some woman five years from now who despises me," Maya says.

"Never," I assure her, meaning the marriage to some random imaginary woman or talking shit about her in front of our son.

After that remark, Maya stares at me silently for a long moment, her eyes searching mine for… something. I hold her gaze, even if I have no clue what she's looking for or what she wants from me. Finally, she sighs and glances toward the kitchen, and the door that leads to the backyard. "Maybe I'll watch you two play for a few minutes today," she says, her tone flat. "But don't expect me to participate. I'm not a superstar with a stick like you."

For some reason, that small concession to come and watch us feels like a victory. One I'll gladly take. I blow out a sigh, hating the fact that despite how cordial we might be now, I know that Maya will be even harder than Preston to win over, and for years he constantly threw punches at my face every time I saw him.

"Come on in," she says, tipping her head toward the other door so I'll cross the threshold into the house. "Finley's already outside, practicing. I think he wants to impress you."

"He shouldn't worry about impressing me. Besides, there's more to life than hockey…" I trail off, thinking about all the times my father told me that shit.

"Not to him there's not," Maya says. "His world revolves around hockey. Always has since he was old enough to walk and hold a tiny stick trying to imitate his uncle."

"No wonder he's already so damn good," I remark. Then I ask her, "How old was he when he started walking?"

"Oh, um, I guess he was about ten or eleven months old. By his first birthday he was running laps around the house."

"Really? Wow. Do you have videos of him at that age?"

"Of course," she says over her shoulder. "I've got most of them saved on the Cloud. I guess…I can put them on a flash drive for you if you want?"

"I would love that," I tell her. "Seriously. Like all of his photos and videos from the day he was born."

Laughing, she says, "Okay. And I also have some of both from before he was born."

"Like photos of you while you were pregnant?"

"The ultrasounds of him, I mean."

"I want to see those, too. And photos of you, like when your belly was all big, looking like it was about to pop. I hate I missed that." God, why does the thought of seeing Maya swollen with my son make me so damn hard? Because everyone would be able to see for themselves that she's mine. That it was me who had been spilling inside her. I've never been as desperate to bury myself deep inside of her as I am right now. Something I never got to do. Something I shouldn't be thinking about while wearing thin athletic shorts.

"I'll give you everything I have tonight," Maya replies just as we reach the back door. It takes me a moment to realize what she's talking about. Oh, right. She'll give me a flash drive of all the photos.

"Great, thank you." My dirty mind was imagining her riding me naked, giving me her body, heart and soul to me tonight, all night, until we collapse together in an uncon-scious, well-sated, tangle of sweaty limbs.

Even better than the sex would be the next morning when we wake up together, then I make breakfast for her and Finley.

Speaking of my son, just outside, Finley's racing around the yard with his stick, chasing the white plastic ball with a look of concentration on his face like his life depends on running faster, until he sees me.

"Hey, Christian! You came back today!"

"Hey, buddy," I greet him, then quietly ask Maya as I head down the porch steps, "He didn't know I was coming over again?"

"At his age...I don't like to make promises that can be easily broken. Canceling plans breaks his heart, so please remember that when you make them."

"I won't break any plans or his heart," I assure her. *Or yours* goes unsaid even though I promise that too, even though Maya was the one who shattered mine. I know I let her down and broke hers too, though.

Grabbing one of the full-size sticks propped up against the back of the house, I shout "Incoming!" and swipe the plastic ball.

Without missing a beat, Finley moves into position so that once the ball reaches him, all it takes is a swing of his smaller stick to send it hurling into the goal.

"Great shot!" I tell him going over with my palm raised for a high five that he jumps up to hit.

Maya stands on the porch, her arms still crossed while we play, but I can feel her watching us. Whenever I chance a glance at her, her face appears to soften as Finley throws his arms up to celebrate every time he scores.

I can feel the weight of her eyes on me too sometimes, and part of me wants to make a smartass remark about her liking what she sees, but I hold my tongue. But I love the attention too much to ruin it, just like in the minor league days when it felt like I was the center of her universe, even though I knew she was there watching her brother too. She didn't constantly track him like she did me, though. I could feel the heat in her gaze, see her own dirty thoughts swirling in her mind whenever our eyes met across the ice. That undeniable chemistry is why, when I picked her up for our first date, I couldn't make the short walk from her dorm to my truck before I kissed her. A near frantic, passionate kiss against a tree that nearly sent me to my knees and lasted a good ten minutes before we could stop. It was like we were both giving in and getting what we had wanted for the weeks before Preston gave his approval for me to ask Maya out.

I later found out it was Maya's very first kiss on her first ever date. More of her firsts that belonged only to me.

But just because she may still be attracted to me doesn't mean she feels the same about me or will admit it even if she does.

If anything, she's probably just keeping an eye on me to make sure I don't screw up and knock Finley down or something.

Still, I want to say something to break the tension.

"Hey, Finley," I say, grinning down at him as we take a break. "Do you think you got your mad hockey skills from your mom or Uncle Preston?"

Finley laughs. "Mommy's good at soccer, not hockey. She hates the ice."

I glance up at Maya, raising an eyebrow. "Soccer, huh? I might have to see that. How come I never knew you played?"

Maya rolls her eyes, but there's a tiny smile tugging at her lips. "I only played a little in high school."

"There are trophies in a box in her closet," Finley informs me.

"Trophies? Really?" Now both of my brows are raised.

"One was for MVP," he goes on to say. "That stands for most, um, most valued person, I think."

"A most valuable player award? That means your mom was the best player the team had, the one person they need the most to win games," I tell him.

"Wow," he says, gazing up at his mother. "So, does that mean she was like really good?"

"Yep. She was the best and she's just being modest," I loudly whisper to him.

Blinking up at me, Finley asks, "What's modest mean?"

"Oh, baby, you're asking the wrong man that question!" Maya calls out with a grin since she can obviously overhear our conversation.

Chuckling while subtly scratching the side of my face with my middle finger in her direction, I explain to Finley, "Modest means you don't go around bragging about how good you are at something, even when you're really good at it. Like, I shouldn't tell people that I'm the fastest player on my team or in the entire professional hockey league, even if it's true. It's better to let all the sports commentators say it instead."

Tilting his head, Finley says, "Are you really the fastest player in the league?"

Plucking the collar of my tee with my fingers, I give him a grin. "That's what everyone says about me, so it must be true, right?"

"Right," Finley agrees with his own smile. "I want to be the fastest one day, too. But I'll probably just be big and slow like Uncle Preston."

I wish I could tell my son that I have no doubt he inherited my swiftness, but I can't because for the time being I'm just his mom and uncle's 'friend.'

Instead, I tell him, "You know, if you work hard, I bet you could be even faster than me one day. You almost have me beat now!"

～

By the time we head back inside that afternoon, Finley's worn out, but seems happy. After lunch and guzzling two cold glasses of water, he plops down on the couch, his eyes glued to the cartoon that's playing on the television. I sit down next to him, but my attention is not on the screen. It's on Maya, who's busy tidying up the kitchen, though I'm pretty sure she's just avoiding sitting in the same room with me.

When she doesn't join us, and continues her scrubbing, I take the hint, standing up and stretching my arms over my head. "I guess I should probably head out."

"When can we play again?" Finley asks.

"Let me talk to your mom about that, buddy. I hope it will be soon," I tell him as I ruffle his hair. "I had fun with you today."

"Me too," he says before his attention returns to the cartoon about a crew of cute little animals who live under the ocean and go on rescue missions together.

Maya's scrubbing the empty, sparkling clean sink when I find her in the kitchen. "So, I guess I'll see you tomorrow?"

She jumps, apparently not hearing my comment about heading out or my approaching footsteps thanks to the running faucet.

Shutting the water off, she turns around, still wearing yellow rubber gloves that come up to her elbows. Shaking her head, she says, "I'm sorry, what?"

45

"I'll see you tomorrow," I tell her rather than ask her permission. "Unless you need some help cleaning up tonight?"

"Well," she says, eyeing the cabinet where the trash bin is located. "The garbage is heavy…"

"Got it," I tell her, happy to help, even in this small way.

Once I return from stuffing the trash into the can next to the side of the house, I come back through the backdoor. Maya's waiting, holding her hand out to offer me…a small, black flash drive. "The photos and videos you wanted."

"Thank you," I tell her, excited to see them as I clutch the device tightly so I won't lose it, as if it holds top secret, world ending documents. I may have to buy a new laptop tonight since I forgot to pack it. I left town in a rush, throwing only the barest of necessities into a bag. Which reminds me, I wonder if Finley has watched The Jungle Book or one of my favs as a kid, The Lion King. Maybe Maya will let me have a movie night with Finley while I'm in town. I want to do everything with him, starting with taking him to a park since he asked about me taking him sometime.

That's why, on my way to the front door, I ask Maya, "Would you and Finley want to meet me at one of the local parks tomorrow?"

"Um, sure, I guess. Just let me know which one and what time."

"How about noon? I'll pack us a picnic lunch."

"A picnic lunch?" she replies with a smile. "Okay, sure."

I won't ever have a picnic again without thinking about mine and Maya's first date, a picnic on the back of my truck because I couldn't afford anything more extravagant. It was one of the best nights of my life. We talked about all sorts of random shit thanks to a game in our date box. We kissed even more than we talked and ended up rolling around in the bed of my truck so hot and heavy that I had to take a cold shower when I got home. All our clothes stayed on the whole time. I only slipped a hand up Maya's shirt for two minutes before stopping so I didn't embarrass myself by making a mess in my pants.

And maybe I'm trying a little too hard to win Maya over now. I can't help it, though. I like spending time with her and Finley. After just two days, it almost feels like we're becoming a family, the one we should've been years ago.

6

Christian

My son was beautiful from the day he was born.

Despite all she was facing on her own, Maya smiled at Finley with love from the second she laid eyes on him.

Those are just two of the many things I learned by looking through photos and staying up all night to watch all the videos of the moments I missed with Finley.

It was a sweet kind of torture I will happily endure again tonight because, while it makes me angry to see the time I lost with my son, seeing all the images helps me feel like I'm becoming a part of his life.

All I know is that I want to be in the photos and videos from now on.

At the park the next day, the three of us eat some pizza, then I push Finley on the swings. His laughter fills the air as he soars higher and higher while Maya sits on a bench and watches from afar, giving us some space. For a while, it's just us — no tension, no awkwardness, just father and son. It feels good; right.

"Christian, can we play hockey in the backyard later?" Finley asks as I slow the swing down and he hops off.

"Sure thing. As long as your mom doesn't mind," I add, steering him back toward Maya. I want to stay on that woman's good side by deferring to her on everything Finley related.

"I wish I had an ice rink out there instead of just grass," he says with a heavy sigh when we're almost at Maya's bench.

"Me too, buddy. But the ice would melt in the summer."

"Oh yeah," he says.

"I have an idea, though," I tell him, since I'm having ice withdrawals myself. "Let me make a quick call, okay?"

"Okay," he says while Maya gets to her feet and arches an eyebrow in question.

I stay close enough for her to overhear the conversation since I don't want her to think I'm calling some other woman.

"Christian?" her brother's deep voice answers, sounding surprised to see my name appearing on his phone's screen.

"Hey, Preston. Sorry to bother you, but I was hoping you could call in a favor for us."

"Us?" he asks.

"Me, Finley, and Maya."

"So, things are going well with the visits?"

"Yeah, so far so good," I tell him. "Finley and I have been playing hockey in the backyard, but he misses the ice. I do too. Do you think you could pull some strings to get us into the Warhawks arena for an hour or two one day this week?"

"I'll see what I can do and call you back," he says.

"Okay, thanks."

As soon as I end the call, Maya says, "You called my brother for a favor?"

"Yeah. Why?"

She shakes her head, making her long raven strands dance in the wind. "It's still odd that you two aren't constantly at each other's throats."

"We've worked things out. Preston's forgiven me for being an idiot and I've forgiven him for hitting me and shit in the past. And stuff, I mean, in the past."

"That's good. I'm glad," she replies. "I know you were his best friend during the minor leagues, when you were roommates."

"Yeah, I actually missed the big oaf over the years," I tell her. "It'll be nice to get to play on the same team with Preston again without him trying to murder me."

Maya's smile makes me weak in the knees.

Clearing my throat, I glance back to Finley going down the slide. "You don't mind if we go to the arena to skate, do you?"

"Not at all. Finley loves the ice," she says. "In fact, I bet he would love to have his birthday party there this year."

"When's his birthday?"

"July twenty-second."

What was I doing on July twenty-second almost five years ago? "I think...I think I was on vacation in Miami. That day, I mean, five years ago while you were..."

"I know," Maya replies softly.

Stepping up closer to her, I ask, "What do you mean?"

She bites her bottom lip and lowers her eyes to her sandals

like they are suddenly more fascinating than the park. "Because…I-I was going to tell you that I was on the way to the hospital. But then I saw the photos of you and your friends on social media at a party on some boat."

"I wish you had called me. I would've swum back to shore if I needed to and then booked a flight. I would've done *anything* to be here."

Maya nods. "I think I knew that you probably would have come. The distance was an excuse because I wasn't sure if I could bear seeing you. Thanks to the hormones, I was bawling like a baby, and in agonizing labor…"

"I'm sorry," I tell her. "For not being there and the agonizing part. But mostly I'm sorry for making you not want me there."

She shakes her head and finally meets my eyes. "That's the problem. I *did* want you there. I wanted it so badly that I wouldn't have wanted you to leave."

"Oh." Not only did she want me with her when she gave birth to our son, she wanted me to stay with them.

"I knew you would have to leave though, to go back to Greensboro to get ready for the start of the hockey season…"

Fucking hockey.

For the first time in my life, I think I'm starting to hate the first thing I ever loved because it likely not only cost me Maya, but my son too. My family.

Every time I've looked at Maya these past few days, I've seen the worry in her eyes. I thought she was just waiting for me to screw up, and honestly, I didn't blame her.

But part of me is wondering if she's also worried about those feelings for me coming back and is trying to keep her distance.

Or maybe they never left.

My feelings for her never faded. I just tried my best to forget they existed.

7

Maya

Christian's been coming over every day for the past week. And I have to admit, I didn't expect him to keep such an enthusiastic interest in Finley for this long. I thought the playboy would get bored after a day or two playing with a four-year-old and use summer training as an excuse to get back to Greensboro.

But to my surprise, Christian has been showing up consistently, staying over a little longer each day. He has taken me and Finley out to eat, the park, and even skating at the Warhawks arena.

In fact, the past two nights he hasn't left until the sun sets, only to return a little after sunrise the next morning.

Which means I'm having to get up earlier than ever to grab a quick shower and try to look halfway awake before he shows up on our doorstep.

The three of us have also been eating all three meals together; breakfast, lunch, and dinner, including tonight.

It's nothing fancy, just spaghetti, garlic bread, and a salad. But the simple, routine activity feels strangely intimate. Christian's sitting at the head of the table, cracking jokes, and making Finley laugh between bites of pasta. The man fits in so easily at our dinner table, as if he's been here all along, like this is how it was always supposed to be.

"So, Finley," Christian says, twirling his fork around his spaghetti. "How would you feel about coming to one of my and Uncle Preston's games in Greensboro this season?"

Finley's eyes light up, his excitement obvious. "Yeah, yeah! I wanna go to a game and wear my Bobcats jersey!"

"We'll have to get you a new one with Uncle Preston's number on it too," Christian replies with a grin. "We can hang out before and after the game. It'll be fun."

I sit in my chair quietly watching their exchange. It's sweet, and I know how much this means to Finley. But there's a small part of me that aches.

Christian makes sliding into this fatherly role look so easy, which is great for Finley. But to me, this familiar version of Christian seems too good to be true. It's the version who swept me off my feet and then ran away. I also know that off-season Christian has all the time in the world for us, for Finley. But during the season, we'll be lucky if he calls even once a week.

"Are you sure you won't be too busy to see us when we visit?" I ask, my voice more pointed than I intended. "With your busy game schedule and all during the season, I mean?"

Christian glances at me, his expression softening. "I'll

make time, Maya. I promise now that I know…I mean, now that we're *friends*, I'll always make time for you two."

I nod, trying to take his words at face value, but my doubts linger. I think Christian means well. But I've seen this all play out before — the amazing, sweet Christian who makes me feel like the center of his world, who then ups and disappears without a word, without any explanation.

Yes, I ended things years ago, but he didn't even take five minutes to say goodbye or ask me what I had decided to do about the pregnancy. He sent a few apologetic texts and voice-mails right after I told him I was pregnant, then he disappeared.

And the reason I called it quits with Christian certainly wasn't because I didn't care about him. It was because of how quickly he disappeared after we finally slept together, leaving me hurt and confused.

At first, I thought that he left me in that fancy hotel room because he had finally got what he wanted all along and had no further use for me.

But over time, the more I've thought about it, the less that explanation makes sense.

Why go to all the trouble of booking the expensive suite, having a romantic dinner, only to bail ten minutes later, after we got into bed together?

Instead of staying and talking to me, explaining what he was thinking or how he felt, he just took off and left me to go to some party with his and Preston's hockey teammates.

I broke up with him the next day because I was angry that he abandoned me when I needed him most. Regardless of the reason, he left me there alone in a hotel room, naked, vulnerable, and with no ride home after the most intimate experience of my entire life. I had to call Preston to come get me, and he was not happy. That's when he kicked Christian out of his apartment, before I even found out I was pregnant.

The whole thing was such a humiliating experience that I told Christian that we were over. I felt so embarrassed that night that I haven't had the nerve to try having sex again with any man.

"What are you thinking about so hard?" Christian asks.

I look up from my plate of untouched pasta I hadn't realized I had been staring at and find Finley has already disappeared from the table.

"I'm just tired," I lie.

Sighing, Christian pushes back his chair from the table, as if frustrated I won't tell him the truth.

While I sit there lost in old memories, he grabs Finley's plate with his own, then goes over and starts running the water in the sink, adding soap suds. A moment later, he's scrubbing a plate with the sponge.

"You don't have to do those by hand. I have a dishwasher," I tell him as I snap myself out of my wretched thoughts and get to my feet.

"No, I've got it. You should finish eating. You've barely touched your plate."

When I just stand there next to the sink and stare at him, watching the veins in his muscular biceps and forearms flexing as he works, he says, "Go eat, woman, since you refuse to tell me what's eating you. Besides, washing dishes is the least I can do to try to make up for a mistake I made nearly six years ago."

"Wh-how did you know that's what I was thinking about?" I ask as I hurry to retake my seat and pick up my fork, determined to put distance between us. I even shovel in a few bites of pasta so my stomach won't growl when I'm trying to sleep.

"I knew because you had the same sad look on your face as you did that night when I got dressed and walked out on you."

"Oh."

"Just so you know, that look has haunted me all these years," Christian says while focusing on the dishes. "I've always regretted my decision to leave you in that hotel room."

"Because Preston made you move out?"

"No. Of course, that sucked, but I didn't blame him. I hate that I hurt you."

"So? Why did you leave, Christian?" I ask him the question I've wondered for over five years.

"Uh, well, because my fragile male pride took a hit, and I think I just...panicked."

What the hell is he talking about?

"You definitely left in a rush, but I don't think I understand the 'fragile male pride' part."

"I was, I *am* very good at...*that* usually. The night with you was a total fluke."

"If you say so," I reply while he scrubs another plate even harder, as if taking out his frustration on it.

"Oh, I do say so! It was a complete fluke that has never, ever happened again."

"You couldn't have explained that to me at the time rather than flee?"

"I should have told you. But..."

"But?" I prod when he pauses.

"You looked so confused."

"I was confused!" Remembering to lower my voice so Finley won't hear us, I go on to remind him, "You were acting like a jackass, and I didn't know why. I thought I had done something wrong. We hadn't even actually done *it*. I didn't take a pregnancy test for weeks after I was late because I didn't think it was actually possible that I could be pregnant…"

Christian groans and leans down, resting his forehead against his dry forearm while his hands drip water over the sink water. "You didn't do a damn thing wrong. Just…please stop talking about it. I still have PTSD from that night."

Giving up on my plate of spaghetti, I dump it into the trash bin, then slip it into the soapy water in front of him. "Tell me now and I'll never bring it up again. I promise," I assure him quietly.

Christian doesn't lift his head, he just mumbles, "There's not much to tell. Touching you, hell, just seeing you like that… so sexy and innocent and eager, I got too…excited."

"What?" He lost me in an unexpected, ridiculous attempt at flattery.

Keeping his voice quiet, his head still resting on his forearm, he says, "I was planning on starting with significant foreplay to make it better for you. But then we got undressed and started kissing and you were so wet and warm. I was barely knocking on the door, but you felt so damn good. And when you wrapped your legs around my waist, pulling me closer, it was all over. I thought I pulled away in time, but…"

Oh. My. God.

"You didn't. Obviously," I finish for him.

Turning his head to look at me, his hazel eyes are distressed when he whispers, "You were technically still a virgin when I left that night."

"Really? I thought so since there wasn't any pain like I was expecting…"

Clearing his throat, Christian lifts his head and stands up straight again to continue scrubbing the silverware while I try to wrap my head around his explanation.

The superstar playboy came before he was barely inside of me, failing to pop my cherry, and then somehow managed to pull out too late, all at the same time.

Holy shit.

Leaning my back against the counter, I mutter, "I gave birth to my son…as a virgin. Wow. I didn't know that was even possible." Christian groans before I go on to add, "And technically, I guess I'm still a twenty-five-year-old virgin…"

There's a loud *plunk* as if Christian abruptly dropped something into the water. "Maya…"

"My lack of experience has nothing to do with you," I lie while running my fingers through my hair, feeling his sympathetic eyes on the side of my face. "I was pregnant and then I was a mother. I don't have time for dating and have had no desire to put myself in that whole embarrassing situation again."

"Oh, Maya," Christian says softly, his voice full of pity. "I'm so damn sorry. I wish I could show you everything that you've been missing all these years."

"You blew your chance. Literally," I point out. "I don't want you to show me anything that you've done with dozens of women you barely know," I say before I walk out of the kitchen, leaving the jackass to at least finish what he started with the dirty dishes.

8

Christian

I've spent years trying and failing to forget that one night with Maya. *Years.* And tonight, she had to drag me back down memory lane to the most embarrassing night of my entire existence.

I regret never getting my tongue between her legs most of all, making her feel good. She never even came on my fingers when we fooled around. Has she ever had an orgasm from a man if she's never had sex with anyone?

My guess is no, and it's all my fault that the beautiful woman has never let a man make her toes curl or her legs shake in pleasure. She's still a virgin because of my fuck up years ago.

Grabbing a towel, I quickly dry my hands and then peek into the living room to make sure Finley's still distracted with his hockey video game. Maya only lets him play for half an hour a day. By my calculation, he still has about ten to fifteen minutes left. There's no way he'll miss a minute of play.

Down the hallway, I go on a mission. One that will probably get me thrown out of the house, but that's a chance I'm willing to take to make up for my mistake.

I step into the dim bedroom just as Maya comes out of her adjourning bathroom, her cheeks flushed.

"Wh-what are you doing in here?" she asks me.

Reaching behind me without taking my eyes off her, those long sexy legs in her short denim shorts and tight tee that stretches across her tits like a tease. I close the door and turn the lock.

"Christian?

"Let me touch you. Please. Just once," I say as I take a tentative step toward her, eyeing the seam of those shorts. Oh, yeah, they'll work just fine. "Over your clothes only."

"What? Why?"

"Please. Please?" I say again as I get close enough to finally touch her. I slide my palm over her cheek, my thumb brushing her bottom lip as she gasps. When Maya's fingers reach for the front of my tee to pull me closer, I press my lips to hers.

The kiss is barely more than a whisper at first. But then it turns into more when I slip my tongue over hers.

From there it's a free for all, just like our first kiss. Maya walks backward, dragging me with her until she's falling back onto the mattress. I had planned to do this standing up, but lying on top of her is even better.

She moans when she feels me hard and long through my jeans, pressing against the seam of her shorts. I grind into that spot as our kiss deepens until I worry I'll come in my pants in an even more embarrassing way.

Reaching between our bodies, I press my fingers to that seam and groan at the heat of her core warming them.

Maya's own hand tries to stroke me through my jeans, but I grab her wrist and press it above her head.

"Come for me," I pant above her, watching the lust fill her eyes as my fingers move between her legs. "Come for me and then you can do whatever you want to me."

A gasp has Maya's head tipping back. A second later and she's undoing the front of her shorts and shoving my hand down inside.

"Fuck, you are so damn hot," I tell her as I tease her through her damp cotton panties, her hand still covering mine, urging me to keep going. Her thighs tighten around our joined hands and then it happens.

Her hips buck as tremors rack her body. At the sound of her first cry of pleasure, I cover her mouth with mine, drowning it out so our curious son doesn't come to investigate.

I eventually release her lips to watch her face as the last of the shudders bring her back down to her bedroom with me.

The haziness in her eyes slowly fades and I hold my breath, waiting for her panic or anger to set in.

Finally, she heaves a heavy sigh, sinking deeper into the mattress and letting my hand go. "Wow."

"Wow good?" I ask.

"So good," she agrees. Grabbing the back of my neck, she pulls my mouth back down to hers. And then it's my turn to cry out when Maya palms me through my jeans.

I'm so damn hard I'm about to explode… right before there's a loud knock on the door.

"Mommy?"

"W-what, baby?" Maya calls out, still catching her breath.

"Is Christian in there too? His car is still in the driveway..."

Maya's eyes widen as she looks up at me, then pushes me off her. "You found us! We were wondering how long it would take. Now it's your turn to hide. I'll start counting. Stay inside the house!"

"Okay!" his excited voice says.

A second later and Maya is climbing on top of me, her mouth claiming mine while her hand finishes what we started. "How fast can you get there?" she asks against my lips.

"Faster if you fist me tight," I tell her. She tugs down my zipper to get her hands on me. As soon as her small fingers wrap around my shaft, I'm ready to blow my load.

"Hurry," she whispers before her tongue is thrusting against mine.

Oh, thank god. This time, speed is of the essence and not an embarrassment. I don't hold back as Maya strokes me so damn good.

A few seconds later, I'm lying on my back, trying to recover, when Maya leaves and returns with a hand towel that she tosses into my face.

"Get cleaned up. Finley's waiting."

My motions are slow, lethargic even, though I'm trying to hurry. I feel like I've just finished playing every second of an entire game without a break, scored ten goals, and won in a blowout.

Maya saying, "This can't happen again," unfortunately snaps me out of my sluggishness. Sliding off the bed, I'm already fastening my pants when I ask in a panic, "Why the hell not? You didn't like it?"

"We can't sneak away again into the bedroom while Finley's awake!"

"Oh," I mutter, since that's not the rejection I thought she was going to throw at me. "But we can sneak into the bedroom again if he's…asleep?" I ask, so hopeful that I'm holding my breath while Maya fixes her shorts and combs her fingers through her hair.

Finally, she says, "If you want to do that again, then yes, it will have to be after he's sound asleep."

"Okay, I want to," I easily agree. "If you do."

"Yeah, sure. It's fine. Whatever," she says in a rush before grabbing the used towel, tossing it into a hamper and going to unlock and open the door. With her hand on the knob, she glances over her shoulder at me, her cheeks still flushed from her orgasm. "Ready?"

"Hell yes. I mean heck yes. Let's go find him." When I'm flush against her back, I splay my palm over her stomach to ask in her ear, "Isn't it about Finley's bedtime?"

"That's all you're getting tonight," she replies, shoving her elbow playfully into my abs. "We'll see about tomorrow."

"H-E double hockey sticks yes, we will," I say, making Maya huff out a laugh.

Maya

After Christian leaves the house with an extra pep in his step, and Finley is fast asleep in his bed, I stare down at my cell phone in my hand.

Elle is probably still awake. If so, her and my brother are likely busy. But I really need to talk to someone, another woman, about what I did tonight. I need someone to tell me that a repeat would be an absolutely horrible idea.

So, despite the fact that my brother's girlfriend was recently spending her nights with Christian, I find her name in my contacts and make the call.

"Hey, Maya! How's everything going up your way?" Elle asks.

"Good. Things are good," I reply. "How are things down there?"

"Ugh, Preston just ran out for some ice cream. He keeps

bringing up me moving in with him even though we've only been dating for a few weeks!"

A smile lifts my lips. "I'm not surprised. My brother didn't move to Greensboro to play hockey; he moved to be near you. It's sweet and surprising for him."

"I know. And I want to say yes, but it's too soon. I know it's too soon, and yet, it's getting harder to refuse him. I'm afraid I'm going to give in soon, then lose my apartment, and be on the streets if things don't work out..."

"I, um, understand the predicament that you're in fairly well, actually."

"Oh yeah? You have a big ass jock trying to woo you too?"

"Yes," I say with a wince.

"Oh, wow," Elle replies softly. "*Christian?*"

"Is it weird to talk about him with you after your history?" I ask.

"No. Of course not. That all feels like a different lifetime ago. I love Preston. He's the only man I think about now," she says. "So, you and Christian may be getting back together? That's wonderful!"

"That's not...it's not like that we're getting back together," I tell her. "But tonight, we were talking, you know, about what happened in our past, the one time we tried to have sex, and I got pregnant. And then he followed me to my bedroom, locked the door and..."

"*And?* You two hooked up?"

"We fooled around a little. Over the clothes. Mostly. But that was it."

"You had fun?" she asks.

"The most fun I've ever had with a man. *Ever,*" I reiterate, smiling with a grin she can't see. While Christian may be under the impression that I had never had an orgasm before, he's only half right. I've taken care of matters on my own. Tonight was just the first time getting there with a man.

"But? It sounds like there's a but coming," Elle remarks.

"We had to be fast since Finley interrupted. We both… enjoyed ourselves. And I told Christian we couldn't hide in the bedroom together again while he's awake or Finley will start asking questions."

"You didn't rule out after he's asleep, though?" she catches on easily.

"Right. And Christian seemed agreeable to that idea. While I liked fooling around with him, really liked it, I'm just wondering if I'm being stupid. I know it doesn't mean anything to him, that he does this sort of thing with lots of women. Tell me I'm being stupid and that I shouldn't do anything with him again."

"Why shouldn't you?"

"Because things are complicated enough as it is with him just finding out he's Finley's father. And it could end badly like before, which would hurt Finley." Rubbing my forehead with my free hand, I say, "I'm an idiot, aren't I? You can be honest, Elle. That's why I called you. I need someone to talk some sense into me."

My brother's girlfriend laughs. "Maya, I don't think you're an idiot. I think it would only be a mistake if you two aren't on the same page, like if you still have feelings for Christian but he thinks it's just physical. Do you still have feelings for him?"

"That's not what tonight was about," I reply rather than think too hard about the answer to that question. "I know we're not going to end up back together. It could end badly, which would only hurt Finley. Besides, long distance wouldn't work with a normal guy, much less a playboy hockey star who travels around the country every week and has beautiful, adoring fans throwing themselves at him."

"So, it's just going to be a casual thing during the summer for both of you? There's no chance that you might move to Greensboro and try to be a couple?"

"I'm going to apply for jobs here. This is where Finley's friends are and…it's time for me to take care of myself without relying on Preston's help. Even if he does own the house."

"Preston loves being able to help you. It's what he lives for. You and Finley could never be a burden to him."

"Even so, I want to try to do this on my own, you know? And if I'm in Greensboro, it'll be too easy to let my brother be a crutch or get my heart broken again."

"So, it's just a casual summer fling with Christian?"

"Yes. That's all this is or will be."

"Then I think that if you explain that to Christian and he's still interested, then there's nothing wrong with having some adult fun after Finley goes to sleep."

Nothing wrong unless I start falling for him again, I think to myself, but don't say.

"If anything, it would be nice to have some experience before I start dating again," I tell Elle. "Because I do want to date. Finley is still young enough to not know what happens between a man and a woman when they're dating, and I won't have to introduce him to anyone unless it starts to get serious. Right?"

"Right," Elle agrees. "He's the perfect age that you can trust a sitter to stay with him for a few hours while you do some adulting. There's no worry about him getting attached to any man you're seeing until you're ready to introduce them. Well, other than Christian. When do you plan to tell Finley that he's his father?"

"I don't know. I told Christian that I want him to prove to me that he could be a dependable, responsible, father-figure this summer before I tell Finley. Honestly, I'm not sure if that will be long enough for me to trust him."

"Well, one way to make sure that things stay casual with Christian, and to see how he handles being a father, is to ask him to stay with Finley while you go out for a few hours."

"Oh. You think I should ask Christian to babysit while I'm on a date?"

"Why not?"

"I can't...Christian and I can't do what we did tonight if I'm dating other people."

"Why not?" Elle asks again. "Unless you want to ensure that he's not seeing anyone else either..."

I don't like the idea of Christian fooling around with another woman when he leaves my bed. I don't like that idea at all.

"You should definitely mention that condition to Christian then, since he requires monogamy to be spelled out in no uncertain terms."

"And if he doesn't want to be monogamous with me while we have fun this summer?"

"Then you'll have to decide if it's worth it or not to keep at it."

"I'll bring it up tomorrow," I agree. "Before we lay another hand on each other."

"I'm happy for you, Maya. Whether you and Christian are

hands on or off, tonight means that you're getting back out there after nearly five years of being single. That's a good thing. You deserve to finally have some fun, with Christian or someone else. Lots of someone elses, if you prefer."

"That's not going to happen. I haven't been asked out but maybe twice since Finley was born. Only one knew about him and was still willing to date a single mother. I turned both down, though."

"Men know when a woman is interested in getting out there or if she wants to be left alone. When you decide you're ready to see what happens, guys will be lining up out the door for a chance to date you."

"I seriously doubt that," I tell her with a snort, even though her enthusiasm puts a bigger smile on my face. "Most men aren't going to want to fool around with an inexperienced mother." I guess that's one good thing about Christian. Since we share a son, he knows that it's a packaged deal. Not that he would want to buy the entire package when he's still so busy sampling so many others.

"You're smart and beautiful in addition to being a great mother," Elle says. "If a man can't handle that, then it's their loss, not yours."

"Thanks for the pep talk, Elle."

"Anytime you need a girl talk, I'm here. I don't mind the nitty-gritty details either, even if he's my ex. Christian never really felt like mine the entire time we dated. I think that was the problem, why deep down I knew it wouldn't ever work between us. With Preston, though, he's everything to me and has never made me feel like he could walk away and never look back."

"Yeah, there's no freaking way my brother would walk

away from you," I assure her. "His anger might try to get in the way sometimes, but you hold his heart in the palm of your hands."

That's what I want someday, too. Someone who I know I can trust to never hurt me, to never walk away.

And since Christian has already done that to me once, why in the world would I think he wouldn't do it again?

10

Christian

"So...about last night," Maya finally says while we're cleaning up dinner dishes. My pants tighten just at the mention of the night before. I've been hoping for a repeat all day and waiting for her to bring it up, even though my palms are sweating anxiously.

"What about it?" I ask, trying to focus on rinsing the salad bowl in my hands and not look too eager.

"This is just physical between us, right? It doesn't mean anything?"

"Right. Yeah," I agree with a nod, since that seems to be what Maya wants me to say.

"And have you, are you going to be physical with just me, or are you hooking up with random women when you leave here?"

Turning off the faucet, I grab a towel to dry my hands

before facing Maya. "No, baby. I haven't been with anyone when I leave you and Finley. I'm not planning on it either. I stopped sleeping around when Elle and Preston messed me up with their ploy. Before that, the women, I was just trying to move on, and that was the only way I knew to do it, you know?"

"Uh-huh," Maya says, giving me a look that says she doesn't know and that she thinks I sound like a complete jackass.

"I'm not…I don't want anyone but you," I tell her as I take her hand, the only contact I'm willing to risk trying while Finley is still awake but getting ready for bed. "Do you want to know what I do at night after I leave here?"

She shrugs, but her pretty brown eyes are filled with curiosity.

"I look at the photos and videos you gave me."

"Yeah, sure."

"I do! Since I didn't bring my laptop, I went and bought a new one the night you gave me the flash drive just so I could look through them all. So, no, I'm not screwing around with anyone in the present or thinking about doing so in the future. Every night I'm stuck in the past, looking back at everything I missed."

Maya's eyes get a little misty, but she doesn't say anything sarcastic, which is a win for me.

"You didn't have, like, one photo of you when you were pregnant on the flash drive."

"I didn't want any memories of when I was ten times bigger than normal all over," she replies.

"Well, I would've liked to see you then. I bet you were ten times more gorgeous."

She playfully slaps at my chest. "You think you're so smooth…"

"Seriously, Maya," I tell her when I seize her other hand in mine. "If you need me to sleepover here in Preston's room at night to prove to you that I'm not sleeping around with anyone else, then I will. I would love to be here with you and Finley than be alone in my hotel room."

"That's not necessary. I doubt we would get much sleep if you stayed here," she says, making me groan at the thought of an entire night in bed with her. "I just wanted to make sure we're on the same page. At the end of the summer, or whenever you leave to go back home, this is over, right?"

"Right," I agree. Unless I can convince her to move to Greensboro.

Something like disappointment fills her eyes, making me want to take back my reply and try again.

But then Finley is barreling into the kitchen in his dinosaur pajamas with a giant shark book in his hands. "Christian, will you read me a story tonight?"

"Absolutely, buddy," I tell him. "Go get comfy and I'll be right there as soon as I finish helping Mommy clean the kitchen."

"I could read you a story–" Maya starts before Finley takes off running without another word. "It's like I'm invisible to him now that you're here," Maya remarks with a smile.

"Why don't you go take a long, relaxing bath while I get him tucked in, and then I'll join you?" I suggest as I tug her closer to me.

Maya rests her palm on my shoulder and shakes her head. "A bath sounds nice, but clothes stay on. For now."

"Fine," I agree, giving her a quick peck on the lips while the coast is clear. "But just remember that it's impossible for me to kiss certain parts of your sexy body if clothes are in the way."

With that parting comment, I leave her to take out the trash and then go read a bedtime story to my son.

Maya

My bath is anything but relaxing since I can't stop thinking about what's going to happen once Christian gets Finley to sleep.

Last night was so hot and unexpected. What if tonight's anticipation leads to a letdown?

Maybe that would be for the best. If things are awkward with Christian, then it won't happen again. But it's never been awkward with him.

After I dry off, I lotion up and then choose my sexiest pajamas—thin, pink satin with skimpy spaghetti straps for the top and shorts small enough that they could be panties for the bottoms.

I brush out my hair and leave it down, apply extra deodorant, and then I'm ready. Or as ready as I'll ever be to fool around with Christian Riley.

It helps to know from our talk last night that I didn't do anything wrong our first time. At least, that's what he claims.

Taking a deep breath, I push aside my nerves and open the

bathroom door to find Christian's big body blocking the way into the bedroom.

There's no chance to overthink things when his eyes rake over my top and shorts a second before he attacks me.

Grabbing the back of my neck with one hand, he pulls my mouth up to meet his in a fierce kiss. His other hand roughly grabs my ass, yanking me toward him and up. My legs automatically wrap around Christian's hips. When he presses my back to the wall, his thick erection lines up right against my throbbing core.

Christian groans as he rocks against me, stealing my breath. When his damp lips lower to my neck, he says, "Let me taste you tonight. I've wanted to taste you for five years."

"I-I don't know," I stammer, my head spinning already with lust. Clothes should stay on, shouldn't they?

"I'll come in my own hand so fast, you won't even have to touch me."

The idea of seeing Christian getting himself off like he did years ago is hot enough for me to agree to anything, even if I'm freaking out on the inside about the…intimacy of such an act.

Back when we were dating, I went down on Christian at least three times to put off losing my virginity. He offered to return the favor with his fingers or tongue, but I was always too chicken to let him.

Tonight, though, I finally say, "Okay."

"Okay?" Christian repeats, sounding surprised as he lifts his mouth from my shoulder.

"Yes."

The word barely leaves my lips before he carries me over to lay me down on the edge of the bed. Only my head and back are on the mattress. I realize why a second later when Christian tugs my shorts and panties down then throws my bare legs over his shoulders putting his face at eye-level with that sensitive part of me.

He swipes a finger down my slit making me squirm. "You're going to need a pillow to scream into."

"I'm sure I'll be fine," I tell him.

"If you say so," he replies with a knowing grin before leaning forward to drag his wet tongue along the same path as his finger.

"Holy shit!" I exclaim as my back arches off the mattress.

"Told you so," Christian says, his warm breath ghosting over my core. He places his big palm on my pelvis to press it down, then starts to lick me so good and fast that I cry out in pleasure. I try to wiggle free, either to get closer or to get away from his tongue, but it's no use with his strong grip holding my hips down.

And after about five seconds, I stop fighting the exquisite sensation. Shoving my fist into my mouth to keep quiet, my hips lift toward Christian's mouth demanding more. His chuckle vibrates over my flesh, making me shiver before the tip of his tongue flicks over the perfect spot.

I'm not sure how it happens but my fingers end up tangled in Christian's hair urging his tongue to go even deeper.

Both hands would've been pushing his head down if I didn't need one in my mouth to muffle my whimpers and moans.

Sound still slips free, getting louder the higher Christian takes me until my toes curl and I finally reach the point of *Ohmygodyesyesyes!*

Good god. Why didn't I let him do this years ago on a daily basis when we were dating?

All I know is that I'll never turn down an offer for oral again. I've never been so wet, so…throbbing and empty.

I'm about to beg Christian to take my damn virginity already when I hear his masculine grunt. Glancing down between my legs, I find him sitting back on his heels, his head thrown back, eyes closed, and teeth clenched tight. The muscles in his biceps strain from the rigorous work he's doing to himself. I lean up on my elbows for a better look of his fist stroking his long hard shaft he at some point freed from his pants, aroused by what he was doing to me with his tongue. When he comes, his release runs over his knuckles. Jesus. The only thing that could make this moment hotter would be if he lost his shirt and the rest of his clothes.

I decide then and there that I hate my stupid 'keep our clothes on' rule as I lay my head back on the mattress.

After giving myself another few seconds to recover, I slide off the bed, scooping up my bottoms and panties on the way to quickly clean up in the bathroom. Once I'm done, I bring a washcloth back to Christian, who is still kneeling on the floor, panting heavily.

"Thanks," he says as he accepts the cloth. His tongue darts out to lick his lips while eyeing my shorts that are back in place. "For the towel and the taste. Guess we're not playing a second or third period after this little intermission?"

"One period was more than enough for tonight," I tell him with a smile as I take a seat on the edge of the bed.

I watch as he cleans himself up, gets to his feet, and fixes up his pants. "Until tomorrow night?"

Nodding, I wet my own lips and tell him, "Tomorrow night, it's my turn for a taste."

"Oh fuck," Christian groans as he throws his head back. "How am I supposed to leave or get any sleep tonight when I'll be counting down the seconds?"

"You'll survive," I assure him. "I'll walk you out." I stand up and head for the bedroom door. If he stays any longer, I have a feeling that things won't end with me going down on him.

At the front door, I unlock it and hold it open for Christian, who wraps an arm around my waist and kisses me good-bye. He kisses me with the enthusiasm of how much he's looking forward to tomorrow in every stroke of his tongue against mine. Even though I can taste myself on his lips and tongue, I'm not embarrassed. How could I be when it's one of the hottest kisses of my life? All of my kisses have come from Christian, and they've all been scorchers.

Finally, he pulls back and places a last soft last kiss on my cheek. "See you tomorrow."

"See you then," I agree breathlessly before he grins and swaggers off to his car, knowing I won't get much sleep tonight either now.

11

Christian

My phone rings as I drive back to the hotel, and I stupidly think it might be Maya calling me to come back to the house and stay the night, even though I know that's a long shot.

I pull into a gas station on the side of the road and finally look at my phone. A missed call from Luke appears on the screen, one of my Bobcats teammates and closest friends off the ice.

"Yo, where the hell have you been all week?" he says when he answers my return call. "I haven't seen you working out and I've been texting you all afternoon without a response."

"Sorry, man," I tell him. "I've been busy. And I'm not in town. I'm actually up in Bethesda."

"Bethesda? Like Maryland?"

"Yeah, it's a suburb near D.C. I drove up here a few days ago."

"What in the world are you doing up there? Reliving our loss?"

"Nah, I haven't even thought much about the championships lately," I admit. Which is a good thing. "I'm up here visiting…someone."

"Someone like who? Who would Christian Riley, a man who fucking loathes driving anywhere, even in his fun, fancy sports cars, be willing to travel that far to see?"

I shove my fingers through my mussed hair, missing Maya's fingers tugging on it. "It's a long story."

"It's a long story?" he echoes me.

"Yes."

"I thought I was your best fucking friend. Give me the long or short version, but I want the deets."

"Fine," I huff, praying I'm not making a mistake by talking about any of this. "Can you keep a few secrets?"

"Can I keep a few secrets? I know you didn't just ask me that, asshole."

"Right. Sorry. I'm not trying to be a dick, but this isn't just my secret," I explain to him.

"Okay?"

"Well, I just recently, like during the playoffs actually, found out that I have a son."

There's a long moment of silence on the other line. "Aw, fuck, man. Some girl got you thinking you're her baby daddy?"

"No, it's not like that. He's definitely my son," I assure him, even though I haven't had a DNA test. "His name is Finley, and he's about to turn five."

"Five weeks old?"

"No, five *years* old."

"Goddamn. So why are you just finding out about him now?"

"You know how Preston Lawrence kept trying to murder me on the ice every game?"

"That's one scary ass dude," Luke remarks.

"He is, and he used to be my best friend when we were playing in the minor leagues together. Then I started dating his sister Maya and it ended badly. I knew she was pregnant, but didn't think she would keep the baby since she was nineteen and just started college. I thought that's why Preston hated me, you know, because I did something stupid that hurt her and knocked her up."

"He hated you because she had your kid?"

"Yeah, she had my kid and her and Preston have been raising him. Maya and Finley both lived with Preston until he recently moved to Greensboro."

"I heard the news. Couldn't believe Lawrence was actually coming to play with us."

"Well, he is."

"And you're fine with having him try to kill you from the bench?"

"No, it's not going to be like that anymore. At least I hope not. We're good now that he finally told me the truth, and I told him Maya dumped me way back when. Maya wasn't too happy about him spilling shit to me without telling her, but we're figuring things out…"

"So, you're up in Bethesda, figuring things out with your baby mama and your son?"

"Pretty much. I'm spending time with Finley all week,

getting to know him. But he still doesn't know that I'm his father."

"Why not?"

"I've got to prove I can be reliable and a good role model before Maya will tell him."

Luke makes a grumbling sound of protest.

"What?" I ask him. "She's not wrong. I up and left her… more than once. And I've slept with a lot of women, very publicly. There's no reason she should just take my word that I can be a good father to Finley."

"I don't know, man. He's your kid. *Your. Kid.* I would've been furious if one of my ex's kept my son from me for all those years, refusing to tell my kid the truth."

"Maya will tell Finley, eventually. I can be patient with this, even if I fucking hate it."

"Let me guess—your easy agreement is all thanks to the fact that you're coughing up lots of hotshot hockey player cash?"

"God no. It's nothing like that. She hasn't asked me for a dime since she has Preston."

"Then what is it? You aren't still fawning over her after all this time, are you?"

"I loved her," I tell him. "And I messed it all up. She ended things weeks before the pregnancy. So, this summer isn't just about getting to know Finley. I also want Maya to trust me enough to give me another chance with her."

"And you've just forgiven her for keeping him from you this long?"

"What choice do I have? I don't blame her. She didn't want me coming and going out of his life and upsetting him. He's a sweet kid. Innocent in all this, you know? And if things work out, I'm hoping she'll move to Greensboro before school starts in the fall. Mostly to be close to her brother, who helped raise Finley, but also so I can see them more often."

"Sounds like you've got your hands full."

"I guess I do. I'm sorry I've been MIA."

"How long are you going to be up there groveling in Maryland?" Luke asks.

"However long it takes," I admit.

"Well, good luck. I'm here if you need to talk. But just remember that you have every right to see your son whenever the hell you want."

"I'm not going to take Maya to court over custody. He belongs with her. She's a good mother and all he's ever known."

"You should have a chance to be a good father to him too, though, not just on her timeline."

"I'm getting there. And we've been closer lately."

"How close?"

"We're not sleeping together, like at night or any other way. But we have been fooling around the past two nights, which has been so damn good."

"And you're ready and willing to give up all other women for this one?"

"Yeah, I am. I would have years ago if she hadn't ended things."

"Well, good for you, man. I hope she's worth it. I just hate that I'm losing my wingman this summer."

"You'll be fine with Tyler and Jason as backup wingmen," I assure him.

"Yeah, yeah. I'll let you go handle your shit. Call me when you're back in town so we can get in some training together."

"Will do," I easily agree before ending the call.

While I wish my best friend was a little more understanding about the situation, it also helps to have an outside opinion about Finley and Maya.

I guess I'm not wrong to have been angry at her for keeping him from me.

At the same time, nothing good will come from me holding on to that anger. Not when I want to prove to her that I can be a good father to Finley and a good man for her.

It's my fault Maya didn't call me when I up and left town and she decided not to end the pregnancy, and when she was in labor, I was out partying with friends. That's why I know that I don't really have anyone but myself to blame for missing out on the first years of my son's life.

All I know is that I won't miss out on anything else with him ever again.

12

Maya

There are no decent job prospects for me within a sixty-mile radius. Not that I would actually drive an hour for a minimum wage job. Even if I wanted to, there's no opportunity that I'm qualified for. The only two potential options are cleaning hotel rooms or working the cash register at a retail store. Both of which have long hours, which would prevent me from picking Finley up from school, few if any benefits, and wouldn't pay enough for me to buy groceries for the month.

Still, despite my lack of education and experience, I decide to fill out the applications online for a few other positions while Christian is outside playing with Finley.

The one job that caught my interest and had a flexible schedule and benefits was the activities director at a senior center. I bet I could even bring Finley in with me in the afternoons or on weekends. The elderly love having cute little visitors. While they want at least a year of experience, they only require a high school diploma rather than a B.A. which I never earned.

Since I also need a few references, I send a quick text message to two of the moms in the neighborhood and then one to Elle.

Elle's response comes back first.

"Of course I'll give you a glowing recommendation! Give Finley my love. I'll call you tonight when I get home from work!"

I've just put my phone down on the coffee table and picked the laptop back up to enter Elle's name and address when the back door opens and closes.

A second later, I hear the hallway bathroom door slam shut.

Christian is chuckling before he steps into the living room wearing nothing but boardshorts. My jaw literally drops. Good lord, his rock-hard abs are delicious and he's so damn tan despite spending most of the year in an arena on ice. He looks more like a surfer than a hockey player.

Seeing me staring at him, he says, "Finley's taking a quick potty break."

"Oh, right," I agree, wondering if letting them play in the sprinkler and slip and slide today was a good idea or if I was an idiot for not joining them. "Y-you should both grab some water while you're inside too," I tell him as I watch the droplets of water trickle down his chest and stomach toward the waistband. "Help yourself to anything in the kitchen. Finley knows where the glasses are in the cabinet. Maybe I could get you a towel…"

Glancing down at his bare chest, Christian says, "Shit. I mean, shoot, I'm dripping all over the floor."

Putting the laptop aside, I hurry to the hall closet and return with two towels. "Here you go."

"Thanks," he replies as he begins drying off right there in the living room. Nodding to my computer that's back in my lap, he says, "Whatcha working on?"

"I'm trying, unsuccessfully, to find a job," I reply.

"Not having any luck?"

"Not really. There are a few positions that I would love to get but probably have no chance of even landing an interview. Which leaves me with few choices since I haven't done anything my entire life except one semester of college before I dropped out and nearly six years of being pregnant and raising a child. Neither is going to be very impressive to a potential employer."

"I'm impressed," Christian says when he takes a seat on the coffee table in front of me. "You were really young and had no experience with kids before you had Finley. He turned out great, so I think that's a pretty big accomplishment."

"Thank you," I say, genuinely warmed by his compliment even if I know he's only saying it to try to get me out of my panties again tonight. Not that he needs to try very hard... "Still, there are tons of women who have done the same thing. Being a mother doesn't gain you any credit career-wise. If anything, I don't want any future employers to even know that I'm a mom."

Christian's blond brow furrows. "Why not?"

"Because single mothers have to miss a lot of work when their kids are sick or have school events. It makes us look like we're less dependable. Oh, and god forbid we get pregnant again while working for a company. That would require time off for doctor appointments then maternity leave. If they hire a man instead of a woman, they know they can avoid all of that."

"That sucks."

"That it does," I agree.

"Well, if you need any references or whatever, feel free to put me down."

"Yeah, right," I snort. "I bet managers would think I'm full of shit if I put down that the oh-so-famous hockey player Christian Riley sings my praises."

"Fine. But the offer still stands."

"Thanks," I tell him. "Between neighbors and Elle, I think I'll have three."

Christian nods and then asks, "So, you and Elle are good friends?"

"She's hard not to love."

"True," he replies with a smile that quickly falls. "Not that I loved her. I mean, maybe I thought I did, but she was just different from the puck bunnies."

"It's fine if you loved her, Christian," I assure him.

"I didn't. I did care for her, though. And I regret how I ended things."

"If you asked Elle now, she would probably thank you for dumping her," I remark. "If you hadn't, she wouldn't have met Preston, and they wouldn't be madly in love."

"I'm glad things worked out for them, not just as a couple, but with Preston moving to Greensboro. I guess it would've been hard for Elle to leave her shop."

"Yeah, it's for the best. Even though I miss him."

"Luckily for you, I know where to find him," he says with a grin. "All it takes is packing up a few boxes…"

"A few boxes!" I exclaim with a shudder. "Do you see all this stuff, all of our furniture, the toys Finley has accumulated thanks to being spoiled by Uncle Preston? It would take no less than half a dozen movers and more than two tractor-trailers to haul all this down to North Carolina."

"It's a price I'm willing to pay," Christian says, his voice sincere just before Finley comes running into the living room and grabs his arm to pull him to his feet.

"I'm ready to go back outside!"

"Hold on a second, buddy," I tell him. "Did you flush and wash your hands?"

Rolling his eyes, his cheeks redden in embarrassment, like how dare I ask such a thing in front of hot shot athlete Christian Riley before he huffs, "Yes, Mommy."

"Good. Now, even though you're playing in water keeping cool, you still need to hydrate and grab a snack before you go back out in the heat."

"Fine," he groans as if I've asked him to give up his entire Lego collection.

"And make sure you check with Christian before assuming that he wants to play out in the heat all day with you!"

"I'm getting some good training in," the hockey star replies with a widening grin. "We're playing slip and slide backyard hockey. It's almost like skating except you fall down more."

"I don't even want to know," I mutter with a shake of my head. "Just don't let him break any bones. And let me know if you need helping making a snack."

"I can handle making a snack, Maya," Christian says tightly

right before Finley runs off to the kitchen. And in his now steely gaze, I know exactly what he's thinking, what he'll probably want to talk about tonight—When am I going to tell Finley that he's his father and not just a famous friend who comes to play with him?

And the answer is, I have no freaking idea.

Once that cat is out of the bag, it's never going back inside.

The only thing worse than having an absentee father is having to constantly see him on television playing hockey, unable to avoid his fame.

~

Christian

Later that night, I refuse to let Maya go down on me, waiting until after she comes on my tongue twice before I broach the subject she's been avoiding.

Lying on my side next to her in nothing but my boxer briefs, I run a slow finger down her chest, right between the cups of her bra she kept on while we fooled around. I didn't object when she tugged off my shirt and yanked down my shorts, even though she still refuses to get completely naked with me, which is so damn frustrating. That frustration is why I find myself saying to her, "So…I think things are going well with Finley, don't you?"

"Uh-huh," she replies, her eyes still hazy with pleasure.

"Do you think we could maybe talk to him, tell him the truth soon?"

Maya blinks at me and that haze completely disappears, making me wish I hadn't opened my mouth. "It's too soon."

"Too soon? Then when? By the end of the summer, at least, right?"

"I don't know," she replies softly, her eyes avoiding mine.

Cupping the side of her face, I tilt it toward mine so she has to look at me. "Baby, it's killing me that he doesn't know the truth. Do you have any idea how badly I want to hear him call me 'dad' or 'daddy'? I want that more than a championship trophy, Maya."

"I know, Christian. I can see how hard you're trying," she replies while stroking her fingertips over my several days' worth of scruff. I usually forget to shave or decide to skip it every morning since I'm in such a hurry to come over here.

Turning to place a kiss on her palm, I ask, "How about on his birthday? It's the first one I'll get to spend with him. Let me tell him then."

Maya looks away and swallows so hard that I know exactly what's coming—a denial.

"It was hard when Preston left. It's going to be just as tough on him when you go back to Greensboro..."

"I'm going to have to leave either way, though, whether he knows I'm his father or not. What difference does it make?"

"I don't know," she says with a sigh as she sits up on her elbows. "I can't explain it. There's just this ache in my chest at the thought of telling him and then having you turn around and leave."

"So, you're not going to tell him at the end of the summer?"

Biting her bottom lip, she finally says what I've known all

along. "I haven't decided yet. He's going to miss you so much as it is…"

As much as I hate leaving, I need some space. I need to get out of this house, this goddamn bedroom that's felt like heaven the past few days, before I lash out and say something I regret.

"You're leaving? I haven't…it was supposed to be your turn tonight."

"I forfeit," I reply as I pull on my athletic shorts and grab my shirt from the floor.

"Christian…"

Once I slip on my shirt, I turn back to face her. Maya's sitting on the edge of the bed, her pajamas already covering her up. "I know you want to protect him. I already feel that same need to keep him safe from…everything in the world. But you know that I'm sticking around, that just because I may live in another state, that doesn't mean I'm going to disappear from his life."

"Finley won't understand the distance during the hockey season."

"There's an easy way to solve that problem, too."

"I'm not moving to Greensboro to keep leeching off my brother! Him and Elle deserve their privacy, and I can't afford a place of my own…"

"You and Finley could move in with me. My huge penthouse apartment has two bedrooms."

Maya shakes her head. "You don't want that, Christian. Not really. Being a father is a huge responsibility. And we are not even a couple."

"We could be."

"We agreed that this was just physical between us, during the summer."

"Why can't it be just physical in Greensboro?"

"Living together is not just physical!" she huffs.

"Fine, I want more, Maya," I blurt out. "I want to be with you. I want you to be mine in every damn way."

She shakes her head. "That's not…I'm sorry, Christian, but I can't."

While I may not be the sharpest skate on the ice, even I'm able to figure out that Maya's refusal to tell Finley I'm his father isn't about whether she thinks I'll hurt him. Her refusal to let me be a bigger part of his life is all because she's scared that I'm going to hurt *her* again.

Maya doesn't fucking trust me not to screw around on her, even though my nights are spent either here with her or alone in my hotel room looking at photos of my son's life from the outside.

Since I know there's nothing I can say to change her opinion, I turn around and leave.

It's frustrating as hell, but I'm not going to give up. It'll take time, more than a single summer together, but I'm never giving up on her, on us, again.

13

Maya

"I just talked to Preston," Christian says without preamble when he shows up at the house the next morning.

"Okay?"

There's a new tension between us after our fight last night. Our argument? I'm not sure what it was exactly. Christian wants to tell Finley he's his father, and he said he wanted more, that he wants to be with me.

But I'm not ready to take either of those steps, especially the first, which makes the second impossible.

Oh my god. Did Christian call Preston about *us* because I haven't mentioned to Preston that we were fooling around!

"Everything's all set for Finley's birthday party," he finally explains.

"Oh, okay," I sigh in relief, glad he's not dragging my overprotective brother into this already confusing situation. "Preston was able to rent the Warhawks arena?"

"He was, but even with his pull, they still asked for a small fee."

"A small fee?" I have a feeling that the pro hockey boys and I have different definitions of small when it comes to money. "How much?"

"Five grand."

"Five thousand dollars?" I exclaim.

"I'll take care of it," Christian says since, just as I expected, five thousand dollars is like fifty bucks to him.

"Are you sure? Finley doesn't even know we were going to have it there. We could just have it in the backyard..."

"We're having his party at the arena," he replies sternly. "This is the first year I'm going to get to celebrate my son's birthday with him. Finley will go nuts to get out on the ice with his friends, and I want to help. If you need like plates or decorations or whatever, I want to pay for those things too."

"You don't have to do that, Christian..."

"It's the least I can do after missing his first four birthdays," he snaps.

"That-that wasn't entirely my fault."

He stares at me like he wants to argue that it was up to me to tell him he had a son and not him to guess.

"I'm sorry," I tell him honestly.

Taking a deep breath, he says, "It's...fine, water under the ice," and even flashes me a half-smile. "So, what do you say? Will you let me pay for this one?"

"I don't need your money."

"I think you meant that you don't *want* my money. But you

do need it, Maya. What's the difference in accepting Preston's help but not mine?"

"I…I don't know. Let me just have time to think about it."

"The clock is ticking. Let me make the arrangements to secure the arena for us. Let's go with what we both know is Finley's first choice. We'll give him a birthday party he'll never forget, including a few surprise guests…"

Oh, I love and hate the way he's using *we* like we're a team now. Still, I'm hesitant to let him help with the planning or financially.

"What? What's that frown about? I just want to help."

"I know that, I do. It's just…letting you help makes me feel like I'll owe you or something."

"You don't owe me. I want to do this for Finley. Please?"

"Fine," I cave, since it's impossible to refuse the man anything when he gives me puppy dog eyes.

That's probably how I got pregnant. Christian was so charismatic and was being so patient, waiting for me to be ready to sleep with him. When he told me, begged me actually, that he wanted to book us the hotel room just so he could hold me all night, I agreed, knowing exactly what would happen. I wanted the same thing, and the dorm and Preston's apartment weren't ideal for sleepovers. I'd hoped it would happen, even though I was so nervous, I nearly puked that afternoon before he picked me up.

"Thank you," Christian says as he leans in to press a kiss to my lips.

"Whoa!" I press my palms to his chest to push him away. "You can't do that…"

"You mean in broad daylight?"

"I mean where Finley could see us and get confused."

"Right. Sorry. I'm just…happy," he says with a grin. "I'll go make some calls."

"Thank you," I tell him. When he turns to leave, I finally concede, "Finley will love a hockey party."

Glancing over his shoulder, his smile widens with pride. "I know he will."

He does know. He's beginning to get to know his son's likes and dislikes. I'm not sure why that scares me so much. Maybe because Christian's proving that he's going to stick around, to step up and be a father to Finley, which means I'll have to figure out how to stop pining for him before my heart gets crushed again and we ruin everything.

The next week flies by as Christian and I stay busy preparing for Finley's party. He even came shopping with me for supplies while Finley had a play date with his neighborhood friend.

While Christian still stays over for an hour or so each night after we put Finley to bed, there's a noticeable difference to our fooling around. At first Christian went slow, eased into things, was gentle. After our fight, though, we don't talk, there's no joking around. There's just plenty of savage kisses, multiple orgasms, and then he leaves me satisfied but still longing for more.

More of him physically and emotionally.

Which I hate.

I know he's only doing exactly what I asked him to do, so I can't complain.

All I know is that I've started looking forward to seeing

him every day, spending time alone together at night, even though I know it's not real. In a few weeks, Christian will be headed back to North Carolina, back to the fame and puck bunnies. Finley and I will barely talk to him and rarely see him except on television.

There's nothing I can do to change what's coming. Even if I up and moved Finley to Greensboro, during the hockey season, I know what to expect from how often Preston is at practice or traveling with the team.

Still, it's so frustrating.

That's why I'm glad that Preston and Elle are coming to spend a few days with us for Finley's birthday. They'll create a nice buffer zone between me and Christian.

I'm so excited to see two of my favorite people in the world that I hurry out to their car as soon as they pull up in the driveway to hug them.

"You made it!" I say when I throw my arms around Preston's neck first. "Thank you so much for getting the Warhawks to let us have the party in the arena."

"Wish I had thought of it, but Christian deserves all the props for pulling this off," my brother replies as we pull apart.

"Yes, but you were the one who had to make calls and ask for favors."

"Anything for Finley," he says with a grin.

Turning from him to embrace Elle, I take her hands when we break apart to examine them with a scoff. "No ring yet?"

Elle laughs and slips her hands from mine. "Don't rush us! It hasn't really been that long since we started dating. You know, like for real dating."

"Time doesn't matter. You two are definitely getting

hitched. I can't wait to help you plan the wedding!" Wincing, I add, "That is, if you want or need my help."

"Of course I want your help! If that day ever comes," she adds quietly.

"It will," I assure her.

"So, where's the birthday boy?" Preston asks. "I can't believe he's already turning five and about to start school."

"Same," I agree. "And he's around back playing with Christian."

"So, this is Christian's SUV?" Elle asks, eyeing the black luxury vehicle suspiciously.

"Uh-huh. Why?"

"I guess I can't believe he bought something other than a sports car for once," she remarks.

It finally dawns on me that Christian must have bought the vehicle since he's been in town, as he arrived in a flashy little car. He probably knew that I would never let him take our son anywhere in a freaking speedster. For one, some of them don't have a back seat, and two, they're too dangerous to be driving around with a four-year-old passenger. Five-year-old tomorrow.

I guess it was sweet of Christian to make the concession and sell the car he drove up here in to buy an SUV.

Not that Christian doesn't have plenty of money to spend, but he didn't have to go to all that trouble.

He did it because he cares about Finley and wants to be a bigger part of his life.

I know he wants to tell our son the truth, to finally hear Finley call him Daddy. But I'm so scared about what comes next.

Will Finley hate me for keeping him from his father his

entire life? There's no way he can understand at his age why I did what I did.

Sometimes I'm not sure why I didn't reach out to Christian sooner.

It's just that he hurt me so much and then went to play for the pros. Before he left, I did tell him I was pregnant, and his first reaction sounded like he expected me to end it, even going so far as to send me money through a cash app.

I thought his reaction meant he didn't want to be a father, not when he was hoping to start his pro career.

Then, seeing him date so many women, I couldn't let my son be a part of *that* life. I want Finley to grow up respecting women, not use them for sex.

But I also, selfishly, wasn't sure if I could handle Christian loving our son but not me.

Christian

Once Preston and Elle show up, I'm old news to Finley. Since I'm so competitive, I'm actually a little jealous of seeing how much Finley loves seeing his uncle and playing with him. Especially while he doesn't even know that I'm his father.

I shove the bitterness down as I search the backyard for Maya. She's standing off to the side of the porch from the rest of us, staring at me in her tempting jean shorts and teasing white tank top.

Unlike usual when there's hesitancy, distrust, or occasionally lust in her gaze, at this moment she's looking at me with almost a smile on her face, like she maybe, sort of, wants to let herself like me.

"What's up?" I ask her when I approach, since my presence in our pretend hockey game is no longer required by Finley.

"Nothing," she says.

"Nothing?"

"I'm just…happy," she replies.

"Yeah?"

"Yeah." She nods and then tips her head toward the front of the house. "Did you buy the SUV for Finley?"

"I didn't think you would let me put him in my Porsche or Ferrari. It's also nice to have some room in the trunk to carry shit if I need to."

"Right. Well, thank you for doing that, because you're not wrong. I wouldn't let him ride with you in a sports car."

"See? I'm learning," I tell her with a proud grin. "Slowly but surely, I'll eventually get the hang of this parenting thing."

"You're doing great for such a short amount of time," she admits. The rare compliment from Maya's lips nearly sending me to my knees.

"You really think so?" I ask her softly.

"I do. And you really knocked it out of the park with the hockey party. Every mom I've talked to has told me that their kids can't wait and haven't stopped talking about it."

"Good, I'm glad Finley will get to have the party of the year for the preschoolers."

"Soon to be kindergarteners. Which is hard to believe."

After a few moments of silence, Maya, her eyes on where Elle and Finley are ganging up on Preston as goalie, whispers, "You can't stay over at night while they're visiting."

Well, fuck. Just when I think things are going great between us, Maya calls a timeout. "Why not?" I ask, wanting an explanation. "You expect me to believe that you haven't told Elle about what we do as soon as Finley's asleep every night?"

Maya's lips part, her cheeks turning rosy red. "How did you know I told her?"

Shrugging, I slip my hands into my jeans. "I figure girls talk about that shit."

"Have *you* told anyone?" she asks softly.

I debate whether or not to lie, but figure honesty is always the best policy with Maya. "Just Luke."

"Luke?"

"My best friend and teammate."

"Oh. Okay," she says then goes quiet, as if thinking that over. "Does he know…everything?"

"About you and me? Not the intimate details. About Finley? Yes, he knows everything." When she opens her mouth, I know a protest is coming, so I tell her, "Luke won't tell a soul. I think he hates the media more than Preston because they always try to bring up his shitty past…"

"God, I hope he doesn't tell anyone," Maya says softly.

"He won't. He would never run his mouth about my business to anyone," I reassure her. Then, I can't help adding, "But it would be nice if I didn't have to hide it from everyone…"

"You *want* people to know you're a father?" she asks, turning to face me.

"Absolutely. Why wouldn't I?" I ask her honestly.

"I don't know, Christian. We're not together or married. The media will twist it all and make it sound like it's all just a ploy for me to get your money. I don't want Finley to get dragged into any headlines. That wouldn't be fair to him. He didn't ask to have a hot shot hockey pro for a father."

"Baby, I know I haven't known him very long, but I'm pretty sure our son loves the spotlight. He's a natural at hockey, too. So, I think you should probably prepare yourself for a future where he's making headlines."

"You think so?" she asks, biting her bottom lip.

"Yeah, I do. I started playing when I was years older than him, and he's a natural. Besides, he's got MVP athletic talent on both sides of his family."

"He has always said he wants to be just like Uncle Preston when he grows up," she remarks with a smile.

"I meant you, Mrs. MVP soccer player."

She waves a dismissive hand through the air with a shy smile. "That was nothing."

"It wasn't nothing. You have serious athletic talent, too. They don't hand out MVP awards to everyone in high school. Finley is going to take after both of us. He's a lucky kid."

"You are so full of yourself," Maya says with a widening grin.

Leaning closer, I whisper in her ear, "When are you going to finally let yourself be full of me?"

Shaking her head, she presses her palm to my chest and takes a step back, putting distance between us. "We can't. We shouldn't. Not yet."

"I'm fine with going slow, but there's no reason for us to let your visitors keep us apart. They don't have to know. And I bet you would miss my tongue between your legs..."

"Fine. I'll think about it," Maya mutters with a smile and roll of her eyes, which I accept as a win.

15

Christian

The birthday party the next day turned out even better than I had hoped.

Thanks to Preston's connections with the Warhawks, he was able to get the bird mascot to attend, along with five current players. Only one is a starter, but none of the kids or their parents seem to care. They're all from a championship winning team.

Seeing Finley having fun laughing with his friends, soaking up being the center of attention and showing off his skills to the other kids, I'm filled with more pride than scoring any goals or winning any games.

Maya and I may not have ever planned to get pregnant, but there's no doubt we created an amazing little guy together. I'm so glad that I finally get to be a part of his life, even if all the time I missed out with him still stings when I look at the photos and videos. Seeing clips of the special moments in Finley's life and him celebrating holidays isn't the same as being there with him.

God, I wanted to tell Finley this morning I was his dad when I gave him his present. He went nuts over the tabletop game with rods like foosball, but with plastic hockey players instead.

My son deserves to know the truth about who I am, and I'm not sure how much longer I can wait, despite Maya's lingering concerns.

"Christian freaking Riley?" Spencer Williams, the Warhawks' backup goalie drawls when he skates up to the goal I'm tending without any pads on. I've only been blocking about a quarter of the kids' shots, letting everyone get a puck in at least once since that shit is good for their confidence at this age. "What the hell are you doing up here at a kid's party in the middle of the summer? Did you lose a bet to Preston or something?"

"No, I didn't lose a bet," I tell him with a grin. I should tell them that I'm just here as a favor, but for some reason, I find myself blurting out, "Actually, I'm the birthday boy's father."

Spencer's jaw falls open comically. "No shit? Hell, now it makes sense why Preston gave you all those beatdowns. I said hello to his sister, and he almost decked me one time."

His outburst makes me wince, worried someone will over-hear. I sort of regret my impulsive decision now. Maya will kill me if the truth gets out before she's ready. "I had no idea until recently," I explain to him. "And, um, Finley doesn't know yet. Neither does the media. So, if you could keep it quiet…"

"I won't say a word," he promises. "Trust me, I don't want to give Preston any reason to kick *my* ass."

"Good," I tell him, letting out a relieved sigh that his fear of Preston, his former teammate, will hopefully keep his mouth shut.

"You and Preston's sister aren't together now, are you?"

"No, we're not together," I admit honestly with a heavy sigh. Maya sadly didn't change her mind about no visiting while Preston and Elle are there. Which means she has no intention of telling Preston, which tells me that fooling around with me is just a little fun for her during the summer.

I let another puck sail past me and into the goal, causing the kids to scream in celebration of their friend's score. To Spencer, I say, "Thanks for coming out today. This is a party none of the kids will ever forget, especially Finley."

"Honestly, Preston wouldn't really take no for an answer, but I don't mind. The off-season gets boring as shit."

"True enough," I agree, since the off-season is usually the loneliest time of the year for me. There are no fans screaming my name, no microphones or cameras being shoved in my face, and no daily practices to keep up with the guys.

"I'll take over goalie duty for you now if you want?" Spencer offers.

"Thanks, man. I know it goes against your goalie instincts, but could you try to let a few pucks slip past you today?"

"Will do, even if I'll have nightmares about those damn goals tonight," he replies with a shudder that makes me chuckle.

Maya

I've just finished getting all the kids photos taken with the mascot near the end of the party when a tall, lean man skates over to me in massive pads, a goalie. He towers over me even though I put on skates for the party too.

"Hey, you're Maya, right? Preston's sister?" he asks. Removing his helmet, his short, brown hair is a little sweaty, and his intelligent eyes seem to lock onto mine with a surprising intensity. I blink, momentarily caught off guard by the random man's sudden attention.

"Yes. Hey. It's Spencer, right?" I manage to say, trying not to sound like a complete idiot.

A small smile tugs at the corners of his lips. "I wasn't sure if you'd remember me."

"Of course I remember you. My brother hasn't been gone from the Warhawks but a few weeks," I say, trying to recover from the surprise of his attention.

He laughs softly, scratching the back of his neck. "Yeah, I know, but I think you and I only met once, briefly, at a family cookout, before he ran me off."

"That sounds like my brother." Nodding my head over to where he's helping Elle clean up the leftover cake, I tell him, "He's not quite as overprotective as he used to be."

"I don't blame him. He's probably spent his whole life beating back guys from you with his hockey stick."

With a laugh, I tell him, "Not really. But he's been a good big brother."

There's a brief silence as we stand there, awkwardly

smiling at each other. It's strange talking to a guy like this, to have a hot, professional athlete looking at me with interest, flirting with me. Well, someone other than Christian Riley. I do remember meeting Spencer before, but only that he was nice before Preston gave him a look that had him scurrying away.

Finley, ever the curious one, comes over and interrupts the silence by tugging on the side of my Warhawks jersey with Preston's number and name on it, matching Finley's smaller one. "Mommy, what's this goalie's name?"

"This is Spencer Williams. He plays for the Warhawks and knows Uncle Preston," I say, smiling down at Finley before turning back to Spencer.

"Backup goalie for the time being," he amends.

"Spencer, this is my son, Finley," I say, knowing it'll likely send him skating away faster than an evil look from my brother.

But Spencer doesn't even flinch. He just smiles and holds out his hand to Finley, "Nice to meet you, birthday boy."

"Thanks for coming to my party. Can I have one of your jerseys?" he asks, making me wince and Spencer cough out a laugh.

"Finley! You can't just ask every hockey player you meet for a jersey!"

"Why not?" my son looks up and asks me.

"Because it puts the players on the spot," I tell him. Then to Spencer, "I'm so sorry. He's a huge hockey fan like his uncle, obviously. And he gets carried away."

"It's no problem. I would love to get you one of my jerseys. Want me to sign it too?"

"Hell yes!" my son exclaims.

"Finley!"

"Oops. I meant, heck."

"Right," I mutter with a sigh.

"How about I get your mom's number and set up a time to get you that jersey? Size youth medium okay to give him some growing room?" Spencer asks me.

"That would be great. Thank you."

"Yes!" Finley cheers before he skates off, no doubt to go tell his friends the good news.

The next thing I know, the hockey player is asking for my phone, putting his number in it, and handing it back to me. His own device buzzes an instant later, like he sent himself a message from it.

"I'll give you a call soon. Maybe we can have dinner too?"

"Dinner?" I repeat in surprise.

"Yeah, like a date? I asked Christian and he said you two aren't together now. Are you seeing anyone?"

"Ah, no, I guess I'm not seeing anyone," I reply, disappointed that Christian told Spencer we're not a couple, even if we're not. I seek him out on the ice, finding him talking to some of the Warhawk players.

"So, how about dinner, just you and me, or with Finley, too. I don't mind either way."

"Oh." He doesn't mind if I bring my son along on a date.

"That didn't sound like a promising *oh*."

"Let me think about it?" I ask rather than turn him down flat after his generous offer.

Spencer flashes me a smile and nods. Then, he clears his throat and starts to skate away backward. "Think about it as long as you need, Maya. It was nice seeing you again and getting to actually speak more than two words to you this time."

"Right," I say with an answering smile. "And thank you for coming to the party on short notice."

"Of course," he says, grin widening. "I love kids. They're my favorite fans, helping me remember why I do this even though I spend most of my time on the bench, you know?"

"Yes, I do," I agree before he skates off.

The flirtation was nice, but I doubt if I'll ever hear from the goalie again.

16

Christian

I didn't follow Maya and Finley back to the house after the party. Instead, I stayed at the arena and played a pickup game with Preston and the Warhawks.

I'm happy to say that smug ass goalie Spencer Williams only blocked two of my shots, missing five of them.

I was trying to respect Maya's wishes not to stay over once Finley goes to bed while Preston and Elle are in town. But I won't deny that I was relieved when she sent me a text around ten telling me everyone had gone to bed and asking if I wanted to sneak in.

Hell yes or *heck yes*, was, of course, my instant response before I drove over from the hotel.

And since Maya insisted that we had to keep quiet, I came up with a great solution—keeping both of our mouths busy at the same time.

"That was it. That's…that's the last time we're going to do this," Maya says when she crawls off me. Her words sound like a bunch of gibberish since I'm still soaring high in ecstasy from having her ride my face while she simultaneously went down on me. It was so damn good, almost as good as sex with her would be, just because it felt less intimate, I guess…

When I finally come back down from the high, though, Maya's words sink into my thick skull.

"You mean the last time tonight or that you're not a fan of sixty-nining?" I ask in confusion. "Because it was fan-fucking-tastic for me, baby," I tell her as I spin around so my head is at the foot of the bed with hers. While I'm completely naked, Maya's still wearing her pajama top, despite my protests. I reach out and dip my finger into the center, tugging it down to get a better look at her beautiful bare breasts.

"Not…I didn't mean. Yes, it was great," she stammers. "All of it has been great, but we've let this go on for too long. We need to stop."

"We need to stop? As in, stop getting each other off?"

"Yes."

Arching an eyebrow, I wait for her to give me more of an explanation, but she doesn't. "I thought you said we could keep it up all summer. So why are you now saying that we need to stop?"

"Because I have to move on," Maya huffs as she sits up to grab her pajama bottoms and to pull them back up her legs. Watching her get dressed almost distracts me from hearing her response.

"You have to move on?" I repeat, not touching my clothes yet because I know my nudity distracts her in the same way. Instead, I prop my head up on my bent elbow, hoping she'll be horny enough to forget what we were talking about, because what the actual fuck made her want to stop?

"Would you please quit repeating everything I say and put some clothes on?" Maya crosses her arms over her chest, a signal that she means business tonight.

Sighing, I crawl up to the head of the bed, resting my head back on the pillow with both my hands behind it, since I'm not planning on going anywhere just yet.

"Does this moving on have anything to do with that jackass Spencer Williams giving you his phone number?" I ask.

Her folded arms drop. "How did you…"

"Well, baby, it doesn't take a genius. I saw the two of you talking and him handing you back your phone. Even I'm smart enough to figure out what happened."

I hate the idea of Maya dating any other man, but especially another fucking hockey player. Why is that? Because it means that all her excuses about me not being around because of the busy schedule and not trusting me on the road are personal. She would endure the hectic months of games and practice, even trust a man she barely knows, but not do those things for me?

While I loathe the thought of another man touching her, I tell myself that Maya's too uptight and inexperienced to hop into bed on a first or even fifth date.

That may be my fault, and I hate that I hurt her so badly years ago, but in this circumstance, I'm thrilled she isn't quick to sleep around with guys.

Although, I'm the last person in the world to be encouraging abstinence thanks to my past. Still, I'm glad Maya has only ever been with me. If only she would give me another chance to take her virginity. Because in my mind she's still a virgin, despite the fact our child came through that whole area without my actual penetration.

Shoving her fingers through the front of her hair to push it back, she eventually says, "Finley asked Spencer for one of his jerseys, and he was nice enough to oblige."

Scoffing, I tell her, "Oh, I'm sure that fucker would love to oblige the shit out of you."

"He also said you told him we weren't together."

"We're not, right? You don't even want Preston to know about us."

"Christian…"

"Maya, I don't get it," I say as I sit up in the bed. "I've spent weeks proving to you that I only want you, that you can trust me to be a good role model and father to Finley and to not hurt you. And now the first time some guy comes up to you, not even a fucking starter for the Warhawks I should add, you're ready to bail on me for *him?*"

"I'm not…I'm not bailing on you for anyone else, Christian." There go the crossed arms again. God, it's like talking to a brick wall whenever that shit happens. "This decision has nothing to do with Spencer asking me on a date, either. You're leaving for Greensboro soon. We both know that long distance won't work between us."

Right, because she'll never trust me not to screw around behind her back, even though I've never cheated on her when we were dating, past or present, and I would never do such a thing to her. I've never cheated on *any* woman. Yes, Elle and I had a miscommunication where she assumed we were both more serious than we were when I thought that we were just occasionally hooking up, having fun, with no strings or commitment. The only real relationship I've ever had is with Maya, then and now. Because this is a relationship, whether she wants to admit it or not. And I know there's only one way Maya will ever trust me—if I'm sleeping in the same bed with her every night. That's why I tell her, "It wouldn't be long distance if you and Finley moved to Greensboro and come live with me."

"I-we can't do that!" she exclaims, most likely loud enough for the rest of the house to hear.

"No, you *won't* do that," I amend for her. "And I have no fucking clue why you won't consider moving. Preston's there too. You could live with him. And you would be closer to Elle, who I know you adore. So, tell me what the real problem is here, Maya."

There's a moment of hesitation before she blurts out, "I…I don't think this, you and I, could ever work."

She could've sliced my chest open with the blade of my skate and it would've hurt less than hearing those words from her mouth.

"This? You and me, you don't think we could ever work?" I ask, needing clarification.

"It didn't work before, and back then you weren't even a hotshot hockey player yet."

"I told you I was sorry about bailing that night!"

"Keep your voice down," she warns me as if she wasn't just yelling too.

Groaning, I scrub both of my palms down my face. "I don't know what else I can do, Maya. I apologized back then by text, in voicemails, hell, even in letters."

"There were no letters," she snaps.

"Yes, there were. A bunch of them. I sent them to your dorm."

"Well, I was so upset that I dropped out of school and moved out of the dorm when I found out I was pregnant," she huffs. "But now we're off topic. You and I, it'll be better for Finley if we stop this now while we don't hate each other."

"I could never hate you," I tell her. "Even after you kept my son from me for nearly five fucking years, I didn't hate you. And I don't think you ever hated me, either."

When she doesn't respond, I'm certain that there's no way to win this fight with her tonight. Reluctantly, I slide off the bed and start slowly putting my clothes back on piece by piece. I'm hoping like hell that Maya will change her mind, that this will turn out like her telling me I couldn't stay over while Preston and Elle are here. But she doesn't stop me.

She'll miss me once I leave and possibly even change her mind after a few nights apart.

At least that's what I tell myself before kissing her cheek goodbye and leaving.

17

Maya

I didn't sleep much last night.

How could I after my argument with Christian?

But it doesn't matter that I want him. It's not enough.

When I became a mother, all my decisions began to revolve around my son. I have to do what's best for Finley, no matter what. I can't be selfish and drag out this thing with Christian, knowing it'll likely end badly.

Christian wants to be Finley's father; he's made that perfectly clear this summer, which means he'll always be a part of my life too. I need to be able to look at him, to be near him, without my heart constantly aching for him to be mine.

Heading down to the kitchen before my shower this morning since I doubt Christian will be showing up early, I fix a pot of coffee to try to wake myself up. I need to snap out of this funk I've been in since he walked out the door last night.

I'm on my second cup when Preston comes lumbering into the kitchen, still half asleep.

"Morning," he mumbles.

"Morning," I reply.

Neither of us say anything else until he sits down at the head of the table in what had started to become Christian's seat…

"You okay?" my brother asks.

I shrug, not really wanting to get into it. "Yeah, I'm fine."

"You don't look fine," he presses. "In fact, you look like you're on the verge of tears," he adds, obviously not buying my lie. And I guess I look as bad as I feel. He stares me down with an expression that says he knows something's up, he's not going to let it go, so I better start talking.

"What's going on, Maya?" he asks, then takes a sip of his coffee.

I sigh and rub my temples where a headache is pounding away. I know Preston means well,but if I talk about it right now, I'll probably burst into tears. If my overprotective brother finds out the tears are because of Christian, he'll go flying out the door to beat his ass without even knowing the man didn't do anything wrong. So, I lie. "I'm just… tired."

Preston narrows his eyes, clearly not buying it. "Is this about Christian?"

I stiffen and blink back tears at just the mention of his name, my heart thumping away in my chest. I don't want to talk about this with anyone, but especially not Preston.

I have to clear the emotion from my throat before I can say, "It's not about Christian. Just drop it, okay?"

"So, you just want me and Elle to pretend like we didn't hear the two of you yelling at each other late last night from inside your bedroom?"

"Oh, god." Crossing my arms on the table, I slam my head into them, burying my face. "You heard us?"

"Yes. Thankfully, just the argument and nothing else."

"Ugh," I groan. At least there's that. "Do you think Finley heard?" I mutter without lifting my head.

"Probably not. He could sleep through a train coming through the house."

"Good. That's good." And it's exactly the reason why Christian and I need to end things now, no matter how good physically it might feel to be with him. I don't want my son to grow up hearing arguments, wondering what we're fighting about.

"Maya, come on. As long as it's not about s-e-x, you know you can talk to me about anything. Save the other stuff for Elle, will you?"

"Don't worry. I will never, ever talk to you about s-e-x," I promise him, before finally lifting my head from the table. "Okay, so, for the past few weeks, Christian has been… spending time with me after Finley goes to bed."

Preston cringes and slumps lower in his chair. "What did I just say?"

"I'm not going to go into details. I'm just trying to explain what our argument was about. Last night, I told him it was the last night, that we should stop."

"And he doesn't want to…stop?" he guesses with a wince.

"He doesn't. But it's for the best."

Groaning up at the ceiling, avoiding eye contact with me,

Preston says, "I hope I don't regret asking this, but why is it for the best?"

"Because he's Christian fucking Riley!" I shout, before slapping my palm over my mouth. Here's hoping Finley is still sound asleep. "You know his reputation as well as I do, Preston."

"You're afraid he's going to cheat on you?"

"Yes."

"That's a valid concern. He's got a reputation as a playboy."

"Right," I agree with a nod.

"Did he ever cheat on you before?"

"Not that I know of."

"And has he gone behind your back with anyone this summer?"

"Again, not that I know of."

"So, he's never cheated on you, but you worry he might in the future?"

"Yes. Exactly. I'm not sure if I'll ever fully trust him when he's traveling with the team or living a state away…"

"How do you know other guys you date won't cheat?"

"I don't."

"But you trust strangers more than Christian?"

I consider his question for a moment, then shrug. "Depends on the person and their reputation, but maybe."

"Wow. That is a huge problem."

"I know. That's why I ended things."

"No, Maya. I meant, there are a lot of cheaters in the world, men and women. The odds of you dating someone who messes around behind your back is extremely high."

"Thank you for that happy little assessment."

"What I'm trying to say is that there's no way for you to

know who is a cheater and who isn't until they prove themselves either way."

"Oh."

"The only way to know for sure is to take a chance on someone, give them the benefit of the doubt, then pray they don't hurt you. That plan doesn't just apply to Christian, it applies to all men."

"So, your advice is to let myself keep falling back in love with him until he screws me over and hurts me again, ruining our relationship to the point that we can't tolerate each other for more than ten seconds in front of our son?"

"I didn't say that was my advice. I said you have to decide if the risk is worth taking or not. Apparently, you don't think Christian deserves a chance to prove that he can be faithful."

Shaking my head, I tell him honestly, "I would go crazy wondering about where he's at or who he's with back in Greensboro while I'm here…"

"So why not move to be closer?"

"Ugh, not you too!" I huff. "That was another part of our argument last night. Christian asked me to move in with him."

"Jesus," Preston whispers. "He really must have it bad for you."

"I'm not moving to North Carolina, and Finley and I are definitely not moving in with him," I tell my brother. "He doesn't seem to want to accept my decision."

"That might be my fault," Preston admits with a frown.

"What do you mean?"

"I may have urged him to try to fix things with you so you and Finley would move to Greensboro."

"Why…how could you do that?" I snap at him.

"Because I miss you and Finley! I worry about you two up

here alone. I'm glad Christian has been around during the summer, but once training starts, you'll be alone."

"I don't need a man to come check on me and Finley," I assure him. "But I am going to consider dating…"

"Yeah? So that's another reason you put a stop to things with Christian?"

"Not really, but it doesn't help. At Finley's birthday party, Spencer Williams sort of asked me out."

"Really?" Preston says, his eyes widening in surprise. I nod, then tap my fingernails on my coffee mug, waiting for his barrage of angry curses about how I should stay away from the goalie, but they don't come.

"What? You're not going to tell me to avoid him or go warn him to keep his hands to himself?"

"Nah, Spencer's a good guy."

"Really?"

"Yeah. He's young, about your age. Since he's not a starter, he doesn't have the same ego and shit as the other players. I approve."

"I wasn't asking for your approval, Preston. Although it is infinitely better than your adamant objection."

"You told Christian about Spencer asking you out?" my brother asks.

"Yes."

"How did he react?"

"Not great. He accused me of bailing on him."

"Can you blame him? How would you feel if the roles were reversed and last night he told you he agreed to a date with some mom he met at Finley's party?"

"I didn't agree to go on a date with Spencer. He's going to give Finley a jersey, that's all."

"Uh-huh."

"And I would hate it if Christian was with someone else. That's why ending things is the right decision," I explain. "I'll have to see that man for the rest of my life. It's better to end as friends than to break-up hurt and end up hating each other."

I don't ever want to be as vulnerable as I felt when he left me alone in that hotel room, or left me alone to handle our unexpected pregnancy.

"I need to try to move on, Preston. It's been almost six years now since Christian and I gave dating a try and it failed. He's the only man I've ever been with because I couldn't bear to let him go yet. But I have to give up on a happily ever after for us, for Finley's sake."

"I'm sorry," Preston says quietly. "I hate that things are so complicated between you two."

"Same," I agree as I blink away tears as I finally admit that last night was about finally letting go of him for good.

Preston sets his coffee down on the table, then gets up to come over to my chair. When he wraps me in a tight hug, the dam breaks. I give up trying to keep it all bottled inside.

Burying my face in his chest, I let go of the frustration, the confusion, the fear I've been holding inside. But worst of all, I let go of that tiny little smidgen of hope I still had left for us.

"It's okay," Preston whispers, stroking my hair. "You're going to be okay, Maya."

I sob against him, my whole body shaking. "I hate it," I choke out. "But I don't know what else to do."

Preston doesn't say anything right away, he just holds me, letting me cry. When my sobs finally start to quiet, he pulls back and looks down at me, his expression soft and understanding.

"I wish I could fix it all or give you some wise brotherly advice, but I don't have any in this situation," he says. "You're the only one who can make this decision. I know you'll do what's best for you and Finley. You always do."

I nod, wiping my eyes. He's right. I will always do what's right for Finley. But that doesn't make this any easier.

The truth is, I'm devastated. I already miss Christian being mine for a few hours a night. I still have feelings for him. Maybe I always will. All I know is that it's time for me to finally move on once and for all.

Preston sighs and rubs the back of his neck, clearly thinking about what to say next. "Look, I'm not sure what else I can say to help, but I will say this—everything happens for a reason. I never expected to meet the love of my life in a rival team's parking lot asking for a selfie that turned into a kiss that went viral. Things were complicated at first with Elle. She was nervous about trusting me after having her heart broken, and I didn't see how I could put a relationship before my family and career. But it all worked out in the end."

"You and Elle…that was fate," I tell him rather than point out that he did have to give up his family, Finley and me, to be with her.

"It was definitely fate," he agrees with a smile. "And one day, I know you'll find that sort of love, too. Maybe it's Christian or maybe it's someone else. When it's right, you'll know because you won't be able to live without them."

"I've lived without Christian for nearly six years, so he may not be the one for me."

"I'm not sure if that's entirely true," Preston remarks.

"What do you mean? I didn't even speak to him again until a few weeks ago."

"True, but you've kept a little piece of him close all these years…"

Finley.

At the reminder of our son, I smile, feeling a little lighter. "Thanks, Preston," I say just before I hear the soft knock on the door.

My brother and I both freeze for a second before Finley comes running through the house yelling, "Christian's here!"

I guess I was wrong about one thing—he's here just as early as usual.

"I need to shower and pull myself together. Do you mind…?" I ask Preston as I push my chair back to get to my feet.

"I'll get the door. Take as much time as you need," he says with a sad smile.

18

Christian

The sun hangs low in the sky, casting long shadows across the courtyard as I make my way into the hotel's gym. The tension of my argument with Maya days ago is still hanging over me.

At least Preston and Elle hung around for a few days to keep the awkwardness to a minimum.

Still, there was a noticeable strain between me and Maya. And so far, she hasn't changed her mind again about me staying at bedtime.

God, I miss kissing her and just having a few minutes to spend alone with her after sharing the day together with our son.

I can't shake the feeling that I blew my opportunity for a second chance with Maya. And the worst part is, I'm not entirely sure what I did wrong.

Even though Preston and Elle obviously picked up on the weird vibe between me and Maya, and probably heard our argument the other night, Preston didn't once threaten to kick my ass. No, he and Elle just gave me looks full of pity, as if they felt bad for me.

Since I need to talk to someone and it definitely won't be Preston about this particular situation, I call up Luke.

"Hey, man. You back in town?" he answers.

"Not yet."

"What the hell, Riley? You've been gone all summer."

"I know. I'm still here in Bethesda."

"No kidding? So, what's up, man?" he asks. "You calling to make sure I haven't gotten myself arrested, or do you have something else on your mind?"

"Yeah, there's something on my mind," I say, as I take a seat on the weight bench in the small, empty hotel gym. "Although I am glad to hear that you're not behind bars."

"Live and learn. What's going on? You sound worse than you did after we lost the championship."

"It's Maya," I admit.

"What happened with your baby mama?"

I exhale, trying to find the words. "We've been great together, no sex but other stuff, and it was amazing."

"Okay, so what's the problem?"

My chest tightens like it's being squeezed in a vice as I tell him, "A few nights ago she said it was the last time, that she's ready to move on, and we should end things because I'm going back to Greensboro soon. And the reason she won't move, won't give us a chance, and won't tell Finley I'm his dad is all apparently because she says things will never work out between us."

Luke lets out a low whistle. "Damn man, that's rough."

"And I didn't really handle it well. I sort of blew up at her and stormed out of the house. Since then, I go over to spend the day with Finley, then I leave to go back to my hotel room."

"So, what's your plan now?"

"That's the thing," I say with the kind of frustration that makes me want to pull my hair out. "I don't fucking know what to do. I don't want to just sit around and do nothing. But I don't know how to fix it if I don't know what I did wrong. I think Maya meant it, about being done with me, like I screwed up my shot at redeeming myself with her."

Luke is quiet for a moment. "You love her?"

"More than anything," I say without hesitation, finally admitting it to myself as well. "She's the mother of my kid. But even if she wasn't, she's… everything."

"Alright, let's break this down. You wanted to show her that you could be a good father, a good role model, and you did that after a few weeks, right?"

"Yes, I think so. Maya told me I was doing great with Finley."

"Okay, and you weren't fooling around with anyone else during that time?"

"I don't want anyone but Maya. Like other women don't even exist in my world now."

"Did you tell her that?"

"Basically, but she just doesn't believe me or trust me."

"Okay, well, you can't just tell her that you're ready to settle down and expect her to believe it. I mean, would anyone believe Christian Riley is head over heels in love? No fucking way."

"What the hell?" I huff.

"It's true and you know it, thanks to your reputation. Words don't mean shit. You need to show this woman that you mean business through your actions. Consistent actions. She's been burned by you before, right? She's going to need to see that you're different, no longer the playboy of the hockey world."

I run a hand through my hair, lying back on the bench as I consider his words. He's right, of course. Maya has every reason to be cautious thanks to my history with puck bunnies. Not to mention that I've hurt her. More than once. I left her twice when she needed me the most. Of course, she's scared of me fucking up again like it's a pattern.

"But what can I do?" I ask Luke, my voice tinged with desperation. "I want to show her that I'm all in, that I'm not going anywhere."

"Well, first off, you need to be present. Not just with the physical shit, but emotionally. Be there for her and for your kid. Every time you say you're going to do something, you follow through. Show her that you're reliable now, that you're the kind of man she can depend on."

"I've been doing that," I say, my voice tight. "But it feels like every time I take a step forward with her, she pushes me back two steps. I don't know how to get through to her."

Luke chuckles softly. "You're not going to get through to her by rushing things. If she's been hurt, then you've got to be patient. If you really want her back, you're going to have to earn her trust all over again. And that's not going to happen overnight or by making her come a few times."

"Fuck."

"Is this woman worth waiting for?"

"Hell yes," I answer without needing to think about it. I

want Maya to be mine, and not just so that we can be a real family for Finley. I love her so damn much.

"Then calm your tits and quit trying to rush shit."

I sigh from the weight of his words settling heavily on my shoulders. I know he's right. Patience has never been my strong suit, but if I want Maya back for good, I'm going to have to give her as much time as she needs.

"You need a game plan," Luke says. "Something that shows her you're serious and in it for the long haul, and that your dedication to her and Finley is just as strong as your dedication to the game."

I nod my agreement even though he can't see, feeling a spark of determination. "Yeah. I need something big, though, something that will show her I'm not messing around this time."

"Nah, man. You've got to think about the little things. Anyone can pull off a big, one-time grand gesture. It's the small things on a consistent basis that will convince her."

"There's no way to do that before training starts, is there?" I ask, already knowing the answer.

"Probably not."

"If I can't convince Maya to give us a chance before Finley starts school here, then my chance of convincing her to move in with me in Greensboro is slim to none."

"Jesus," Luke mutters. "You asked the woman to move in with you?"

"Yes. It's what I wanted years ago, but she wouldn't return my calls or texts. And I swear I sent her so many cheesy ass letters, but she said she never got them."

"Well, maybe her not moving in is for the best. You don't want to jump into this too fast and screw it up, right?"

"Right."

"Then you're going to have to work on building her trust, all the way from North Carolina."

"Fuck." Putting that much distance between me and Maya feels like the bane of my existence, like it's going to cost me everything.

And unfortunately, Maya's made it clear she's not ready to move and I don't have a choice in going back to Greensboro. I have to show up for my team, keep earning money that maybe one day she'll accept for herself and Finley.

19

Maya

After my talk with Preston about ending things with Christian, and a whole lot of tears, I'm ready to move forward. To try to move on with my life after being frozen in time for nearly six years. I want to be more than a mother and I need more than Christian can give me, even if I crave him at night so much it hurts.

Sure, fooling around with him was great, but afterward I couldn't help but think about how he's done the same thing with so many other women, that our time together doesn't mean anything to him. Or at least not the same thing it means for me.

I missed Christian for so long that I think I got ahead of myself when he started coming around, spending time with Finley. When we kissed and he touched me, it felt so good to be wanted again after feeling invisible to men, to Christian, for years. But we need to set boundaries for Finley. Someday, he's going to find out he's his father, and I'm the one who kept him away. I can't cut Christian out of our son's life again, no matter what he does to me. We have to be a united team on solid ground. Which means I have to get over my feelings for him and have a co-parenting relationship only with the hockey playboy.

And who knows, maybe Preston is right, and I haven't met the man I'm meant to spend my life with yet. I never will if I keep pining for Christian.

That's why, when Spencer Williams sends me a text message asking if I want to meet him for dinner tonight and get Finley's signed jersey, I decide to say yes with one caveat—I told him the date is contingent on me finding a babysitter on such short notice.

And I think I know just the person who should be free tonight and has more than earned the opportunity.

Not only will it be good for me to go out, but it'll also give Christian a chance to prove to me that I can trust him alone with Finley. It's what he's been working toward for the past few weeks, moving a step closer to telling Finley the truth.

Walking outside to the hockey game in the backyard, I tell Finley, "Time to refuel, buddy. Go grab a snack and some water."

"But Mom…we're in the middle of a game!" he whines, his narrow shoulders drooping.

Christian makes a loud buzzing sound. "Great timing since it's intermission!" he tells our son, pointing his stick at him. "Even if it wasn't, you have to do what your mother tells you to with no complaining, right? You wouldn't whine to your hockey coach if he told you to take a water break, would you?"

"No," Finley mutters before he tosses his stick down in the grass and stomps up the steps to the porch past me, heading inside.

Smiling at Christian, I tell him, "Thanks for backing me up."

"That's what we do, right? Show a united front when it comes to our son?"

"Christian!" I hiss, turning around to make sure Finley had made it inside before he said that so loudly.

"Sorry. It slipped out. But god, I really do want to tell him soon."

"I know you do, and we're getting there," I promise him. "We might get a little closer if you can do me a huge favor tonight…"

"Anything," he says. "Whenever you or Finley need me, I'll be happy to help if I'm here or in Greensboro. It's not that far, but I wish I could be closer…"

Before we get into another argument about us moving, I tell him, "If that's true, then how about you stay and babysit tonight."

The hockey hotshot blinks at me with what looks like surprise on his face. "You mean, you want me to watch Finley, like all on my own?"

"Yes, Christian. All by yourself for a few hours. Do you think you're ready for it?" I ask because despite his best intentions, the man still has no clue what it means to be a father. It's not just hanging out and having fun every second of the day.

"Okay, well then, yeah. I can do that. Definitely."

"Great. Thank you. You can stay this afternoon or go to

your hotel and come back. I'll need to leave here at around six-thirty at the latest."

"I'll stay, if that's okay?" he says when he comes over and leans his forearms on the porch railing to look over it at me.

"Sure. And you'll be responsible for dinner. Either making something or ordering in, but I hope you'll stay here with Finley and not take him out anywhere."

"We'll stay inside the house if that will make you feel better," he replies with a smirk.

"Great. Thank you. I know you two will be fine, but promise me that you'll still call me if you need me?"

"I promise," he agrees, then clears his throat. "And I should probably know where you're going just in case I can't get you on your phone or you don't come home..."

Oh, the nosy bastard is so full of shit. But he's not entirely wrong. "I have a date," I tell him.

"You *what?*"

"I'm going to dinner with Spencer."

"Wow," he mutters as he pushes away from the porch and starts to turn away.

"Does that change your mind about babysitting? If so, one of my neighbors is probably available."

Turning back to me, his golden, unshaven jaw clenches as if he wants to refuse, but then he finally says, "No, I can handle it."

"Great. Then, I better go start getting ready."

I start back inside when Christian says, "It's only four o'clock!"

"I want to look nice," I tell him over my shoulder.

~

Despite trying to act confident about this date in front of Christian, my stomach is in knots as I shower, put on a little makeup, blowout my long black hair, and then try to decide what to wear. I finally pair a red floral dress that sits just above my knees with a pair of red strappy sandals. It's an outfit that I hope says I wanted to look nice but doesn't look like I'm trying too hard.

Christian and Finley are sitting at the dining table enjoying their hamburgers that Christian cooked himself out on the grill. The charbroiled scent smells delicious and reminds me of all the times Preston would cook out on the patio for us in the summer.

My stomach growls loud enough for them to hear and they turn towards me. The half-eaten burger in Christian's hands falls with a thud to the plate as his jaw literally drops open.

"Do I look okay?"

"You look pretty, Mommy," Finley says before he turns away to toss another potato chip into his mouth.

"Well?" I ask Christian.

"I…you…wow, Maya."

The fact that he can't speak in a complete sentence instantly boosts my confidence and makes me smile. "Thanks, I guess? Anyway, I appreciate you staying over tonight. I shouldn't be home too late."

"Good," Christian replies. "I mean, I'm glad you're not planning to stay out late on a first date."

"Uh-huh," I mutter. "Finley, bath and bed by nine, even if I'm not home, okay?"

Our son looks at Christian, who raises a single blond eyebrow before he says, "Yes, ma'am."

Ma'am is a new one that I assume is Christian's influence.

Going over to him, I place a kiss on Finley's forehead, leaving behind a lipstick stain. "Love you. Behave."

"I will," he agrees.

"Oh, I know you'll behave," I say to Finley. With a wink and whisper, I tell him, "I was talking to Christian."

Both guys grin at me before I wave goodbye, grabbing my purse and keys on the way out the door.

I drive myself to the restaurant Spencer chose, rather than have him pick me up and encounter the hockey player in my house. The nervous flutters in my belly grow stronger with each mile.

The last time I had a date was so long ago, years ago, with Christian.

While I barely know Spencer, he's probably the least intimidating man I could've picked for the first one getting back on the horse. Even Preston likes the goalie, and Preston doesn't like anyone.

It feels good to be wanted; for Spencer to be interested in me. He seems like a nice guy, so I'm not sure why I'm so nervous.

If that's even what I'm feeling.

I guess I'm also a little sad, as if going on this date, moving on with another man, might close the chapter on Christian for good.

That's what I want, though, so I'm not sure why the thought nearly brings me to tears.

When I arrive at the restaurant, I'm a little taken aback by how fancy it is. Spencer picked one of the nicest restaurants around, and I suddenly feel underdressed. At least I wore a dress and not jeans that would be way too casual.

Inside, the place is all warm lighting and polished wood, with white tablecloths and soft music playing in the background from a man sitting at a piano. It's intimate, classy, and definitely not the type of place I'm used to going to with Preston and Finley on the rare occasions we would go out to dinner. Preston hated the attention, and Finley is a picky eater, so takeout was usually a better option for us when nobody wanted to cook.

I spot Spencer at a table for two right away. He stands up when he sees me, a broad smile on his face. He's certainly not underdressed. The tall, lean goalie looks good in his blue suit, but he also has a tight smile on his handsome face that makes him look almost as nervous as I feel.

"Hi Maya," he says in greeting. "You look amazing."

"Thank you," I say, feeling a blush creep up my cheeks. "You look pretty great yourself."

He pulls out my chair for me, and I sit down, still trying to shake off the nerves. It's just one date. It doesn't mean it's the beginning of anything, or necessarily the end of anything either.

"I'm glad you came," Spencer says as he takes his seat across from me. "Even if it was just to get a jersey from me."

"Me too," I admit with a smile. "But I'm not just here for the jersey."

"Good," he replies. "And the jersey is in my truck, so don't leave without it."

"I won't, thank you. Finley will be so excited," I tell him. "And I should warn you right now that it's been a long time, years, since I went on a date."

"I don't do this much either." He gives me a shy smile, and for a moment, it feels like we're both able to relax a little bit.

We start with the usual small talk—what we've been up to this summer, hockey, living in the area. It's a simple, easy conversation.

By dessert, a raspberry cheesecake I can't resist trying, the conversation deepens into how life doesn't always turn out the way you think it will, but we should still be thankful for what it gives us.

I enjoy every delicious bite as I listen to Spencer talk about the challenges he's faced, the risks he took, the injuries he overcame to be a part of the Warhawks. It's inspiring, really, to see how far he's come, and how he never gave up on his dream even when the deck was stacked against him.

"I hope you get to be the starter soon," I tell him. "I know how much that would mean to you."

"It was hard at first, watching from the bench when I got picked up from the minor league. But now I'm just glad to be part of a pro team. A team that just won the championship cup. I still get paid to play the sport I love, so I can't ask for much more."

"That is great. I wish I knew what I loved, what I was good at, so that I could try to find a job doing it," I admit. "I *need* to figure it out fast so I can get a job like yesterday."

"I'm sure you will. Tell me more about your hobbies, what you enjoy in what little free time you have as a mom," Spencer says, his voice softening a bit as he leans closer, as if genuinely interested.

I really don't have time for any hobbies. Once Finley's in bed asleep, I enjoy taking long baths and then streaming old sitcoms.

My fingers play with the stem of my wine glass as I tell Spencer the truth. "I… well, my life is so busy, I don't have a lot of free time to figure out what I *enjoy* doing. That's what I had hoped to do at college. But then before the end of my first semester, I got pregnant..."

Spencer watches me closely, his expression gentle and understanding. "That must have been hard," he says quietly. "And you don't have to talk about it if you don't want to. I still can't believe Christian Riley is a father..."

I gasp at his casual mention of our secret. "How did you..."

"Oh, ah, Christian told me, at Finley's birthday party," he explains. I vaguely remember him mentioning that Christian told him we weren't together. It should have occurred to me that Christian would've had to have mentioned being Finley's father for the subject of our relationship status to come up.

At what I'm guessing is my stricken expression, Spencer lowers his voice further and says, "Don't worry. I would never tell anyone. It's none of my business or anyone else's. That does explain why Preston hated him so much and brutalized him on the ice."

"Right," I agree. "It was all a long time ago, obviously."

Maybe it's the wine, or maybe it's just that being around Spencer feels comfortable and easy in a way that I didn't expect. Whatever it is, I find myself telling him about how I ended up pregnant, about Christian, and how it became harder each day to tell Christian he had a son. It's really nice to be able to open up to someone about our past.

As I talk, Spencer's expression shifts from curiosity to concern. He listens intently, not interrupting, just letting me get it all out.

"Christian said you're not together, but it sounds like there's a lot of history."

I nod and can feel tears prickling at the corners of my eyes.

I hadn't expected our light conversation to get so intense, or to veer off into this awkward topic.

"Christian and I…we're definitely not together," I manage to say, though my voice cracks a little. "We haven't been for a long time. I didn't even see him for years, which was my fault. But now he's a part of Finley's life, trying to get to know his son. We both need to focus on being great parents to Finley and nothing more."

Spencer nods slowly, his expression thoughtful, but I can see the wheels turning in his mind. He's probably trying to figure out where a date with him fits into all of this, and I can't blame him. I've been trying to figure that out myself. The timing isn't great.

"Thanks for telling me," Spencer says softly, reaching across the table to take my hand. "I can't imagine how challenging that would be, to have a child with someone and have to let them be a part of your life, even when it hurts."

One of the tears spill over, and I hate that I'm crying in the middle of this beautiful restaurant, but I can't help it. The weight of everything—Finley, Christian, the uncertainty of my life—is all too much.

Spencer doesn't seem bothered or embarrassed. He just keeps holding my hand. "It's okay," he whispers, his thumb rubbing gentle circles over my knuckles. "It's going to be okay, Maya."

For a moment, I let myself enjoy the comfort of a stranger. But as much as I appreciate his kindness, I already know that I have no romantic feelings for him. I pull my hand away from his after a moment, wiping my tears with the back of my hand.

"Sorry," I mutter, feeling embarrassed now. "I didn't mean to… break down like that."

Spencer gives me a small, understanding smile. "You don't have to apologize. I shouldn't have brought it up. It's none of my business and obviously burdening you. I bet you try to put on a brave face all the time for your son and brother."

I nod, but I still feel awkward. This was supposed to be a date and now it's turned into a freaking therapy session.

"Do you want to go home?" Spencer asks, his voice gentle. "I can drive you if you're not feeling up to staying."

For a moment, I consider it. Going home sounds safe and familiar, or it used to, before Christian showed up. Now, it's impossible for me to hide from these messy emotions for long. I also don't want to run out now, further ruining the night. Spencer's been nothing but kind, and I am nothing but a mess.

"No," I say after a moment. "I think I'm okay."

Spencer looks at me with a hint of uncertainty, as if he's not sure if I'm being honest, but eventually, he nods. "Alright then."

We spend the next hour sipping wine and talking about much lighter things. Spencer's humor comes out more, and he easily makes me laugh. It's fun, and a nice little escape as I temporarily forget about everything else.

Eventually, though, the conversation comes back to future plans.

"What I really want is to be able to take care of myself and Finley on my own," I admit. "For once. I also need to find some sort of purpose with my life once Finley's at school for the entire day. I've been trying to find a job, but you can imagine how that's going with no degree and no actual experience doing anything but helping out at the preschool when they asked for volunteers. My only job for years was to make sure he's happy and taken care of, so I'm sort of feeling a little lost now that he doesn't need me all day and night."

Spencer nods, his expression thoughtful. "You're doing a great job raising Finley."

"Preston was a huge help," I admit, unable to take credit for him on my own.

"You both raised a happy kid. He knows you, Preston, and Christian love him and would do anything for him. Your job there is secure."

"I guess so," I agree. I've always known how much I love Finley, but hearing someone else recognize it, someone outside of our little bubble, is a relief, like maybe I'm not failing as a mother. "Thank you," I say, my voice thick with emotion. "That means a lot."

There's a comfortable moment of silence between us. Spencer's eyes are still on me, searching as if he's trying to figure out the right thing to say next. "Can I ask you something?" he says after a beat.

"Sure," I say, though I can tell by the fact that he asked that I may not like his question.

"Are you still in love with Christian?"

His question stuns me. And for a second, I'm not sure how to respond.

Am I still in love with Christian? I don't know! It's complicated. I care about him, and he's Finley's father, but love? That's a whole different thing.

"I don't know," I finally admit honestly, feeling my throat tighten. "It's so… complicated. I'm trying to move on…"

Spencer doesn't push, but I can see the flicker of disappointment in his eyes as he leans back in his seat. "I get it," he says softly. "Life's messy."

It is messy. So messy. And as much as I appreciate Spencer's understanding, I also feel the weight of the situation pressing down on me. There's so much uncertainty, so much I still haven't figured out.

"I didn't mean to put you on the spot," Spencer adds quickly, his tone gentle. "I just wanted to know where things stood."

I shake my head, forcing a small smile. "No, it's okay. It's just… I'm still trying to figure it all out myself."

He nods, and for a moment, neither of us says anything else. "I had fun with you tonight. I hope we can do this again if you feel the same."

"I had fun too, Spencer," I admit, my voice quiet. "But…I have to warn you that there's a lot going on in my life. Finley's about to start school, I need to find a job like ASAP, and then there's Christian who I think is serious about being a part of our life, Finley's life…"

He smiles, but I can see the disappointment settle in his handsome features, though he tries to hide it. "I understand. You're busy. I will be too soon when the season starts," he says, his tone gentle. "How about we just take things slow, as friends for now?"

"Okay," I agree.

We sit there in silence for a few more moments, the weight of the conversation lingering between us before he changes the subject. "So, you need a job?"

"Yes."

"Well, I grew up not far from here, which is why I was so damn happy the Warhawks wanted me. I know tons of people in the area. Maybe I can help you find a job. If you could do anything in the world, what would it be?" he asks.

"I honestly have no idea."

"None at all?"

"I really don't know. I've never had a chance to explore any careers. I just know I need a job with flexible hours. That's why I applied to one job I didn't have the experience requirement for but would potentially work with Finley's school day."

"Which position was that for?"

"Oh, um, an activity director at a senior center."

"Really?" Spencer asks. "You want to work with seniors?"

"Yes. I can't imagine leaving your home behind and being stuck in a place like that for years, away from your family that can only visit when they're not working or raising their own families. I'm so lucky I have my brother, but if I didn't, I would be all on my own. I guess I would like to be there for someone else to make their day a little better."

"I get it. And I actually have an aunt who is a nurse at a retirement home near here."

"Really?"

"Yeah. I could ask her if they're hiring and let you know."

"That would be so great, thank you. But no pressure. I don't have any experience, and I might be awful at it."

"You won't be awful at it," he replies with a grin. "But I can't promise anything."

"Understood."

"Well, what do you think? Are you ready to call it a night?"

"I think so." Ready to get home, I check my phone before I start driving. "No calls from Christian, so things must be going well on his first time alone with Finley."

"That's great," Spencer says. "I like kids, but I'm not sure if I would trust myself to be completely responsible for one."

"Oh, I'm sure you would be fine," I tell him with a smile.

Spencer picks up the check and we leave the restaurant. We stop by his truck for the jersey before he walks me to my car.

"Thank you for dinner and the signed jersey," I tell him, lifting the black and red sweater. "Finley will adore it."

"You're welcome." He gives me a warm smile, and for a second, I think he's going to say something more, but he doesn't. Instead, he leans in and gives me a gentle hug, his arms wrapping around me in a way that feels comforting without asking for anything more.

I hug him back, closing my eyes for just a moment as I let myself sink into the warmth of his embrace. It feels nice and safe, but there's also a part of me that knows this isn't where my heart will ever lie. Not just with Spencer, but any man who isn't Christian Riley.

As much as it hurts, I think I still love Christian. Maybe I never stopped. I don't think I ever will either, no matter how much time goes by. God, that's really depressing.

When we pull apart, Spencer looks at me with a mixture of affection and uncertainty. "Don't forget to take time to take care of yourself, Maya," he says softly. "Let me know if you need anything now that Preston's gone, and since Christian will be going back to Greensboro for training. I'll check in with you soon, if that's okay?"

"Sure, Spencer. And thanks again for tonight," I tell him, offering him another smile before getting into my car.

As I drive home, my mind is a whirlwind of emotions. I replay the night over again in my head. It was a good evening.

Nice. But only at a friendly level. There's no spark with Spencer. No desire for anything with him but friendship.

When I finally pull into my driveway, I sit in the car for a moment, staring at the house. Finley should be asleep by now, and Christian is probably on the couch, scrolling through his phone or watching TV, wishing I would hurry up and get home so he can leave.

As soon as I finally step inside, Christian stands up from the sofa to greet me, his face blank when I walk into the living room lit with only the screen of the flickering television. "Well? How was your date?"

I force a smile, but I can tell he sees right through me. "It was… nice," I admit, sinking down onto the couch.

He raises an eyebrow. "Just nice?"

I let out a sigh, leaning back against the cushions. "We talked and got along great. Spencer is a sweet guy, but I'm glad it's over."

"Me too," Christian agrees with a smirk as he sits back on the sofa next to me.

"So, what are we watching?" I ask before slipping off my shoes and curling my legs underneath me, trying to adjust to my new normal—being next to Christian without touching him or kissing him the way I really want to.

I lie awake that night after my date, staring at the dark ceiling, feeling the weight of his voice as if Christian were standing outside my door, asking me to let him in. The desperation, the sincerity—it's all there. I want to open that door. God, I almost did. But something held me back, something deep and familiar.

Fear.

Fear that letting him in would mean inviting all the pain from the past back into my life and Finley's.

But then, there's this other part of me—a quieter, softer voice that whispers maybe—maybe he really has changed. Maybe this time, things could be different.

That voice is dangerous because it's hopeful, and hope is exactly what led me down this road before. I fell in love with Christian once, and I got hurt. Can I risk doing it again?

The house is quiet. Finley's asleep, oblivious to the turmoil in my heart. I know I should sleep, too, but my mind is running a marathon of doubts and what-ifs. Every time I close my eyes, I see Christian's face—his eyes pleading with me, his voice cracking just a little when he said, *"Fine, I want more, Maya. I want to be with you. I want you to be mine in every damn way."*

I sigh heavily and roll over, squeezing my eyes shut, wishing I didn't believe him.

20

Christian

After Maya's date with Spencer last night, which she didn't seem too excited about, I still feel like the space between us is growing even wider. And I don't know what the fuck to do.

So, that morning, when I come over and Maya says, "Since you did such a great job last night, would you be up for babysitting this afternoon?" I almost lose my shit.

"Why? You have another date with the fucking bench warmer?" I snap.

Maya rolls her eyes, and warns me, "Watch it with the swear words."

"Sorry," I mutter.

"And no, it's not a date. I have a job interview!"

"Oh wow. Congrats."

"All thanks to the *bench warmer*," she replies.

"Great."

"It is great. Spencer told me about his aunt who works at a retirement home. Her boss agreed to meet with me about an activity director position. I sent over my resume an hour ago and she emailed to ask if I could come in for an interview at four today!"

"That's…wow." Shit. Maya might get a job here in Bethesda, which means the chances of her and Finley moving to North Carolina are dropping even lower.

"Right? It's exactly what I had hoped to do."

"So, if you get the job, you're definitely staying here?"

"I've told you from the beginning that we weren't moving," she replies. "So? Can you stay with Finley for a few hours again today?"

"Yeah, I can stay with him. We had fun last night," I tell her. "Good luck, I guess?"

"Thank you!" she says excitedly before running off. "Now, I have to figure out what to wear!"

Later that afternoon, I'm eating pizza at the table with Finley, who is still, unfortunately wearing his new, signed, Spencer Williams Warhawk's jersey, feeling like a dick for hoping Maya doesn't get the job when Finley asks me, "Did you always want to play hockey?"

"Yes," I answer, pausing with my next slice halfway to my mouth. "Even though my dad wasn't ever thrilled with the idea. Still isn't."

"Why not?"

"Because he's a professor, a genius with a doctorate who

teaches at a university. He thinks it's stupid for grown men to chase around a puck on ice skates. For years, I thought he was just being an ah… being difficult." I barely catch the swear word in time. "But then when I got older, I realized he mostly just didn't want to see me get hurt."

Finley nods as if that all makes sense to him. And he's a smart kid, so it probably does. His intelligence all came from his mother.

"I wonder if my dad's a professor. Or maybe he's an astronaut," he says softly. "That would be cool too."

"That would definitely be cooler than him being a hockey player," I agree before biting into my slice of pepperoni.

His eyes widen. "You think my dad could be a hockey player? Like you and Uncle Preston are, playing in the big arenas full of people?"

I swallow, then tell him, "Yeah, I do, so you got your skills from both sides of your family."

Tilting his head to the side, Finley says, "How do you know?"

"How do I know what?"

"That my dad plays hockey. Do you know him?"

"Ah, well…" I pick off some pepperonis while I struggle to figure out how to answer his question. Having him ask me about his father while wearing another man's hockey jersey makes me so fucking angry. And jealous. God, I'm just tired of lying, of pretending that he's not my son and I'm not his father. While I know Maya wanted to wait and tell him on her own timeline, Finley deserves to know the truth. He deserves to know that I'm not just some random hockey player he looks up to babysitting him for a few hours, but that I love him so damn much I would do literally anything in the world for him.

"You've already met your father, actually," I tell Finley, swallowing around the sudden tightness in my throat. Not out of fear of Maya's reaction, but a new fear of how Finley will handle it. I didn't even know to worry about that before now, but it still doesn't stop me from saying, "In fact, you've spent the whole summer playing hockey in the backyard and eating pizza with him."

"But…" Finley trails off as he bites into his cheese pizza, chews it up, takes another bite, all while thinking that information over. Finally, he swallows and tosses the crust down on his plate. "You're the only one I've played with this summer. You and Uncle Preston."

"That's right." I nod my head in agreement, letting him put the pieces together.

He blinks at me, staring at my face. "Are *you* my father?"

Holy shit, the waterworks instantly turn on and I have to blink the tears away after hearing him use that word in reference to me.

Giving him a smile, I say, "I am, Finley. I'm your father."

And those are the last words I get to say before he storms off to his room and slams the door.

I imagined having this conversation with him so many times, and this is not at all how I expected it to go.

In the best scenarios, Finley would immediately throw his arms around my neck to hug me and tell me that he's glad I'm his dad.

This version is definitely the worst. I should've expected the anger for lying to him for weeks. Just because he's a kid doesn't mean that he wouldn't be hurt by the betrayal.

After wiping off my greasy hands on a napkin, I go after him. I knock on the bedroom door and try the doorknob that's locked. "Finley, please let me come in so we can talk about this, okay buddy? I'm so sorry I didn't tell you sooner…"

"You lied to me! Every day! You're a big fat liar!"

"I wish I had told you sooner," I reply. "And I'm sorry I didn't. Your…family thought it would be best if we got to know each other as friends first, and that was all my fault. Your mom and uncle weren't sure if I was up to the job of being your dad, so I had to prove it to them. That's what I've been doing all summer. Not lying to you, but proving to your mom that she could trust me to take care of you."

He doesn't respond to a word I say the rest of the afternoon through the door.

And when Maya comes home from her interview, I lie and tell her Finley was tired and went to bed early before leaving. I just don't have the energy to fight with her, too.

21

Maya

My interview went great. At least I think it did.

Spencer's aunt Justine was invited in for most of it as well. She and her boss gave me a tour of the center and we talked for over an hour before her boss said she would be in touch soon.

I don't know if she'll be in touch in a day or so or a week. All I can do now is wait.

Which sucks, and meant another night I couldn't sleep worth a shit.

By six-thirty the next morning, I'm sitting in the kitchen drinking a cup of coffee when Finley shuffles into the kitchen just as early. His energy is at the lowest level ever, as if picking up his feet would be too much work. That's how I know something is off with him.

"Good morning," I say cheerfully as I get to my feet to

make him his favorite breakfast. "Are you hungry? How about some blueberry pancakes?"

"I guess."

I smile weakly at his unenthusiastic response. He must still be waking up and is just sleepy. I start gathering up all the ingredients, trying not to let him see the worry on my face.

Finley watches me closely, his little face scrunched up in thought. "Mommy?" he asks, his voice unusually soft.

"Yes, baby?" I reply, turning to face him fully.

"Is Christian really my father?"

His question hits me like a freight train.

My breath catches in my throat, and for a moment, I can't speak. The container of blueberries slips from my hands, spilling all over the floor.

Finley's big, innocent eyes are staring right at me, waiting for an answer, and I have no idea what to say.

I always knew this day would come, but I wasn't ready for it to be today. Not now. Not like this.

And I'm going to kill Christian Riley!

Last night when I got home, I knew something was wrong. Finley rarely goes to bed early without a fight, and Christian is never in such a hurry to leave, barely asking me about my interview before running out.

"Wh-why do you ask that, sweetheart?"

Finley shrugs, looking down at the table. "Last night he said he's my father and that he lied to me all summer!"

I swallow hard around the lump in my throat. "Christian cares about you so much, Finley," I say slowly, carefully choosing my words when I take a seat next to him at the table. "He...yes, he's your father. But at first, you didn't know him, and he didn't know you. So, I asked him to get to know you as friends this summer. I wanted you to spend time with him before we told you."

"Why didn't he come play with me before this summer?"

I can't lie to him. I won't. Even if I'm furious with Christian for not warning me about the bomb he dropped on our son.

"That was my fault, not Christian's," I tell him. "You see, Christian left. He moved away to play hockey when I found out I was pregnant with you. And then I didn't see him again until recently. You remember the day he came to the championship game with a jersey for you?"

Finley nods his head.

"That was right after he found out he was your father. He didn't know before then or he would've been around more, I promise. So, that's my fault for not finding him to tell him sooner so you could spend time together."

"But...you and him aren't married."

"No, baby. We're not married. Christian was best friends and teammates with Uncle Preston, and we were friends too. I cared about him so much before he had to leave."

Finley stares at me for a moment, processing my words. Then he nods as if he understands more than I expected him to. "Does that mean he's gonna keep coming over?" he asks, his voice small, like he's afraid of the answer.

I feel my heart tighten. "Of course he'll keep coming over. But he'll have to go back to Greensboro soon to play for the Bobcats. We'll go visit him when we visit Uncle Preston. And I bet he'll call you whenever he can."

Finley seems to accept that answer for now, but the question lingers in the air, heavy and unresolved about how much of a presence he'll have in our life.

"Do you have any other questions about Christian?"

He shakes his head, so I give him another moment just to be sure. Finally, he asks, "Is Christian coming over to play today?"

"Do you want him to?"

"Yes. But I'm still mad at him."

Oh, I know that feeling well.

"It's okay to be mad or sad or anything else you feel right now," I tell him as I give him a hug, thankful when he hugs me back. "It's okay to be all those things and still want to spend time with Christian. He loves spending time with you."

"I like playing with him too," Finley says when I let him go. "And it's pretty cool that out of all the dads in the world, he's mine."

"Yes, that is very cool," I tell him before I get up and finish making him pancakes.

While I'm still a little uneasy about how Finley will handle this monumental revelation, I'm so damn relieved that it's finally out in the open, off my shoulders.

For years, I was so focused on protecting myself, on keeping my heart locked away, that I didn't think about what's best for Finley.

He deserves to know Christian is his father. He deserves the chance to have that relationship with him.

I've known that for years.

The only problem was that I wasn't sure if I was ready for what that meant for me as well.

Am I ready to let Christian back into my life in such a big way?

Once Finley scarfs down his pancakes, he goes to brush his teeth and clean his room. I pick up my phone, staring at the screen for what feels like forever, before finally dialing Christian's number.

"Hey, I'm on my way over," he answers softly, sounding gutted. That's the only reason I don't lay into him.

"You should've told me."

"I know," he replies with a heavy sigh. "I'm sorry, Maya. I wasn't planning to tell him last night, I swear. You know I wanted to, but I was trying to be patient. Then, the topic of dads came up and Finley was wishing he knew more about his father, about the kind of job he had. So, I caved and told him the truth."

Based on his distressed tone and Finley's sluggish demeanor this morning, I say, "I assume it didn't go as well as you hoped?"

"It did not. Finley ran off to his room, slammed the door, and refused to let me in or talk to me."

"Oh. Well, welcome to the parent club," I tell him.

"What do you mean?"

"That's pretty much our son's normal reaction to anything and everything that upsets him."

There's a long pause. "So, I didn't ruin everything? You think he'll forgive me?"

"No, Christian, you didn't ruin anything. I'm sure he'll forgive you like he always forgives me," I explain to him. "Finley asked me this morning to confirm that it was true. I also told him that you staying away for so long wasn't your choice, that it was mine."

"Maya...you didn't have to do that," he says softly.

"No, I did need to say it, to be honest with him. He should know that it wasn't your fault for not being a part of his life sooner. I take full responsibility for that. I'm so sorry my issues kept you from him for so long."

"You did what you thought was best for you and him. I hate it, but I can understand where you were coming from. All is forgiven, okay?"

"Okay," I agree. "And I promise you that Finley will be fine with you when you come over."

"You think he still wants me to come over today?"

"Of course he does. He's already asked if you were coming."

"Good. That's…god, I thought he might never speak to me again," Christian says in a rush, his voice hitching with emotion.

"It'll be fine," I assure him. "I'll see you soon?"

"Yeah, I'll see you soon."

22

Christian

It takes me twice as long as usual to get to Maya's. Most of that time was spent when I pulled over to get my shit together.

All night long, I thought about calling her to confess what I had done. Even though I knew she would be angry, I wanted to beg for her help to convince Finley to speak to me again, to forgive me.

And it turns out, everything is going to be fine.

At least that's what Maya said.

Even after bawling like a baby, the tears falling in relief, there's still a nervous twist in my guts when I walk up to the front door. Maya opens it before I have a chance to knock.

"Hey," she says with a sad, half smile as she stands in the doorway in her pajamas, her long hair tussled from sleep. She's never looked more beautiful.

"Hey." After I blink to ensure that the waterworks have been forcefully turned off, I say to her, "Thank you for not hating me for telling him."

"I'm sorry I made you wait so long. I really thought it was best, though, at first…"

"I know you did. And you had good reasons. Honestly, I was a little relieved to just be his friend at first, to take some of the pressure off being the perfect dad when I was so clueless about what that meant. Now…now it's like everything's changed, become more intense. There's no room for error, you know?"

"I know," she replies. "Come on in. Finley just went out to the backyard." She holds the door open for me to step through, like I've done so many times before this summer. Still, this time is definitely different. "I'll go shower and give you two a moment alone."

"Thanks," I tell her before I walk straight through the kitchen to the back door.

Unlike usual, Finley isn't running around the yard with a hockey stick in his hand. He's sitting on the steps, his narrow shoulders hunched.

Going over, I take a seat on the step next to him and he glances over at me. His big brown eyes are full of pain. That would've been enough to bring me to my knees if I wasn't already sitting down.

"How are you doing, buddy?" I ask him softly. "Are you okay? I mean, after what I told you last night? It's okay if you're not…"

"I'm sorry I got mad at you," he says, which is the last thing I expected. "Mommy said you left town before she had me."

"Right. That-that is true."

"She said…she said that you would've come around sooner if you had known you were my dad. Is that true?" he asks hesitantly.

"I swear on all that is hockey that I would've been here as much as possible if I knew sooner. Finding out you were my son was the best day of my life."

He nods as if he believes me. "And you'll keep coming to play with me until you have to go back to Greensboro?"

"Yes, absolutely. And I wish you could come with me, but your school and friends are all here. Hopefully, you and your mom can come visit. I'll call you every night if I don't have a game. It would be too late to call you on those nights, but we can talk before, in the afternoons then. Would that be okay?"

"Yeah, sure."

"Even if I don't get to see you every day, I'll be thinking about you," I promise him. "I love you, buddy. I've loved you since the second I found out you were my son."

He stares at me, letting that information sink in. Then asks, "Do I have to keep calling you Christian or can I call you dad?"

"Sure, yes. You can call me whatever you want. Whatever you think feels right, okay?"

"Okay," he replies with a nod.

"Any other questions?"

He shakes his head, so I say, "Race you to the goal?"

A smile spreads across his face before he shoots up from the step and takes off with a five second head start.

And then we spend the day playing like every other day, as if nothing has changed, which is a huge relief.

Finley doesn't call me daddy or dad, which is a little disappointing, but I don't want to rush him. One day, though, I hope to earn the privilege of being his dad in every possible way.

Maya

"Hey, how are you and my favorite nephew doing?" Preston asks when he picks up my call.

"Ah, well, things have been better," I confess, which is the reason I'm calling him.

"What's wrong? Do I need to come up there?"

"No. Although, I did consider having you come kick Christian's ass for a few seconds this morning."

"Seriously? What the fuck did he do?"

"Everything is fine now, I think," I admit, leaning back against the kitchen counter with the phone pressed to my ear. "Yesterday, while Christian was babysitting for me to go to a job interview, he came out and told Finley that he's his father. Then, he didn't even give me a head's up before he left the house last night!"

"Oh, shit."

"Yeah, exactly."

"And how did Finley take the news?" he asks.

"Well, he didn't come out of his room last night. Then this morning he looked so pitiful when he came into the kitchen and asked me if it was true, catching me completely off-guard."

Preston is silent for a moment, and I can practically hear

him thinking on the other end of the line. "And you told him he was?"

"Yes," I reply quietly, the weight of the question still hanging over me. "I told him the truth and explained that the reason Christian hadn't been around was because he didn't know he was his father until recently, the day he met Finley and gave him his jersey."

"Well, it's nice of you to take the blame off Christian, even though he spilled the beans before you were ready. Why have you been waiting?"

"I don't know! I just...I wanted to make sure Christian understood how important this was and that he was all in."

Preston sighs, and I can hear the rustle of him shifting in his chair. "Maya, just admit it. You were scared, right?

I roll my eyes, even though he can't see me. "Of course I was scared. I wasn't ready to deal with the fallout yet. I wanted Christian to prove that he was devoted to being here for Finley."

"And he hasn't done that by coming up to Bethesda, living out of a hotel, and seeing him every day of the summer?"

"I just don't want Christian to break Finley's heart like he broke mine."

Preston's voice softens when he says, "Look, I'm not going to tell you it's going to be easy now that Finley knows the truth. It's not. But you've already taken the first step by letting him be part of Finley's life. I'm sure Christian will make an effort to see him and talk to him as much as he can during the season, too."

"Yeah, I think you're probably right about that."

"So then, why do you sound so depressed?"

"Because…because now Christian is a part of my life, our life, forever and…it's not easy to be around him."

"Oh. You weren't just scared for Finley's sake. You were scared for yourself," Preston mutters. "You still have feelings for him, don't you?"

"I wish I didn't, but the more time he spends here the worse it gets."

"So, the real question is whether you're going to take a chance on him as more than Finley's father, right?"

I bite my lip, feeling the sting of those words. "I would love that. But I don't know if I can trust him again in a romantic relationship. And if it ended badly, it would hurt Finley."

"Trust isn't about certainty, Maya," Preston says gently. "It's about taking a risk. Do you think Christian's earned another chance with you or not? You know he's earned the right to be Finley's father in every way, so that just leaves one question. Has he earned back the right to be with you?"

I pause, thinking back to the nights we fooled around together, how he looked at me and worshipped me. Then, when he asked me to not just move to Greensboro but to move in with him. The old Christian would've probably run from the idea of such a huge commitment, not practically begged me for it.

"I think he has," I admit quietly.

"Then maybe it's time to follow your heart," Preston says. "Not just for Finley, but for yourself."

I close my eyes, letting his words sink in. "What if I get hurt again? What if we have a falling out and can't stand to be in the same room again? How can we raise Finley together if we hate each other?"

Preston's voice is firm but kind. "Finley didn't know

Christian was his father for weeks. I'm sure the two of you could give things another try without him realizing what's happening. And you'll never know unless you do exactly that —try."

I swallow hard, feeling the tears prick at the corners of my eyes. "I'm just so tired, Preston. Tired of being strong when I'm so scared. Tired of not knowing what to do or what the future holds. It's all great now, but how long could that happiness last?"

"I get it," my brother says softly. "But none of us know what the future holds. And you're stronger than you think, Maya. You've already been through the worst with our parents, having Finley so young, and you came out the other side. Don't let fear keep you from something that could turn out to be great. It's not just Finley who deserves to be happy. You deserve it too, you know?"

Preston's words hit me hard, like a wave crashing over me, dragging me under. I want to believe Christian. And Preston. I want to believe that I deserve happiness too after all the loneliness. But the fear, the doubt—they're still there, lurking in the background thanks to how much it hurt when Christian left and my parents abandoned me rather than love me because I was pregnant. If I had told them I got pregnant but didn't technically have sex, they would've accused me of lying.

"Just think about it," Preston adds. "And take your time. You're right not to rush into anything for Finley's sake. But don't shut Christian out forever out of fear of the unknown. You owe it to yourself to at least give it a chance if you still have feelings for him."

"You're that certain Christian still has feelings for me, too?" I ask, while chewing on my bottom lip.

"Maya, that man might be a pain in my ass most of the time, but I think he always loved you. You broke his heart too, remember?"

I smile. "Fine, I'll...think about it."

"Good," Preston says, his tone lightening. "And if you still need me to come kick his ass, I'll come right up there no matter the time or day. You know that, right?"

I laugh despite the tears in my eyes. "Yes, I know that. Thank you, Preston."

"Do you need me to come up there for all the daddy drama?" he asks again.

"No. No, we're fine. I'm sorry to bother you."

"Call me anytime, Maya. That's what I'm here for."

We hang up, and I'm left standing in the kitchen, my mind swirling with everything he said. He's right. I can't let fear rule my life forever. But letting Christian in again—it's terrifying. The stakes are so much higher now with Finley involved. We can't afford to mess this up a second time.

23

Maya

That night, after Christian left without even attempting to stay with me once Finley goes to bed, I find myself sitting on the sofa, watching our son play with his Legos on the floor. He's completely absorbed in his blocks, his little face full of concentration. Every now and then, he glances up at me with that same innocent curiosity, like he's still thinking about the conversation we had this morning.

"Mommy?" Finley asks, his little eyes filled with a mix of curiosity and something else—something deeper.

"Yes, sweetie?" I manage, trying to sound calm, but I can already feel that this conversation is about to head in a difficult direction.

"Why doesn't Christian live with us?" His question hangs in the air like a ticking bomb. God, why didn't it occur to me that he would wonder why we're apart?

I take a deep breath, my mind racing for a way to explain things to him without overloading his little heart. "Because Christian and I… like we discussed this morning, we aren't married."

"You and Uncle Preston lived together and weren't married," he points out.

"Yes, but Uncle Preston is my brother. We're family."

"Christian's not our family?"

"Of course he's our family, but we're just not as close with him as we are with Preston."

Finley frowns, clearly not satisfied with my answer. "But why? All my friends live with their mommies and daddies together. Some of them have two mommies and two daddies."

My heart clenches at the innocence of his words, at the way he's trying to piece together a world that doesn't make sense to him. I reach out and gently ruffle his hair. "Sometimes mommies and daddies don't live together, baby."

"But Christian's going to leave soon and then we won't see him or Uncle Preston except on TV." His voice rises slightly, filled with the urgency of a child who's trying to understand why his life isn't like all his friends'. "Why can't we live where they live?"

I struggle to keep my voice steady. "It's complicated, sweetie."

He looks down at his Lego bridge, his small hands fidgeting with it. "Christian said he loves me and that I could call him dad if I want to."

I didn't know Christian had said that to him, but I'm so glad he did. "You can call him dad or daddy or just keep calling him Christian. That's totally up to you."

"Does Christian love you too?"

The question pierces through me, and for a moment, I can't breathe. I want to give him an easy answer, something that will make everything make sense in his little world, but the truth is so tangled up in past hurts and present uncertainties that I don't know how to put it into words.

I bite my lip, trying to hold myself together. "Christian… cares about me a lot, Finley. I care about him too."

"But you don't love each other?" Finley's voice grows louder, more insistent. "If you loved him, could we go live with him?"

I can feel the frustration building up inside me, bubbling over from my own doubts and fears. I know he doesn't mean to push, but every question is like a little dagger poking at a wound I've been trying to keep closed.

"Finley, I'm sorry that this is so complicated…" My voice wavers slightly. I'm supposed to be strong for him, to be the one who has the answers, but right now, I feel as lost as he is. "But it's not that simple."

"Why not?" His voice breaks, and there's a tremor in it that tells me he's about to cry. "I want to live with him, not you!"

"That's not going to happen!" I snap, sharper than I intended, mostly out of sadness, and instantly regret floods through me.

Finley's eyes widen, and his lower lip quivers as he looks up at me, startled by my tone. Tears well up in his eyes, and before I can say anything else, he bursts into sobs, covering his face with his small hands.

"Oh, sweetie…" I whisper, reaching out to pull him into my arms. I hold him tightly, my heart aching at the sound of his cries. "I'm so sorry, Finley. I wish it was as easy as it sounds to up and move and all of us live together, but it's not."

His little body shakes with sobs, and I gently rub his back, trying to soothe him. "I know you're confused, and I'm so sorry. Please don't cry."

"I'm going to…miss him…like I miss…Uncle Preston."

"I know. I know you will."

God, seeing him so upset, maybe I should just cave and move us to North Carolina. I want to do just that, I do. But then there will not be any excuses to give Finley if Christian stops coming around, or if I can't find a job. I'll be right back where I started, being dependent on my brother thanks to my parents throwing me out and refusing to pay my tuition. At some point, I have to stop letting them, life, hold me back from finding my own happiness.

Besides, during the hockey season, we may as well be living in a different country than the players who constantly stay busy on the road.

I wish there was a simple way for me to decide, to know for sure, what's best for us in the long run.

Then it hits me.

If I get the perfect job I want so badly, working at the retirement home before Finley starts school, then that means that we're meant to stay in Maryland. It's fate. This is where I can stand on my own two feet for the very first time, and Finley can keep his routine, his friends.

If I don't get the job, well, I can't let Preston keep paying for two houses, one here and one in North Carolina. I'll only be putting more of a burden on him, so I'll enroll Finley in a school down there for fall, even if the thought of packing up our things and leaving our life here behind makes me nauseous.

God, I hate change. I hate empty boxes and saying goodbye to my home with so many happy memories.

Finally, Finley's sobs begin to quiet. I continue holding him, rocking him gently, whispering soft words of comfort. "It's okay, Finley. Everything's going to be okay."

He pulls away slightly, his red, tear-streaked face looking up at me with so much innocence, and my heart breaks all over again. "I just… I don't want the summer to end, Mommy," he whispers, his voice small.

"I know, baby," I say softly, brushing a tear from his cheek. "I don't either."

Maya

Later that night, I've just tucked Finley into bed when there's a knock on the door. I glance at the clock, realizing that it must be Christian returning. Maybe he forgot something, or he's going to beg us to move in with him again. Who knows with the playboy.

I open the door and try to keep the disappointment off my face when I find my brother standing there with Elle by his side, her warm smile and her gentle presence already making me feel a little more grounded.

"What in the world are you two doing here?" I greet them quietly, then hug them both before stepping aside to let them in. "And why didn't you just come on in since you still have a key?"

Preston walks in first, his usual confident swagger replaced with something softer, more concerned. "I was worried about you after we talked this morning. Elle thought we should come visit and check on you and Finley. How are you holding up?" he asks, his brow furrowed as he looks at me.

I give him a weak smile. "It's been…a long day."

Elle, always the intuitive one, places a hand on my shoulder and gives it a light squeeze. "We brought ice cream," she says, holding up a local grocery bag. "Thought you might need a little comfort food."

I'm grateful for their thoughtfulness. "Thanks. I could also use the company."

"Finley already out for the night?" Preston asks as he leads the way to the kitchen.

"Yes, you just missed him. He might still be awake…"

"No, that's okay. Let him sleep. We'll see him tomorrow. That is, if you don't mind us staying in my old room?"

"No, of course not. It's your house, your room. You can stay here whenever you want."

A short while later, we settle into the living room, each of us with a pint and a spoon, and for a moment, I feel like I can breathe again. But as soon as we dig into our ice cream, Preston's sharp gaze fixes on me.

"So," he starts, leaning back against the couch. "How are you really doing?"

I hesitate for a moment, not sure where to begin. But then I remember how comforting it was to talk to my brother earlier, how much I trust him, and the words just start spilling out.

"Finley had more questions tonight," I say, my voice a little shaky. "Then he said he would rather go live with Christian."

Preston's eyebrows shoot up in surprise, and Elle's eyes widen as well. "And what did you tell him?" Preston asks.

"I told him that wasn't going to happen," I reply. "He doesn't understand why Christian and I don't live together like all his friends' parents. Or why we can't move to be near him."

Elle frowns, her face full of sympathy. "I'm so sorry, Maya. Those are big questions for such a little boy."

"I know," I sigh, running a hand through my hair. "I just… I told him it was complicated. I don't want to confuse him, but I also can't explain it to him, not yet. Maybe not ever."

Preston puts his pint with the spoon sticking out of it on the coffee table to lean forward, his elbows resting on his knees. "What about you? Where are you at with all of this?"

I pause, feeling the weight of his question settle over me. "I don't know," I admit quietly. "Part of me is relieved that it's all out in the open…"

"But you're scared of what happens next?" Elle finishes for me, her voice gentle.

I nod, swallowing the lump in my throat. "Yes. I'm scared," I say, giving my brother a pointed look. "Even if I was ready to give Christian another chance, I know I couldn't handle the away games that are about to start, wondering if he's hooking up with women while he's away."

Preston is silent for a moment, his expression thoughtful. "You've been through a lot, Maya. No one would blame you for being cautious. But… do you really think Christian will hook up with strangers as soon as we hit the road?"

I look down at my already half-eaten ice cream container, as if the pieces of cookie dough hold the answer. "I honestly don't know. I hope he wouldn't, but hope won't help me sleep at night or help me trust him while he's gone."

Elle reaches out and takes my hand, her touch warm and reassuring. "Maya, you don't have to jump right into anything. You and Christian could take it slow, see how it goes…"

Preston nods in agreement. "And you can do that without Finley finding out you two are dating or whatever. I know you worry about what happens if it fails, but what if it works out? Then Finley would get to know his father even more, and you three could all live together one day as a family."

I swallow hard, feeling the weight of their words. I know I should try to focus on the positives, to be optimistic, but I'm a worrier. It comes with the territory of being a mother. "It's not that easy."

"It is that easy," Preston says, his voice soft but steady. "But you'll never know how easy and great it could be if you let the fear win."

I close my eyes, feeling the tears welling up again. It's terrifying, this idea of letting Christian back into my life, of opening up to him again. But maybe it's time to stop running from this relationship. Maybe it's time to take that risk—for Finley's sake and for mine.

"I'll think about it," I say quietly, my voice barely above a whisper. "And I've decided…if I get the job I interviewed for here, we're staying. If I don't, we'll move to North Carolina."

Preston nods, a small smile playing on his lips as if contemplating tracking down the hiring manager to dissuade them. "Good."

We sit there in silence for a while eating our ice cream, the weight of everything still hanging in the air, but somehow, it feels a little lighter with Preston and Elle here, and with a plan for how I'll make such a huge decision that could completely change my and Finley's lives.

25

Christian

The sun is warm but not too harsh, and there's a soft breeze blowing as I push Finley on the swing at the park.

I was surprised to see Preston and Elle at the house this morning, but I shouldn't have been. I know why they're here —to give Maya moral support.

Since I wanted some more time alone with Finley, I asked Maya if I could bring him to the park for an hour or so. I was a little shocked at how easily Finley agreed to leave his visiting uncle behind. I know Preston wants to spend time with his nephew, so I won't keep him out long. I just want to make sure everything is okay between us now that the truth is out.

Finley's laughter echoes through the park, and for a

moment, I forget everything else. It's just him and me—no stress, no history, no mistakes. Just a father enjoying the summer day with his son.

The word hits me like a punch to the gut. It's what I am, what I should've been all along. And now my son knows the truth.

Finley looks up at me, his little face lighting up with joy, and I swear, I'd give anything to hold on to this moment forever.

"Higher, Christian!" he shouts, his voice filled with excitement.

I give the swing another push, and he soars higher, the wind rushing through his hair. His giggles fill the air again, and my chest tightens with a mix of pride and something deeper—something I can't quite put into words. I watch him, and for the first time in a long time, I feel like I'm right where I'm supposed to be, something I haven't felt since those few days Maya and I had together before I screwed it up. Back then, being with her was the best part of my day, helping me forget all about trying to get picked up by a professional hockey team.

Thinking of Finley as my son feels more real now. There's no more pretending to just be a cool friend or hockey player he looks up to.

I'm his father. And he's…everything I never knew I wanted, everything I've been missing in my life. And he seems to love spending time with me, as if there's no other place he would rather be.

As the swing slows down, Finley drags his feet along the grass and dirt, stopping himself. "Can we go play on the jungle gym?" he asks, hopping off the swing.

"Of course, buddy." I follow him as he sprints toward the apparatus, his little legs carrying him as quick as they can. He really is fast for his age.

I watch as he climbs up the bars, his hands gripping them with confidence. My son is damn strong too, which makes a smile tug at my lips. He's so strong and fearless. It's incredible to think that I had a hand in making this amazing little human. Not that I think he got his strength and fearlessness from me…

"Look, Christian! I made it to the top!" Finley calls out from the highest platform, waving at me with a wide grin.

"Yeah, I see you! Great job, Finley!" I call back, my heart swelling with pride.

He beams at my words, his face lighting up even more, and I realize just how much my approval means to him. I'm not sure why I'm surprised since my father always held that same power over me. Still, it's a sobering thought—how much power I have in his life, how much influence. And I've wasted so much time. But I'm not going to waste it anymore.

Finley runs across the adjoining rope bridge, heading for the slide. I move closer to catch him at the bottom. He slides down with a squeal of joy, landing in my arms with a giggle as I scoop him up.

When I set him down, he glances up at me with those big brown eyes of his—Maya's eyes—and something in his expression changes. He looks serious and thoughtful in a way that makes him seem older than five.

"Christian?" he says, his voice soft.

"Yeah, buddy?" I crouch down so that I'm at his level, my heart beating a little faster for some reason.

"I think I want to call you 'Dad'."

His words hit me like a freight train. And for a second, I can't breathe. My heart pounds like a drum in my chest, in my ears even, as I stare at him, this little boy who is so much a part of me, and I feel like the ground underneath my feet is shifting.

He wants to call me 'Dad'.

I swallow hard, emotions surging through me so fast I can barely keep up. "Of course, Finley," I manage to say, my voice thick. "I would love that."

His face breaks into a huge smile, and he throws his arms around my neck, hugging me tight. "Okay, Dad," he whispers, and this time, it's not just a word. It's real. It's everything.

I close my eyes, hugging him back. For the first time in what feels like forever, I feel whole.

When Finley pulls back, his face is still glowing with happiness. "Can we go get ice cream, Dad?"

Dad. He said it again. My chest tightens, and I nod, forcing myself to keep it together. Part of me knows it was probably a ploy to get some dessert, but I don't mind. "Yeah, buddy, let's go get some ice cream. How many scoops do you think you can eat?" I ask him.

"Three!" he replies, holding up three fingers.

Maya is going to kill me for letting him have ice cream before noon.

We walk over to the stand near the park. This moment, this day, it's everything I've been working toward, one I'll never forget.

But the summer isn't just about me and Finley. It's about Maya, too. It's about showing her that I'm here to stay, that I can be the father Finley deserves and be the man she needs. One day, the boyfriend or husband she deserves.

I have to make this work. I have to make her see that I'm ready for the life we should've had all along. The life I want now more than anything, even hockey.

For once, my own father's words start to make sense to me.

He always told me that there's more to life than chasing a puck with a stick. I think this, having a family, is what he meant in his own grumpy way. We were that perfect family, until my mom died, my father shut down, and I lost myself in girls and hockey to escape the sadness.

Finley and I order our ice cream—chocolate, vanilla, and strawberry scoops for Finley, vanilla for me—and then we sit on a bench, watching the other kids play. Finley chatters away, telling me about his favorite games and the friends he's made at preschool who will be in his kindergarten class. I listen carefully, hanging on to every word like it's the most important thing I've ever heard.

"When do you think we can do this again?" he asks, licking his dripping cone. "Like, go to the park and stuff when you go back to where you live? Do they have parks in Greensboro?"

"There are tons of awesome parks in Greensboro," I assure him. "And I'm not sure when," I tell him honestly. "But as soon as we can, we'll visit them all."

My son grins, his face smeared with chocolate ice cream, making me laugh. I reach over to wipe it away with a napkin. He looks so happy, so carefree, and it hits me again just how much of his life that I've missed.

But I'm here now, and I'm not going anywhere.

Well, I am, but it's not for good.

Hockey may no longer be my priority, but it's the only way

I can earn a living to make sure Finley and Maya have every-thing they could ever need.

As we finish our ice cream, I start thinking about Maya again, about how I need to talk to her, to show her that I'm serious about being hers in every way. I've been trying, but I need to do more. I need to confront her fears and her insecu-rities and prove to her that I'm not the same guy who left her twice. I'm not going to run this time. I'm not going to hurt her ever again.

Once Finley is full, he trashes his leftover cone and runs off to play on the swings again. I pull out my phone, staring at Maya's number for a long moment. I want to call her to tell her how much today has meant to me and how much Finley means to me. But I know it's more than just words. She needs to see it, to believe it.

After a while, Finley comes back, tired but happy, and we start walking back toward my new SUV. He's holding my hand in his sticky one, swinging it back and forth, and the simple act makes my heart ache in the best way.

"Dad?" Finley says again, and I still can't get used to hearing it. I don't think I ever will.

"Yeah, buddy?"

"Can Mommy come with us to the parks where you live?"

I smile down at him, ruffling his hair. "Of course she can. I think she'll love them too."

Finley grins, and we climb into the car. I fasten him into the booster seat I bought just in case, right after I purchased the SUV, then drive us back toward Maya's.

When we get to the house, Finley runs ahead, opening the front door and barging inside. I stand there on the porch with my hands in my pockets, trying to steady my breathing.

"Hey, sweetie! How was the park?" I hear Maya ask him.

"So much fun! Me and Dad got a big ice cream cone too!"

I wince at how fast he sold me out to her. Of course, it's my own fault for caving. Besides, he called me dad again.

"Really? Ice cream? Before lunch?" Maya mutters.

"I'll still eat all my lunch, promise!" he assures her, then, "Uncle Preston, you want to play the hockey game?"

"Heck yes," Preston's deep voice agrees. "I bet Elle wants to play, too."

I'm so lost in eavesdropping that I startle when Maya appears in the doorway. "Are you going to come in or just stand out there all day?" she asks.

"Hey, yeah, I'll come in," I say, my voice a little rougher than I intended. "We had a good time."

"Sounds like it," she replies. "Ice cream this early, though? Really, Christian?"

"He called me dad," I tell her in explanation.

Her eyes soften, filling with emotion. "Okay, fine. But you can't spoil him every time he says it."

"I know. Just the first time," I tell her with a grin.

"I'm happy for you."

"Thanks. I'm happy too."

When I step inside, Maya's eyes flicker to Finley, who's telling Preston and Elle, "We went to the park and played on the swings and the slide. Oh, and I called Christian 'Dad' today!"

"That's…great, Finley," Preston tells him, and even his voice is a little shaky.

Maya looks at me then, and I can see the uncertainty in her eyes, the fear that has nothing to do with my bonding with Finley. But there's something else, too—something that tells me she's thinking about us—me and her.

There's a long, heavy silence between us, but I decide to break it.

"I know you still don't fully trust me," I start quietly. "But, Maya, I will do anything, absolutely anything in this world… to hear you call me daddy."

She puffs out a laugh and shakes her head, causing Preston and Elle to glance over their shoulders at us. Then Maya smiles and crosses her arms over her chest, her guard going up.

"But seriously, I love Finley," I continue, my voice quiet and shaky. "I love him, and I want to be a part of his life. And I want to be a part of your life, too. I know I screwed up before, but I'm asking you to give me a chance to make it right. To be the father he deserves and the man you need me to be."

Maya's brown eyes fill with tears, and she looks away, biting her lip.

"I'm not asking you to forget everything that's happened," I say, taking a step closer. "I know it's not going to be easy, especially during the season, but I'm willing to put in the work. Whatever it takes. However long it takes. Don't give up on us."

Her gaze drops to the ground, her lips pressed into a thin line. For a long moment, she doesn't respond, and the silence is a weight pressing down on me. I feel my heart pounding in my chest, each second dragging longer than the last.

Finally, she exhales, her voice barely above a whisper. "Christian…I don't know. Once you leave…the away games… even if you told me that you were faithful, I'm not sure if I would believe you."

Her words hit me hard, but I don't flinch. I know this is part of it. I know I can't just expect her to put all her trust in me and it's my own fault for earning the playboy reputation. "I get that," I say, my voice steady but filled with sincerity. "I know I hurt you, and I'm sorry for everything, especially for my…reputation over the past five years. But I never stopped caring about you. And I'm not asking for a second chance today or tomorrow. I'm just asking for the opportunity to show you that I'm here, that I'm fully committed to you and Finley, for however long it takes. There could be a million women on the road, and I would only want you."

She looks at me then, really looks at me. And for the first time, I see the conflict in her eyes. She wants to believe me, I can tell. There's a part of her that still holds on to the good memories, to the trust she gave me to be her first, and the love we could have had before everything went wrong. But the hurt is there, too, and it runs deep.

"What happens when things get hard again?" she asks, her voice trembling slightly. "What if you decide it's too much and you walk away? What if I let you back in and you break my heart all over again? Making things a mess with us is the last thing Finley needs."

I take a deep breath, my chest aching. This is it. The moment of truth. "I'm not going anywhere, Maya. Not this time. I'm ready to face the hard stuff. I want to face it with you as a team. For Finley. For us."

Her shoulders slump slightly, and she wipes at her eyes, looking more vulnerable than I've seen her in a long time. "I don't know, Christian," she whispers. "I just…I don't know."

I reach out, gently placing my hand on her arm, and to my relief, she doesn't pull away from the touch in front of her brother and Elle, and in front of Finley. "I'm not asking for answers right now," I say softly. "Just promise me that you'll think about it."

Maya's eyes flicker, and I see a flash of something—hope, maybe?—in her expression. She nods, though it's hesitant, and for the first time, I feel like we've taken a small step forward.

"I'll think about it," she finally says, her voice barely audible. "But Christian… no more empty promises. If you want this—if you really want to be part of our lives—then you have to mean it. No more disappearing when things get tough. No other women."

I nod, my chest swelling with determination. "I mean it, Maya. I'm all in."

She doesn't say anything more; just gives me a small, uncertain smile before I turn and walk back to my car. I can't rush her, and I know she needs to know that I have patience. The door closes behind me as my heart still races, but this time it's different. There's a spark of hope, and I'm not going to let that go.

From the driveway, I can still hear Finley's chatter as he plays with Preston inside the house. I can still see the way he looked up at me today—calling me 'Dad' for the first time, like he's been waiting his whole life to say it, to find me. And I know, without a doubt, that I'll do whatever it takes to make sure I never let him down again.

I'll prove to both of them that I'm worth this second chance.

I climb into the SUV, gripping the steering wheel tightly for a moment, letting the weight of the day settle in. This is just the beginning. I know there's still a long way to go, but for the first time, I feel like I'm moving in the right direction.

I'm about to start the car when my phone dings in my pocket with a new text message. I take it out to read it before driving off…and thank god I did because it's from Maya.

Do you want to stay for a while?

I don't bother responding by text. I'm out of the car a second later and hurrying up to where Maya's holding open the front door for me.

26

Maya

The next day, Elle and Preston leave, heading back to North Carolina as the sun dips low in the sky. It casts a warm glow over the living room where Christian helps Finley with a puzzle. Their laughter fills the air, light and carefree, and it tugs at something deep inside me. Seeing them together like this, everything out in the open, makes my heart swell with a strange mix of hope and fear.

Finley fits a piece into the puzzle and cheers. "I did it, Dad!"

Every time he calls Christian "Dad," it feels like a jolt straight to my heart. Christian, for his part, looks like he's about to burst with pride and bawl like a baby every time Finley says it. I can see it in his shimmering eyes—the way he's trying so hard to be everything for our son.

But when Finley calls him Dad, I'm reminded that we're

still not the family I dreamed of as a teenager. Not yet. Not fully. I want Christian to be here every day and every night. Which is why I caved on letting him stay until the morning.

The gorgeous man glances over at me, a soft smile tugging at his lips, either from Finley's use of the fatherly term or because he's still thinking about last night.

God knows I am.

We made out and fooled around for hours after everyone went to bed, unable to get enough, but not crossing that final line before he held me, and we fell asleep together.

I feel a pang of guilt for keeping him at arm's length in the bedroom, even though I've let him back into Finley's life. I know he wants more. He wants to be with me again, to make up for the failed first try. But that's easier said than done.

As I pour myself a glass of water, my phone buzzes on the counter. I glance at the screen, and my stomach twists when I see Spencer's name. I hesitate, knowing that right now isn't the best time to answer the call, but I can't just ignore him. After all, he's been nothing but kind to me and Finley, and he may have helped me find a job.

I swipe to answer and press the phone to my ear. "Hello?"

"Hey, Maya," Spencer's voice comes through, smooth and a little uneasy. "I heard your interview went well."

"It did! Thank you. Your aunt told me her boss would make a decision soon."

"After hearing her rave about you, I have no doubt you'll get the job."

"Thank you," I tell him with a smile.

"So," he starts. "I was wondering if you're free this week-end. You, me, and Finley could grab dinner or something on Saturday? As friends, just casual…"

I glance at Christian and Finley. Christian's attention is still focused on the new puzzle they're starting, but I feel his presence in the room like an anchor. I swallow hard, torn between the two men in my life. Spencer deserves to know the truth, that I'm still hung up on my ex.

"That sounds nice, Spencer," I say quietly, unsure of the words as they leave my mouth. "But, um, I can't Saturday."

"What about Sunday, then?" he asks, his voice filled with hope. I hate to hurt him, even if we've barely got to know each other.

"I'm sorry, and I know you said we could just keep it casual, but I'm actually seeing someone at the moment. I don't want to upset him by having dinner with another man," Christian's gaze meets mine, relief in his eyes. "Especially since it could be turning into something more serious."

"Oh," Spencer says. "Well, I'm disappointed, but I'm happy for you. You have my number if you change your mind. And you know that I still hope the job works out, too."

"Me too. Take care," I tell him before ending the call, knowing Spencer isn't the type to be petty enough to urge his aunt not to hire me just because we're not going to be dating.

Grinning over at me, Christian mouths "Thank you" and I nod back at him. If I'm going to expect him to be faithful, to not see any other women, then I can't be going out on any dates, even friendly ones. Not that I ever really wanted to…

When I return to the living room, Christian is watching me. His eyes flicker with curiosity, and I can tell he wants to ask about the call, but he doesn't. Instead, he stands up and stretches, giving Finley a pat on the back before he comes up to me.

Speaking low enough that only I can hear, he says, voice

light, "Do you want me to head out tonight or do you want me to stay?"

I smile and tell him equally quietly, "Stay. If you want."

"Of course I want," he whispers, his heavy-lidded eyes lowering to my lips, warming my belly.

"Until the morning like last night?"

"Heck yes," he quickly agrees. "Last night was…better than perfect."

"Finley, sweetie, it's time for you to get your bath and get ready for bed," I tell him.

"Already?" he complains.

"Maybe Christian can read you two stories after the bath if you don't take too long."

"Okay!" he says as he runs off down the hall.

"You don't mind, do you?" I ask Christian.

"Absolutely not."

"Good, because otherwise, he will spend an hour playing in the tub until the water is ice cold," I explain.

Slipping his hand around my waist to pull me closer, he says against my lips, "You're not in a hurry to get him tucked into bed tonight, are you?"

"Nope. Not at all. Are you?"

"Hell yes. He runs me harder than my coach. I'm fucking exhausted."

"Oh really? I'm sorry to hear that you're so tired," I remark with a grin.

"Don't worry, I'm not *that* tired, baby."

"Join me for a bath first?"

Christian's lips press a kiss to my bare shoulder where my tee has slipped. "I wouldn't want to be anywhere else than in a warm bath, naked with you. Will there be bubbles?"

"What kind of bath would it be without bubbles?" I ask before I head down the hall to check on Finley.

A long, forty-five minutes later, Christian and I finally get to soak in the tub together.

~

Christian

I'm not sure I've ever undressed quicker than I do when I see Maya sitting in the bathtub filling up with steamy water. Suds cover everything from her shoulders down, and I can't wait to get under them with her.

"About time," she says.

"It's hard to tell our son no," I reply with a smile as I pull off my socks and stride over to the tub to climb into it, taking the spot Maya left behind her back.

"Jesus, woman!" I exclaim when I submerge myself in the scalding hot water.

Maya laughs. "I want the water to stay warm for more than five minutes."

"You want to peel a layer of my skin off too?" I grumble as I settle in, sweat already beading on my forehead from the fiery temperature.

My discomfort is quickly forgotten though when I wrap my arm around Maya's waist to pull her to me so she's sitting between my legs, her soft, round bottom rubbing against my swollen dick, making me groan.

Since Maya's dark hair is piled up on top of her head, I

have full access to her bare neck, so I can lean forward and kiss, making her shiver. One of my palms gripping her waist slides up, cupping her breast, while the other lowers to that magical spot between her thighs.

"Yes," Maya whispers in a moan as she presses back against me, grinding against my dick that's trapped between our bodies. I want nothing more than to have her sit all the way down on it, but I know she's not ready for that yet.

I'm more than content to have just my hands and mouth on her beautiful body, stroking her between her legs while squeezing her breast. When her head falls back limply onto my chest, I know she's close. So am I, thanks to all her sexy gasps and squirming against my aching cock.

Needing to feel her tight heat clenching around my fingers, I slide my hand lower, continuing to apply pressure to her clit while thrusting two fingers inside of her. That's all it takes to set her off.

"Oh! Oh god!" she exclaims before I release her breast to cover her mouth. The sounds of her moans are so loud in the echoing bathroom, I know she wouldn't want our son to hear.

"Fuck, yes, baby," I whisper into her ear as I place a kiss near it. "You're gonna make me come just from all your wiggling."

"Mmm," Maya moans when her trembling body begins to relax, though her core still grips my fingers. She eventually grabs my hand to pull it free from her even though I was planning on getting her off on my hand at least one more time.

Surging forward, Maya puts enough space between us to turn around. Kneeling in the tub between my legs, her hands grip either side of the tub before she leans forward and kisses me deeply.

My right hand is lowering to my dick to give myself some relief when she grabs it and places it where hers was on the tub. She does the same with my left hand, then holds hers over them to keep them there.

"Come on, baby. I'm so close already," I tell her, my balls agonizingly heavy. "Only you can make me come so damn fast."

"Do you remember how much I used to love to swim?" she asks quietly while still kneeling between my legs, her cheeks flushed, so gorgeous it hurts.

"Huh?" I ask, since there's not enough blood flowing to my brain to keep up with the sudden change in topic.

"I loved swimming, and I can still hold my breath for a really long time."

"That's…great, baby," I tell her. "We'll take Finley to the pool someday. But right now, I'm hurting so—" That's the last word out of my mouth before Maya's face disappears under the water and… "Holy shit!" I shout. Her head is almost entirely submerged in the deep tub as she wraps her fingers around my cock. She takes me into her mouth, applying that heavenly suction.

Her head begins to bob, nearly breaking the surface before diving back down, taking me to the back of her throat.

My grip on the sides of the tub tightens a little more with each pleasurable second until I'm holding on with a white-knuckle grip. I don't dare reach for her head to hold it down and chance drowning her. Besides, she's doing just fine without my…

"Fuck, I'm coming! I'm coming!" I warn her when my entire body jerks with the first pulse of my release. My hips thrust upward on their own over and over again, chasing the cresting waves of pleasure, drawing them out, trying to make them last as long as possible as Maya strokes me and swallows every drop of my cum.

I throw my head back onto the rim of the tub when the shudders come to an end. A moment later, I realize Maya's face is still underwater. Grabbing her now soaked, messy bun, I pull her head up by the strands.

Lips parting in a gasp of much-needed oxygen, water droplets pour down her face from her soaked hair until she reaches up and wipes it away from her eyes. My mouth claims hers as soon as she's sucked in a few breaths of air.

Returning the kiss with as much enthusiasm, Maya straddles my lap without breaking it. Oh, and her soft folds stroke over my half-hard dick, making me wish I was ready to go again.

Pulling her back by her hair to see her face, I tell her, "That…was fucking amazing."

Smiling, she says, "You've never had an underwater blowjob before?"

"God, no. I can't believe you held your breath for that long…"

"It wasn't that long," she mocks me with a grin.

Gripping her hips, I press her body down on that exhausted part of my body. "It was definitely long. I just couldn't last more than two minutes in your mouth."

"Right," she agrees with a laugh.

"You know, I can hold my breath for a while too…" I tell her.

"Oh, really?" she asks, her eyes widening when I begin to slide down into the water. Wrapping each of my arms around her thighs, I hold my breath and disappear under the water, underneath Maya's spread thighs, keeping her body lowered to my face so she can't move when I swipe my tongue through her folds.

Her moan above me is muffled as I flick the tip of my tongue over her clit. Opening my eyes under water, I look up and see a blurred Maya shove her fist into her mouth to keep from screaming louder. That only makes me work harder to get her off.

And I overestimated how long I could hold my breath. I have to break the surface to suck in some air twice. Unlike me, Maya has no problem pushing my head back under the water, making me chuckle before I get back to work. As soon as I suck her swollen bud into my mouth, her thighs tremble then rock rapidly toward my face.

My lungs are ready to explode before the tension finally leaves her body and I break through the surface again.

"*Jesus*, Christian," Maya gasps as I wipe the water from my face.

"That was one hell of a baptism, baby. I thought you were going to let me drown," I tease her.

This is what has always been missing with every other woman—fooling around is fun with Maya. It's not about rushing to the finish line. I just love being with her in every way possible.

27

Maya

After our ridiculously hot bath, Christian and I dried off but didn't dress before climbing into bed to pick up where we left off.

It's the first time we've both been completely naked together since we started fooling around weeks ago. The only other time was the night I was supposed to lose my virginity.

As we kiss, my thighs bracket Christian's hips with his erection poking me insistently. Tonight is the night we'll have a redo.

I want Christian, all of him.

Based on his low groan between kisses to my neck, I'm pretty sure he feels the same.

Reaching down between our bodies, I fist his shaft and line it up…only for Christian to grab my hand and peel my fingers off him.

"You…don't want to?" I ask, holding my breath to brace for the rejection.

"Oh, baby. I want you. So damn bad. But I think I should tell you this first."

"What?"

"I'm…well, I-I've been meaning to tell you," he stammers hesitantly, making me worry. I brace myself for the worst, for him to admit that he has been picking up women since the night I told him it would be our last time, before I went on a date with Spencer. Not that I could blame him, but still, I hate the thought of my Christian with anyone else.

"Just tell me," I nearly scream at him.

Exhaling a breath, he does in a rush. "Practice starts Monday morning."

Practice? He's been putting off telling me about practice? Oh, right.

"You have to leave us?"

Wincing, he says, "I've got to head back Sunday afternoon. And I don't want us to finally do *this* tonight after waiting for a redo for so long, and then have you regret it once there's distance between us…"

Dammit. He's right. All the heat from earlier instantly cools inside of me.

He's leaving.

Again.

And while I know it's different, I've known all summer he was just visiting temporarily, I had tried not to think about when that time would end.

Our time, his time with Finley this summer, now has an official expiration date.

Sunday.

"Have you…have you told Finley?" I ask while trying to pull myself together and not burst into tears.

"I was going to tell him tomorrow morning. Hopefully, during breakfast if you'll let me stay and help make it?"

"Yeah. Sure," I agree. Lowering my eyes, I notice that while he's still hovering above me naked, I'm not the only one who is no longer aroused.

It's a sad sight to see his perfect cock so unenthusiastic.

While I know I could probably use my hand or mouth to get Christian in the mood again, I'm glad he stopped us before taking that final step tonight.

"How soon can you and Finley come visit?" he asks from above me.

"I-I don't know. I guess, any time before school starts. I'm sure he'll be happy to visit Preston, too." The truth is, I should've gone down to visit my brother before now. I think I've been putting it off because I'm afraid I'll love his new town so much I'll never want to leave, losing out on making my own decision.

"Good. Maybe next weekend? We should have Saturdays and Sundays off."

"I'll have to think about it and talk to Preston, so don't tell Finley yet?"

"I won't," he assures me as he rolls off me, climbing off the bed to grab his clothes. Or at least his navy-blue boxer briefs. "Can I still spend the night?"

"Yes," I easily agree.

God, I should've let him stay all the other nights too, now that I know he's leaving so soon…

That familiar ache in my chest makes me want to cry. I already miss Christian and he's still here, in my bedroom.

Once he's gone, the longing for him is going to be so much worse.

And the doubt, well, it's inevitable. I can feel it already setting in.

Everything is about to change again.

I fucking hate change.

~

Christian

I wake up early the next morning, a sense of anticipation and sadness bubbling in my chest. Today's the last day I get to spend with Finley before I leave, and I'm not going to waste a second of it.

Maya, well, I'm trying not to think about leaving Maya, or about how I was the one who put the brakes on to stop things last night after waiting for so long to be with her again.

It just didn't feel right. Physically, yes, the night was perfect, but emotionally, I know Maya's not ready yet, even if I weren't about to leave.

By the time the pancakes are sizzling in the pan, Finley comes bounding down the stairs, still in his pajamas, his hair a wild mess. "Morning, Dad! What's that smell?" he asks, waking right up.

"Pancakes," I say with a grin, flipping one of the golden-brown discs. "You ready for our big day?"

Finley nods enthusiastically, practically bouncing on his toes. "Yeah! Where are we going?"

"I was thinking we could go to the arcade first," I suggest, plating the pancakes. "And then maybe grab some lunch, go to the park, then hit the community pool once it's smoldering hot outside. What do you think?"

His face lights up. "Yes! Can we play the racing games at the arcade?"

"Of course," I say, ruffling his hair as I set the plate of pancakes down in front of him. "We'll play whatever you want."

Maya comes downstairs just as we're finishing breakfast, her hair pulled back in a loose ponytail, freshly showered and in a red, sleeveless cotton dress. She gives me an easy smile, leaning against the counter as she watches Finley devour his pancakes. "You two ready for an exciting day?" she asks.

"Yep," Finley says through a mouthful of food. "We're going to the arcade and park and pool! Dad said I can play the racing games!"

Maya smiles, her eyes flicking to mine. "Sounds like you've got a full day planned."

I return her smile. "Yeah. We're going to have the best day ever."

I'm torn between wanting to invite Maya and wanting to make the day solely about Finley. As if understanding that, she leans down and kisses the top of Finley's head before turning to me. "I'll go pack up a bag for him with his swimsuit. Have a good time today. I'll be here tonight when you get home."

28

Christian

The arcade is exactly the kind of chaotic fun I remember from when I was a kid. The flashing lights, the sound of coins clinking in machines, and the laughter of kids running from one game to the next. Finley's eyes are wide with excitement as we walk in, and he immediately pulls me toward the row of racing games.

"Come on, Dad! Let's race!"

I chuckle as we sit side by side, and Finley picks the biggest, flashiest car on the screen while I opt for something more modest. Not that it matters — I'm going to let him win, anyway.

The race starts, and Finley is a bundle of energy beside me, leaning into every turn as if he's really driving. I keep pace with him, but I make sure to fall behind just enough so that he crosses the finish line first.

"I won!" he shouts, jumping out of his seat and pumping his fist in the air. "I beat you, Dad!"

Laughing at his enthusiasm, I get up from my seat and give him a high-five. "You sure did, buddy. You're a natural."

We spend the next couple of hours bouncing from game to game — basketball hoops, skeeball, even a few rounds of air hockey. By the time we're done, we've racked up a decent amount of tickets, which Finley exchanges for a bag full of candy that Maya is probably going to hate.

As we leave the arcade and head out to get lunch, I can't help but feel a sense of contentment settle over me. This is what it's all about. Spending time with my son, being there for him in ways I wasn't before.

When we arrive at the park, the afternoon sun is casting long shadows across the grass, and the air is filled with the sound of children playing and birds chirping. Finley runs ahead to the jungle gym, and I follow at a slower pace, watching him climb up the bars with the energy of a kid who just had too much sugar. I couldn't help it. I let him have three pieces of candy after lunch.

As he plays, I sit on a nearby bench, my thoughts drifting. I think about how far we've come — me, Maya, Finley. We're not perfect, and we've still got a long way to go, but for the first time in a long while, I feel like we're headed in the right direction.

I'm committed to this. To be the father Finley deserves and the partner Maya needs. And it won't be easy — I know there will still be challenges and times when it feels like everything could fall apart again once I'm in a different state. But I'm not going to let that happen. Not this time.

As I watch Finley swing from the monkey bars, laughing and calling out to the other kids, I feel something inside me shift. It's a deep sense of peace, the kind that settles into your bones and lets you know that, even with all the chaos and uncertainty, you're exactly where you're supposed to be.

Finley glances back at me from across the playground, his face flushed with excitement. "Dad! Look at me!" he shouts, waving his arms dramatically as he lets go of the monkey bars and jumps down to the ground.

I give him a thumbs-up, smiling as he runs over to a group of kids who are playing tag. He fits in so easily, so naturally, and it's moments like this that make me realize just how much he's grown even since the first day I met him.

I settle back on the bench, watching him play, and my thoughts inevitably drift back to Maya. She's been through so much, carrying the weight of raising Finley practically on her own. She's made mistakes, like not telling me sooner that she had our son, or letting me share the news with Finley, but I know she did those things to protect him, and herself. It may have sucked, but it was the right thing for her to do until I proved myself to her.

I had to prove to myself I could be a decent father, too. And I want to be the man who's always there for his family, the one who steps up when things get tough instead of running away. I want to give Finley the kind of childhood he deserves, one where he knows without a doubt that his dad loves him and is always going to be there for him.

As the sun heats up the day, casting a warm golden light over the park, Finley runs back over to me, breathless and grinning. "Dad, can we get ice cream before we go to the pool?" he asks, bouncing on his toes in excitement.

I ruffle his hair, knowing this will be the best time to tell him I'm leaving. "Sure thing, buddy. Let's go find the ice cream truck."

We walk together, hand in hand, toward the truck parked near the park's entrance. The line is short, and within a few minutes, Finley is happily licking away at a chocolate cone, his face smeared with the sticky sweetness. I opt for a vanilla cone, then we sit down on a nearby bench to enjoy our treat.

As Finley eats his ice cream, his eyes flick up to mine, thoughtful. "Dad?" he asks between licks. "After you leave… you're going to come back again, right?"

The question hits me square in the chest. It's going to be even harder to tell him I have to leave.

"Don't worry, buddy," I say softly. "I will definitely be back. And you and your mom can come visit me soon. I have to go back to North Carolina to start training for the hockey season tomorrow, but even when I'm not here in town, right beside you, I promise I'll still be close enough to come whenever you need me, okay? I'm just a phone call away."

He nods, satisfied with my answer, and goes back to his ice cream. But the weight of the promise I just made settles over me like a heavy blanket. It's not something I take lightly. I've rarely made promises before, and this one I'm going to keep.

After we finish our ice cream, we walk back toward the car and go to the local pool to swim. Some of Finley's friends from the neighborhood are there, so they take turns jumping off the diving board to see who can make the biggest splash. I swear my son can swim better than I can.

When we get back to the house, Maya is in the kitchen, her

hair pulled back and her hands busy with something on the stove. She looks up when we walk in, her eyes lighting up at the sight of us.

"I missed you two," she says with a smile, wiping her hands on a towel. Finley runs over to her, wrapping his arms around her waist. "Looks like you had fun."

"We did," I say, giving her a warm smile in return. "Arcade, lunch, park, ice cream, and pool. The whole package. Oh, and a few pieces of candy." I offer her the bag. "Next time, maybe you'll come with us?"

"Mommy, Dad said he's got to leave for training, but he promised that he'll come back again," Finley tells Maya.

Maya's eyes meet mine over his head, and for a moment, the air between us is heavy with unspoken words. She gives Finley a soft smile, stroking his hair. "I know he will," she says quietly. "And we'll go visit him and Uncle Preston soon."

There's a tension in the room, but it's not the kind that feels like everything's about to fall apart. No, it's more like feeling something good is going to happen, but you don't know when, so you just have to be patient and wait for it.

Later that evening, after Finley has been put to bed, I join Maya on the sofa. She's curled up beside me, her head resting on my shoulder, and I can feel the steady rise and fall of her breathing against my side. It's such a small, ordinary thing that feels good.

It's moments like this that remind me of the times we had before everything fell apart — the quiet moments when we were dating, the ones where we didn't need to say anything because we already understood each other.

"He's going to miss you so much," Maya's voice is soft, barely above a whisper, but there's a weight to her words.

I tilt my head to look down at her, brushing a strand of hair away from her face. "Yeah, I'm going to miss him too," I say, my voice just as quiet. "And you. You and Finley are my world now. Even if I'm not here with you, you're with me."

Maya doesn't say anything for a while, but I can feel her relax a little more against me, like maybe — just maybe — she's starting to believe me. Starting to believe in us again.

"I was thinking," I begin, my voice hesitant, "maybe we could plan a weekend trip. Just the three of us. Somewhere close, nothing too fancy. Just... some time away together before Finley starts school. What do you think?"

Maya lifts her head, her eyes searching mine. "A trip? Just the three of us?"

"Yeah," I nod. I need something to look forward to now that the summer is ending. "I think it would be good for us. To get away, spend some time together before the season starts too."

She looks at me for a long moment, her gaze thoughtful. "I guess it depends on if I get the job or not, but if we can make it work, then I'd really like that," she says finally, a small smile tugging at the corners of her lips. "I think Finley would love it, too."

Leaning down to press a soft kiss to her forehead. "I'll start looking into it tomorrow."

～

The next morning, I wake up early, my mind already buzzing with ideas for our trip. It's a small thing, really, but it feels like the first step toward something bigger, like we're a family.

I head downstairs, making a mental list of places we could go — somewhere with a beach, maybe, or a cabin in the mountains. I'm not sure yet, but I'll figure it out. All that matters is that we will get to spend some uninterrupted time together, just like we did this summer.

As I sip my coffee, I hear the sound of small footsteps, and I look up to see Finley standing in the doorway, rubbing his eyes sleepily.

"Morning, buddy," I say with a smile, setting my mug down. "How did you sleep?"

"Good," he mumbles, shuffling over to throw his arms around me, giving me a hug. "I didn't know if you would say bye before you left." He rests his head against my chest, and I wrap my arms around him, holding him close.

"Of course I'm going to say goodbye to you. I don't have to leave until late this afternoon."

"Okay, good."

"And don't tell anyone if I cry a little, okay? I'm going to miss you so much."

"I won't tell anyone," he agrees. "Is it okay if I cry because I'm going to miss you, too?"

"Absolutely." I press a kiss to the top of Finley's head, my heart full.

I just wish I could have it all – Finley, Maya, and hockey all at the same time. Then my life would be perfect.

29

Maya

Christian's last day with us goes by way too fast.

It seems like I barely blink and we're having dinner, which means he better get on the road soon so he can get a few hours' sleep before tomorrow's training starts.

I tell him as much. "I'll leave after I help you clean up the kitchen and read Finley a bedtime story."

There's no way for me to argue with either of those things, so he stays another hour.

I wait out in the hallway while he's finishing reading a book about dinosaurs who wear pants.

"This is goodbye, but not for long, okay? I'll call you tomorrow and tell you all about the first day of training and you can tell me all about going school shopping with Mommy. I wish I could go too. We'll have to do a video call so I can see all your cool supplies."

"Okay," Finley agrees, his voice soft and shaky as if he's trying to hold back tears. I try and fail to do the same.

"I love you, buddy. Sleep tight."

"Love you too, Dad."

A moment later, Christian comes out of Finley's room, pulling the door shut behind him. He's swiping the back of his knuckles over his cheeks before he sees me. Rather than be embarrassed about showing emotion, he just says, "You think the Warhawks would trade Spencer Williams for me?"

I smile and shake my head.

"Too bad," he says as he takes my hand and leads me into my bedroom, shutting and locking the door once we're inside.

"I thought you were leaving," I remind him. "It's getting late…" He lifts my dress over my head, stopping my protests.

"There's one more thing I have to do before I go," Christian tells me as he dips a finger into the waistband of my panties and pulls me over to the bed. "Lie down and get comfortable. I want to lick you until you fall into an orgasm coma. I want to taste you on my tongue all the way home."

"Okay," I agree as I sit down on the bed and he kneels before me, pulling my panties down my hips and legs. "I just have one request."

"Anything, baby."

"I want you to come on me down there like the first time…"

Christian groans and leans forward, pressing his face between my legs. There's no slow teasing tonight, either. He has me flat on my back, back arching as I throb around his fingers in record time. Again and again, he takes me over the edge until I can barely move a muscle and my eyelids are heavy, begging for sleep.

I keep them open long enough to watch as Christian, now completely naked, climbs on top of me. His lips claim mine in a fervent kiss while he settles himself between my spread, damp thighs. I gasp at the feel of his long, hard shaft sliding over my sensitive flesh. My fingernails dig into his muscular ass cheeks, wanting him to bury himself deep inside me. But he doesn't. As if worried he might accidentally slip inside, Christian reaches between us, thrusting two fingers inside me to send me soaring again while hot, thick seed spills over my lower belly. Our lips separate for us to both moan and gasp through our releases.

Feeling brazen, and sexy, I remove his two fingers from inside me, drag them up and through his cum, coating them, before bringing them to my mouth to suck them clean.

"Jesus, baby. You're killing me. How can I leave you, when you go and do that?"

"I want you in my mouth," I tell him, making him hang his head with a groan.

"Fuck, baby. I want to say yes, but then I may never leave. And it could take me a few minutes…"

"Roll over," I say, pressing my palms to his chest. Christian quickly hits his back, caving that easily. His eyes darken as I move lower, until I'm straddling his legs. Curling my fingers around his half-hard cock, I lick the moisture from the tip.

"That feels…so damn good," he groans. "But I'm not ready to go again."

"I don't mind," I remark before running my tongue up and down his length. "This is the only time I can fit all of you in my mouth. And I want to do that until you finish again."

"God, yes," Christian grunts as I do just that. He lifts his hands to tuck them under his head, as if to keep them from guiding my movements, and to get comfortable since we're going to be here for a while, my mouth working him up. His hips occasionally thrust upward, and I love all the garbled sounds he makes – half swear words, half growls of pleasure. I want to make him feel so good that he can't think about another woman because he'll be too busy remembering this night with me, and the time in the bathtub.

This is where he belongs, here with me.

Christian

I think Maya is trying to kill me. Or trying to convince me to stay. Either way, she's doing a hell of a job.

It's been five, maybe ten minutes since her mouth started suckling me and I'm so aroused, so turned on, that I had to wrap both of my arms around the headboard behind me to hang on, trying not to come out of my skin.

I can taste the blood from where I've been biting down on my lip to keep from shouting down the house.

Maya hums around me again and I whimper like a wounded animal. The pleasure is growing so intense it almost hurts, but in the best way. It's torture. And I love it. Love her.

"I'm close…don't stop, baby," I beg her, hoping her jaw isn't getting too sore because I need this, need her so much.

Another happy hum is her response, making me snap.

Releasing the headboard, I grab Maya's ponytail and do what I swore I wouldn't do – my hips buck up as I push her down, fucking her mouth. Her eyes widen and water as she stares up at me, looking like a degraded angel. Oh, I'm such an asshole. This is the woman I love, the mother of my child, and I'm treating her like a…

Maya's eyes close and she moans long and low, setting me off.

"Fuck!" I shout as I guide her mouth all the way down my shaft until I'm pulsing down her throat. Before the last twitch of bliss leaves my body, I release my grip on her ponytail. Maya's mouth pops off my cock an instant later. Instead of yelling at me, she licks up the sides of me, cleaning me up. "God, I love you…your mouth," I quickly amend, causing her to glance up at me.

She's not ready to hear those words, and especially not for the first time during sex. Besides, she would never believe that I love her because she's an amazing woman, an incredible woman, who just so happens to suck me off like a pro.

I know exactly what she's doing – trying to ruin me for other women before I leave. I'm guilty of doing the same since that's why I wanted to make her come a few more times before I hit the road.

Maya's staking her claim on me, and *that* is why I love her.

I cup her cheek so she'll look at me when I tell her, "There will never be anyone but you. Ever. And it's not because I love your mouth."

"That's not…" she starts then she sits up, kneeling between my legs. "Promise me you'll be honest with me if anything happens with another woman."

"I promise. Now, will you promise me that you won't assume I'm keeping shit from you if I don't confess to any hookups?"

"I'll try," Maya replies, which is all I can hope for at the moment until time helps build up her trust in me. "You should go. Text me when you get home, even if it's late."

"Sure, thing," I easily agree. Before I leave her, I tell her, "Just to warn you, Preston gave me your checking account numbers."

"Why would he do that?"

"Because I wanted to make a transfer. Just a little spending money for you and Finley…"

"Christian, no!"

"It's too late, it's done. Buy a house, save it for his college fund if you want, but it's there if you need anything."

With a heavy sigh, she says, "Thank you. Even though it's completely unnecessary."

It is necessary, though. I want to support my family and she's being stubborn about it.

Then, with a sigh of my own, I get up and get dressed because it really is getting late.

Giving Maya one last soft kiss on her lips, I leave her.

30

Maya

Christian kept his promise, calling Finley every night to talk on video so they can see each other. Then we flirt a little once he's tucked into bed.

I knew I was going to miss him, but I had no idea it would hurt so much.

Finley's handling the separation better than I am, likely thanks to the daily calls and my intentionally scheduled play-dates with his friends.

But one week apart is too long for me. That's why we made the five-hour drive down today, the first Friday after training week.

Finley skips ahead of me, his tiny sneakers scraping against the pavement, obviously happy our long car ride is over as we approach Elle's salon, our first stop since getting into town other than lunch and a bathroom break. His excitement at seeing Preston and Christian tonight is palpable.

For the millionth time, I second-guess surprising everyone this weekend, hoping Elle and Preston won't mind our visit. If they have plans, Finley and I can always get a hotel room for two nights.

And Christian, well, part of me wanted to surprise him for a different reason, to see if he's keeping his promise. I still can't believe he dumped two million dollars into my checking account as if it was "a little spending money" for me and Finley. I refuse to touch a cent of it, though, leaving it for Finley to use for college one day.

Elle's shop is so cute and girly, all pretty in pink, exactly what I imagined as I push open the door, making a bell jingle in greeting.

Elle's standing behind an older gray-haired lady, a brush in one hand, hair dryer in the other. When she glances up and sees us, she raises both straight up in the air.

"Finley! Maya! You're here!" Her smile is warm and genuine, which is a relief, as she powers off the dryer.

"We're here," I agree, unable to help my own grin.

"Aunt Ellie!" Finley exclaims, using his nickname for Elle as he runs over and throws his arms around her waist. He also bestows the title on her for the first time as she puts down the brush and hair dryer to hug him back.

"Oh, I've missed you, cutie. Preston has too," she tells him.

The rest of the salon is buzzing with activity, the usual sounds of hair dryers and chatter filling the space from the other side where a brunette is clipping a client's damp hair.

"I just had to come see your shop," I tell her. "It's so cute!

I'm sorry to drop in unannounced, though. We'll let you get back to work and catch up with you tonight, if that's okay?"

"No, stay! I'm almost finished up and then I'm free for the next hour. There are restrooms in the back and a sitting area with some snacks if you can wait?"

"As long as we're not imposing."

"Never," Elle replies. "Help yourselves!"

A few minutes later, as promised, Elle finds us hanging out in the little sitting area. "So? What do you think?" she asks, her hands braced on her hips.

"I love it. I should've given you a heads-up to try to get an appointment for a trim."

"Well, come on back," she says with a smile. "Audrey can keep an eye on Finley since she's sweeping up and he seems to like watching Animal Planet."

"I don't know. Are you sure? You shouldn't have to work during your lunch break."

"I've already had lunch, so it's just an empty spot," she explains, then waves me forward. "Come on."

"If you're sure," I tell her, then to Finley, sitting next to me on the small sofa, "Stay right here, okay?"

"Okay," he replies easily enough.

As I sit down in one of the salon chairs and Elle starts combing my hair, I try to remember the last time I had a haircut. Last year? Year before?

"What are we thinking? A little trim or a big change?"

"Ugh, no. I hate change," I tell her. "Could you just take as much as you think it needs for the dead ends? I actually can't remember my last cut," I admit sheepishly while she fits the black cape around me.

"Then you are due one today." Wetting my hair with a squirt bottle, she says, "I'm so glad you decided to come down. Are you staying the weekend with us?"

"Oh, Elle. I'm an awful sister-in-law," I confess. "I should've warned you we were coming and asked if we could stay with Preston."

"You know the answer is always going to be yes. Besides, it's his apartment, not mine. I just stay over occasionally."

"Occasionally?" I ask, grinning at her in the mirror's reflection.

"Fine. I stay with him most nights. But there is more than enough room for you and Finley. He's been so worried about you two."

"Of course he has," I mutter with a roll of my eyes. "We've been fine. We miss him, not his overprotectiveness or his wallet. I'm actually still waiting not-so-patiently to find out about that activity director position."

"Right. The one that will decide your fate; get it and you stay in Maryland, don't get it and you move here. Tell me more about it," Elle says as she breaks out the shears.

We spend the next fifteen minutes catching up before Elle uses the hairdryer to dry my hair and blow away the loose hair from my cape. In the silence, my mind wanders over to thinking about Christian, how to tell him we're visiting, and whether or not he'll be invited to Preston's.

"Penny for your thoughts?" Elle says, meeting my gaze in the mirror when she puts the dryer away.

I force a smile. "It's nothing, really."

Elle gives me a look. "Girl, part of my job is to gossip and find out what's going on with all my customers while I work. And I can practically see your thoughts churning."

I let out a sigh because Elle is so easy to talk to, it's hard to resist sharing. But I'm not sure if I want to talk about him. "It's just… complicated," I say, my voice quiet.

"Christian?" she asks, her hands pausing from brushing out my hair.

I nod. "He's doing so great with Finley and with us, but I just… I can't shake the feeling that it won't last. At least not with me. That he'll get bored or distracted or… forget about us, me, once the season starts."

Elle turns me in the chair to face her, her eyes serious. "I know it's hard to do, but you can't hold on to the past forever, not if you want to move forward. It's going to take some trust, though."

I cross my arms over my cape, a little defensive. "But what if he hasn't really changed? What if he hurts me again? I still haven't recovered from the first time."

Elle lets out a sigh, leaning back against the counter. "Look, I get it. I really do. You've been burned by him before, and it's hard to trust someone who's hurt you. But Christian… I think he missed you, even when he was sleeping around. I'm certain of that, actually. He missed you before he knew you two had a son together."

I bite my lip, thinking back to the way Christian's face lights up every time he sees me and Finley. He's making an effort, not just for our son but for me too. There's definitely something deeper, more genuine there, just like when we were dating. But still, the fear lingers.

"I just don't know, Elle. What if I take the leap and we end up hurting Finley, too?" I whisper. "Or seeing him after he moves on is too hard? I can't drag our son through a nasty breakup."

Elle studies me for a moment. "You know, I used to feel the same way about Preston."

That catches me off guard. "Preston? Really?"

She nods, her expression softening. "Yeah. When we first got together, I was so sure he would never make room for me in his life. I mean, you know what he's like. He's this big, tough guy who loves his family more than anything. Then, I didn't think we had a future because of the distance between us. But it all worked out." Elle smiles, shaking her head. "Now, I can't imagine my life without him. He changed our complicated circumstances. He uprooted his life for me, Maya. And while Christian may not be able to up and leave this city right now, I think he would do it for you if he could. Are you willing to do the same for him?"

I look down at my hands, her words sinking in. I've seen Preston and Elle together, how solid they are, how they balance each other out—her sunshine to soften his grumpiness. They weren't perfect, there were distance and obstacles between them, but they made it work. And maybe… maybe Christian and I could, too.

Glancing over at the sitting area where Audrey and Finley are watching some penguins play, I say, "If we move, I want it to be my decision for once. And what's best for Finley. I just wish I knew exactly what the future holds."

"I get it," Elle says, her tone gentle. "But here's the thing—you're never going to know unless you give it a chance. You don't have to jump in with both feet, but maybe… maybe you could take a step."

"A step?" I ask, glancing up at her.

Elle shrugs. "Yeah. Like… visit him while you're here or

when he's on the road for a preseason game. See how he is after you two are forced to be apart. Maybe that'll give you some clarity."

I laugh lightly. "What, you're encouraging me to spy on him?"

She grins. "I'm just saying, sometimes seeing someone in their natural element gives you a better idea of who they really are. Plus, it's a good excuse for you to go on a little road trip with me."

I roll my eyes, but the idea sticks with me. Visiting Christian on the road wouldn't be the worst idea. Maybe it would help me figure out if he really has changed or if I'm just setting myself up for more heartbreak.

Elle returns to my hair again, working her magic on the annoying little flyaways. But I needed more than a trim from her. I needed all the heart-to-heart she could muster.

After we're done, Finley happily shows off the cookie Audrey gave him as a reward for being so "good" which is fine with me, since he deserves it for being such a trooper on the long drive.

Still thinking about Elle's advice, I ask her, "Do you know what time training usually ends?"

Elle gives me a knowing look and grins. "Usually around six."

"Six."

"Uh-huh. And I'm closing up here at four today, you know, if you were to need a babysitter."

"Are you sure?" I ask with a wince, already imposing on her for dropping by.

"Absolutely! I'll give you a key to go to Preston's apartment so you two can get settled in, then I'll be there a little after four."

"You really are the best, Elle. I am so freaking glad your breakup with my ex led you to my grumpy brother."

"Same, girl," she replies with a wink.

31

Christian

After spending the summer with Finley and Maya, I can't shake the weight sitting on my chest during our first week of practice. Being back in Greensboro without them feels like someone's ripped the ground out from under me. I'm off-balance. And I hate it.

The last thing I wanted to do was walk away from Finley and Maya, but since she won't budge on moving, and I have an obligation to the Bobcats, I didn't have any other choice.

Still, not being able to spend the day playing with my son or in bed with the woman I love feels like I'm getting daily beatdowns while serving a prison sentence. The only thing that helps is the phone calls at night. Finley gets on the video call first, then while he's getting his bath, I talk to Maya. She even lets me stay on the phone while she reads a story and tucks him into bed so I can say goodnight.

Just when everything was going so well over the summer, Maya was beginning to trust me, we're right back to where we started with her doubting everything again.

Training today was the last thing on my mind. I go through the motions, trying to focus on drills and strategies, but my head is still in Bethesda. My teammates notice, too. They threw me a few odd glances when I dropped the barbell on my throat and nearly killed myself during weight training, but no one says anything directly. I guess they can tell I'm not up for conversation. They probably assume I'm in a shit mood because Preston has joined the team. Nobody would ever believe it's his sister that has me tripping over my own two feet.

"Yo, Christian! You with us, man?" Luke asks from the treadmill next to mine when I stumble. He's the only one who knows the truth.

I give him a half-hearted smile. "Sorry, just distracted."

He raises an eyebrow. "You've been MIA all week. Snap out of it, *Captain*," he says, emphasizing my leadership role on the team. "Coach isn't gonna go easy on you because you're daydreaming about a woman."

I nod, trying to force myself to focus as I turn up the speed to finish my third mile.

The Bobcats are getting ready for a hell of a season, one where we make another run at the playoffs and the championship. As a team captain, the last thing I need is to let my teammates down.

But as much as I try, Maya's face keeps flashing in my mind, distracting me. Her hesitation to move down here with Finley, to give us a real chance, to trust me, is killing me slowly from the inside out.

After practice, I head for the locker room, peeling off my sweaty clothes with a sense of detachment. The only thing worse than practice is my lonely ass apartment.

The adrenaline from training doesn't hit me like it usually does. Instead, there's just this dull ache in my chest. I don't even want to know what the guys would say if they knew how torn up I am about a woman. They'd probably tell me to suck it up and focus on the game.

As I head for my SUV in the arena parking lot, I hear someone, a woman, call my name from the gate. At first, I ignore it, since there's only one woman I want to talk to. But then I hear it again, and I'm certain I'm imagining it. I turn around, my heart doing an odd flip, and there she stands.

Maya.

She's waiting with two guards just outside the entrance, looking hesitant, her arms crossed over her chest, wearing a light blue dress that shows off her sexy tan legs. For a moment, I can't quite believe she's here in North Carolina. She told me she would think about coming to visit this weekend, but never confirmed and I didn't want to push her.

I jog over, my pulse picking up speed, a mix of hope and dread swirling in my chest. "Hey, baby," I say, trying to keep my voice steady. "What are you doing here? Where's Finley?"

She smiles, but it's a small, uncertain smile. "He's with Elle. I... I wanted to talk to you alone first."

My mind races as I lead her away from the security guards. "Okay. Let's talk. I'm so fucking happy to see you."

She takes a deep breath, looking up at me with those brown eyes that always seem to see right through me. "I've missed you this week. So much. Finley has too, of course, but..."

"But you missed me too?" I say with a grin.

"Yes." Maya bites her lip, clearly struggling with what to say next. "I know that things are…complicated between us, but maybe we could give this a real try?"

"You want to give us a try?" I repeat, uncertain I heard her correctly. I mean, that's already what I was doing, even after she tried to end things and said she didn't see us ever happening.

"We would have to take things slow…"

"Consider me a sloth," I tell her, making her smile, loosening her up a little

"And make sure Finley doesn't find out about us…"

"I'm a sneaky fucking sloth."

"I'm serious, Christian."

"Baby, I'm serious too," I promise her. Stepping closer, it's nearly impossible to be near her and not touch her, but I'm waiting for her to initiate it. "I'm not going anywhere. I'm going to be here in Greensboro, either training or sleeping, or alone in my apartment every single night. I want to be in Finley's life and yours, baby. Permanently. All you have to do is let me in."

She looks up at me, her eyes filled with uncertainty. "And what if things don't work out between you and me?"

"We will," I say confidently. "But if we don't, we sure as shit aren't going to go five years without seeing each other again. If you agree to date me, to take this chance, then you can call it quits whenever you want. I'll still be around in Finley's life, even if you're not mine, no matter how much it hurts. I can promise you that if we split, it won't be my decision."

When Maya doesn't speak, I cave, reaching for her arm to

uncross it and take her hand. "I'm Finley's father. *Nothing* will ever come between me and my son, not even us."

There's another long pause between us, the air thick with unspoken fears and emotions. I watch as she processes everything, her face a mixture of conflict and hope.

"Then, I want to try again," she finally says, her voice soft but determined.

Relief floods through me at her words, but I know this is just the beginning. We still have a long way to go. But she's here. She's ready to give me the chance I've always wanted.

"I'm so excited to give us a real shot, baby."

"Me too."

"Where is Finley now?" I ask her.

"At Preston's apartment. Elle got off work early," Maya explains. "Am I a bad mother for coming to see you without him? I didn't want him to overhear…"

"No, baby. You could never be a bad mother. And I'll see him soon enough. In fact, do you think Elle could watch him for another hour or so?"

"Why?"

"Because, even though I can't wait to see him, I want to take you on a date tonight. A real date. It'll be easier to do it now instead of you trying to sneak out later."

Maya smiles, and this time, it reaches her eyes. "I'll check with Elle, and if she doesn't mind, then yes."

"Good," I say, leaning in to press a gentle kiss to her cheek. "You won't regret this, baby. I promise."

As I pull back, Luke and Tyler come walking out of the arena.

"Give me one second?" Maya asks as she holds up her phone.

"Absolutely," I agree as she walks away, and Luke and Tyler come over. He looks between the two of us and claps me on the back. "Everything good with your lady?"

"Yeah," I reply, feeling a lightness in my chest I haven't felt in weeks. "Everything is good. I'm taking her out on a date."

Tyler raises an eyebrow in surprise while Luke grins. "About time, man. Maybe next week you'll be worth a shit on the ice again."

I flip him the finger and shake my head as he strides off with Tyler.

A moment later, Maya returns. Pushing a strand of her long black hair behind her ear, she says, "Elle told us to 'take our time' and that Preston and Finley are catching up. How did he get home so quick?"

"I told you, I'm a sloth," I joke. "Seriously, Preston was in a hurry to get home while I was taking my sweet time, dreading my lonely apartment."

"Really?" she asks.

"Really. If I had known you were here, I would've been out before Preston," I assure her. Then, taking her hand, I lead the way to my SUV. "I'll drive since you don't know your way around town yet."

With her hand in mine, this whole afternoon feels like a dream. But Maya is really here, and she said the sweetest five words ever: *I want to try again.*

I don't know what the future holds for us as we drive away, and I debate where to take her for dinner. But I'm more determined than ever to make things work—with Maya, with Finley, with everything. I'm all in.

I just hope that she is too.

Maya's scared, and I understand that. Hell, I'm scared too. Scared of screwing up and losing her again.

But the fact that she's willing to try gives me hope and confidence in myself that I won't miss on this shot.

32

Maya

"So, where are we going?" I ask Christian from the passenger seat of his SUV as he drives us around town. "Are you sure I look okay wearing this?"

"Maya," he says quietly, his gaze moving from the road to sweep over my pale blue dress for a quick second. "You look beautiful."

I smile at him before he looks away, and some of the nervousness leaves me. "Thank you. But that doesn't answer my question."

"I thought we could go to a steakhouse in a hotel if that's okay? The food is great, and it's casual."

"That sounds perfect," I agree.

"I wish I had known you were coming, that we were going on our first date in almost six years, so I could've actually planned for perfect."

"No, this is great. I like seeing you just…wing it."

"So, we're winging it, huh?"

"Yes. No expectations, no commitment."

"Well, I want commitment, and you exceed all of my expectations."

"Oh please," I laugh with a roll of my eyes.

The hotel Christian picked is on the edge of town, away from the busy streets and noise of the city. It's quiet and intimate—exactly the kind of place where we can escape for a few hours and just be us. Or at least that's what I hope.

But the moment we step inside and wait at the hostess stand, I see the familiar looks. A few tables of guests are already watching us, whispers spreading through the room as people recognize him. Christian's fame comes with a price, and even on what's supposed to be our first date, we're not really alone.

It doesn't take long before a group of three women approaches. Hockey fans, obviously—one of them is even wearing a Bobcats tee.

"Christian Riley!" one of them squeals, her eyes wide with excitement. "Oh my God, I can't believe it's really you!"

He gives the women a polite smile, clearly not wanting to cause a scene. "Hi, yeah. Just here for a quiet dinner date with my girl, but it's nice to meet you."

I'm relieved he was so quick to publicly claim me as *his* girl.

The women, though, ignore the hint that we want to be left alone. "Can we take a picture with you?" another one asks, stepping closer, her gaze a little too sultry for my liking. "Pretty please?"

I take a step back, standing off to the side, and trying not to let the attention bother me, but it's hard. This is supposed to be our night, our first date in nearly six years. One Christian worked an entire summer to convince me to give him, and they're already intruding on it.

Christian glances at me, his expression apologetic. "Just one group photo," he says softly, stepping away for a moment.

I watch as they swarm around him, laughing and giggling like teenagers. One of them even puts her arm around his waist, and a spark of jealousy flares inside me. I'm still working on trusting him, and these women—they're practically throwing themselves at him. And superstar Christian Riley is too polite to push them away.

When the picture is finally done, Christian gently but firmly reminds them that he's here with me. "I'm on a date, so if you'll excuse us, I want to get back to it," he says, his voice kind but firm.

The disappointment on their faces is obvious, but they eventually back off, leaving us alone once again.

Christian walks back to me, a sheepish grin on his face, and takes my hand in his. "Sorry about that."

"It's fine," I say, though I know he can tell I'm more than a little annoyed. "It comes with the territory."

"Ignore them," he says, his tone softening as he reaches for my hand. "You and me are all that matter tonight."

We finally get seated at a table. The soft glow of candlelight casts a warm glow over the menus as we quietly look over them. I can feel Christian's occasional gaze on me.

Finally, I take a deep breath, breaking the silence. "Christian, I need to ask you something."

He looks at me, his expression suddenly serious. "Anything."

I hesitate, my fingers fidgeting with the edge of my napkin. "Why…why did you sleep with so many women?"

He looks away before answering. "Because…after things ended with us, I missed you and wanted to try to get over you. Which didn't work. I realized right away that no one could make me feel what I do with you. It all felt so…empty. I think mostly, I did it because I could, but also I was hoping to find that feeling again. I was lonely, bored, and stressed out. It was a decent distraction from all those things, from being a rookie, needing to make a name for myself in the pros, to prove to my father I had what it takes. All stupid reasons, really."

When he's finished speaking, and I don't say a word, Christian leans across the table, his lips brushing softly against mine in a kiss so tender, so careful, it feels like a promise to stop my worry. I don't pull away. Instead, I lean into it, letting the warmth of his touch wash over me, melting some of the tension that's been coiled tightly in my chest. It's not like before when everything between us was rushed and filled with the heat of new passion. This is slower and more deliberate. It feels like he's trying to tell me something, something deeper than words. The night he left, he almost said he loved me. Granted, my mouth was on him at the time, but I think he meant it.

When he pulls back, his hand is still wrapped around mine, his thumb gently stroking my skin. "Maya," he whispers, his forehead pressed against mine, "Thank you for tonight, for coming this weekend."

I nod slowly, my breath catching in my throat. "Sure."

"I know you'll probably never look at me the same way

you did before, before I screwed up," Christian says after a moment, his voice soft but sure. "But I hope you do someday."

I look down at our hands, feeling the warmth of his palm against mine. "Me too."

"I'm going to be a part of Finley's life no matter what happens between us," Christian says, his voice steady. "I want to be there for him. I missed so much already, and I don't want to miss another second of his life. I hate living so far away."

I look up at him and all I see is sincerity, along with a deep longing that mirrors my own. He's not the same man he was when he up and left me, and maybe—just maybe—I'm not the same timid woman I was, either. We've both changed, and that change has brought us back to this moment, this possibility of something real.

His expression softens, and he leans in closer. "Whatever you or Finley need, I'm here for it. You're only a few hours away."

I swallow hard, feeling the weight of his words settle over me. "Right now, I just need you to be patient with me. I can't move to Greensboro. I know that's what you want, but it has to be my decision this time. And I also need to know that you're really in this for the long haul, even if we're not always here with you."

"I am," he says firmly, his grip on my hand tightening slightly. "I'm in this, Maya. For you. For Finley. For us."

There's something about the way he says it, so sure, so confident, that makes me want to believe him. And maybe I do. Maybe, for the first time in a long time, I'm starting to believe that we could actually make this work.

"I hope we can do this," I whisper, my voice trembling slightly. "I really do."

Christian smiles a slow, genuine smile that lights up his whole face. "Me too. All we can do is try. Both of us."

For the rest of the evening, the tension between us melts away, replaced by something lighter and hopeful. We talk quietly, our conversation flowing naturally, the way it used to when we first met and were inseparable. Christian tells me about his week of training, how he's ready to get back out on the ice, and about some of the guys on the team—Luke, his wild best friend and the team's tough guy, Tyler, his shadow, a shy rookie forward, Connor, the goofy, funny guy who never sits still, and Jason, the veteran goalie who's been like a big brother to him, a part of the team for the past six years.

I find myself laughing at his stories, feeling more relaxed than I have in weeks. It's easy to get caught up in the way he talks and the way his eyes light up when he's passionate about something. This is the Christian I fell in love with—the one who's funny and thoughtful, who knows how to make me feel like I'm the only person in the world when he's with me. The man he was before he became a famous hockey star.

When dessert arrives, a rich chocolate cake that we share, I finally feel like I can breathe again. The weight of our past and the unfortunate physical distance between us is still there, but it doesn't feel as heavy anymore. It feels like something we can work through together.

As we finish our meal, Christian leans back in his chair, his eyes soft as they meet mine. "I've been thinking," he says, his voice thoughtful. "We should definitely do this more often."

"Go on a date?" I ask, raising an eyebrow.

"Spend time together, just the two of us," he clarifies. "Like we used to. Don't get me wrong. I adore my time with Finley, but I love being alone with you, too."

I smile, the thought of spending more time with him warming something inside me. "I'd like that. I love him so much, but it's nice to have a short break from being a worried mom for a few hours."

"I'm glad you get it."

It's a simple moment, but it feels significant—like we're finally moving toward something real, something lasting. And for the first time in a long time, I feel a flicker of hope.

When we leave the restaurant, Christian wraps his arm around my waist as we walk to the car. The night air is warm, but I still lean into him, savoring the warmth of his body next to mine. It feels right—like we belong here, together.

As we drive back to Preston's apartment, the conversation is light, and the heavy emotions of earlier are now behind us. It feels good to be with him like this, without the weight of the past hanging over our heads.

When we pull up in the parking lot, I hesitate for a moment, unsure of what to say. Christian must sense my hesitation because he turns to me, his expression soft.

"I had a great time tonight," he says quietly.

"Me too," I say, smiling at him.

There's a beat of silence, and then he leans in, pressing a soft kiss to my cheek. It's a gentle, lingering kiss, one that sends a warm shiver down my spine.

"That was my goodnight for you. Can I come in? Just to see Finley, I mean?" he asks, his voice hopeful.

"Yes, of course," I whisper, my heart fluttering in my chest. "I wish you could stay the night..."

"No, I get it. This is Preston's place. Maybe you and Finley can stay with me one night this weekend?"

"That would be great," I agree.

Later that night, after Christian and I put Finley to bed in Preston's guest room, he leaves. Preston and Elle have gone to bed too, so I sit on the couch in the dark, my phone in my hand. I scroll through Christian's recent messages, short and sweet updates about his workouts, practices, and asking how Finley is doing, to tell him he said hello. It's nothing fancy, nothing dramatic, but the messages are there. They're consistent.

I hesitate, my finger hovering over the keyboard. Should I text him to say goodnight again? Should I bring up the idea of visiting him on the road? Or would that make me seem… desperate? Or worse, remind him that I still don't trust him?

But I think I want to surprise him.

Before I can second-guess myself, I type out a quick message.

Will we see you tomorrow? I ask, so I can pretend I'm inquiring for Finley's sake. After all, we didn't discuss plans for the weekend tonight.

I stare at the screen, waiting. I hate that my heart speeds up just from sending a simple text. After what feels like an eternity, but is only moments, my phone buzzes.

Absolutely.

I smile and the dots appear as he types and then sends, *How about we go to one of the parks? I told Finley about them over the summer and he asked me to take him to all of them.*

The park sounds fun.

I hit send before I can overthink it. There's a pause and then another message.

I've missed him. And you. I want us to spend the entire weekend together.

I bite my lip, my fingers tapping against the phone as I contemplate my next move.

Are you sure? What if someone sees us out in public and posts a photo? People will ask questions...

Let them. I don't care if the whole world knows I have a son, or that you and I are together.

His confident message is followed by, *Shit. I should probably tell my dad first.*

You haven't told your father about Finley? I ask in surprise and disappointment.

He's going to be so pissed at me. The lecture about how immature and selfish I am will last years. But he'll be excited to be a grandpa.

Oh. So, his hesitation sounds like it's more about how his father will treat him, not because he's ashamed.

I'll tell him soon. He'll probably want to meet Finley.

Of course, I agree. *We could plan a visit to see him.*

He'll love you and Finley, Christian says. Then, *What about your parents? Finley doesn't ever mention his grandparents.*

Because he's never met them. They don't want to know him.

WHAT?

I don't really want to talk about it.

Well, I do. Who the hell wouldn't want to know my incredibly awesome son?

His defensiveness makes me smile despite the overwhelming sadness.

Assholes, I respond.

Assholes, Christian agrees, making me feel like we're a team, that we're on the same side no matter what comes.

33

Maya

The Carolina sun beams down. It's warm, but not oppressively humid yet this morning, as we spread out on the checkered blanket for our picnic. We're in the middle of a grassy park in downtown Greensboro, a spot Christian picked out. Elle sits next to me with Audrey reclining on the other side of her, casually flipping through a magazine. It's a laid-back Saturday, and I think we could all use a day like this —the kind of day where you let go of the stress and just enjoy being together. It smells like summer—freshly cut grass and the chlorine from the nearby fountain. Kids run in and out of the water whenever it bursts upward from the ground.

I glance over at Christian, who's playing frisbee with Finley a few feet away. Finley's giggles ring out each time Christian exaggerates a missed catch, stumbling or tripping for comedic effect. My heart does that little thing it's been doing lately—fluttering between happiness and anxiety. I'm glad Christian's been making an effort, and I love how much joy Finley gets from these moments, but I can't shake the worry that things could get complicated.

Elle nudges me gently with her elbow, a knowing smile on her face. "He really is a natural," she says, nodding toward Christian. "Finley adores him."

"I know," I murmur, watching as Finley throws the frisbee just a little too high, and Christian stretches to catch it before tossing it back with ease. "He's good with him. Really good."

Elle takes a sip from her water bottle and eyes me cautiously. "How are you holding up?"

"It's…a lot," I admit, pulling my knees to my chest. "I'm happy Finley has his dad in his life. But, at the same time, it's all happening so fast. The summer has flown by and school starts soon…"

Finley will be starting kindergarten over three-hundred miles away from his father and uncle. And I'm not sure how I'll do everything on my own.

Preston returns to us with a fresh lemonade, and sits down beside Elle, wrapping an arm around her shoulders. "Everything okay over here?"

Elle gives him a reassuring smile. "Maya just mentioned that school starts soon."

"Gah." Preston shakes his head and leans back on one arm, his long legs stretched out in front of him in his athletic attire. "I can't believe he's old enough to go to school. I mean, pre-school was really more like daycare. To think that he's going to the real deal in a few weeks blows my mind. I remember holding him when he was barely bigger than my palm."

"Time flies," I agree.

Finley and Christian come back over to the blanket, both of them smiling. Finley's cheeks are flushed from the sun and running around, and he flops down beside me. Christian sits next to him, a little out of breath but grinning from ear to ear.

Preston grabs the cooler and opens it, handing out sandwiches. "So, I've been meaning to ask," he says, biting into his ham and cheese. "Elle and I were talking about our honeymoon plans, and we've narrowed it down to two spots. Bali or Santorini. Thoughts?"

Elle chuckles, rolling her eyes. "Ignore him. We're not even engaged!"

"Yet," my brother remarks.

We all know it's only a matter of time.

"Well, I think they're both beautiful," Audrey chimes in from her spot, putting her magazine down. "But Santorini has those amazing views, and you could get those Instagram-worthy sunset shots."

"Bali's got the beaches, though," Christian adds, reaching for a sandwich. "Plus, the diving is incredible there if you're into that."

I listen as the conversation flows easily between everyone, laughter and lighthearted banter filling the air. It feels good—natural, even. For a moment, I allow myself to relax and enjoy this little piece of normalcy.

"So, Maya," Elle says, a mischievous twinkle in her eye. "We have great schools around here too, and Finley seems to love it…"

Her question hangs in the air, and I stiffen slightly. I knew this topic would come up eventually, but I wasn't prepared for her to ask it now, in the middle of a peaceful picnic, where they can all gang up on me. I glance at Preston and Christian, who are suddenly very interested in their sandwiches, though I can see the tension in Christian's jaw.

Preston, always quick to read the room, clears his throat. "Yeah, I mean, I know you want a place of your own, but you could stay with me until you find a place. Or with Christian…"

"He offered but…" I start.

"He offered up his bachelor pad?" Audrey asks in surprise. "I barely recognize this Christian. The one who broke Elle's heart is long gone."

"He is," Christian says, finally looking up. His eyes flicker toward me for a brief second, but he quickly turns back to his sandwich. "And Maya said no to all of it, so can we please just drop it?"

There's a shift in the air, subtle but unmistakable. The conversation lingers dangerously close to what we've all been skirting around—the question of what's really happening between Christian and me.

Elle shoots me a supportive smile in apology for bringing up the topic.

"I think fatherhood has been good for you," Audrey says, breaking the silence. "Forcing you to grow up."

Christian smiles warmly, his gaze softening as he looks at Finley. "I won't deny that."

Finley beams, proud of the attention on him, and scoots closer to me, leaning against my side. "Mommy," he says, his eyes sweet and innocent when he looks up at me. "Could we please move in with Christian? I mean, with Dad?"

I can feel everyone's eyes on me, and I wish I could explain it to my son, our son, but I can't. And I hate that I have to figure out how to refuse his request in front of everyone.

I swallow hard, trying to find the right words. "That… would be a big change, buddy. One I'm not sure we're ready to make yet."

Finley tilts his head, his bright eyes looking up at me, full of curiosity. "Why not?"

I glance at Christian, who winces as if he knows it's hard to describe.

I take a deep breath, reaching for Finley's hand. "We are going to visit Christian and Uncle Preston as much as we can on weekends. You'll get to see your friends and them this way."

He seems satisfied with that answer for now, and he turns his attention back to his sandwich, happily munching away like it wasn't a heavy conversation. But the tension between Christian and me is palpable. It's like a giant elephant sitting in the middle of our picnic blanket, and neither of us knows how to address it.

Elle clears her throat, clearly sensing the shift in mood. "Well, we'll give you three some time to talk. Preston and I are going to take a walk over to the fountain. Audrey, you coming?"

Audrey looks between us, then nods. "Yeah, sure. A walk sounds nice."

The three of them all stand and wander off, leaving Christian and me alone with Finley. The sun is still shining, and the air is warm, but suddenly, I feel cold. I can sense Christian shifting beside me like he wants to say something but doesn't know how to start.

We sit in silence for a moment, watching Finley eat his small bag of chips, completely oblivious to our tension.

"So," Christian begins, his voice low. "How do you really feel about the city?"

I swallow hard, my heart pounding in my chest. "You know that the city was never the issue."

"I know," he says gently, turning to face me. "It was stupid for me to think that you would come down to visit and fall in love…"

His words hang in the air, heavy with meaning. I know he's not just talking about me falling in love with the city.

I don't have a job while Christian is a professional hockey player making millions here in Greensboro. If he could move up north to be with us, I know he would in a heartbeat.

So why can't I move down here for him?

Part of me wants to say yes. Part of me wants to jump in with both feet and trust that everything will be okay. But the other part—the part that's been hurt before, brutally even by my parents—holds me back.

"I want Finley to have his dad in his life," I say quietly. "And you are a great father. But we have to take this slow for now. It's not just about us anymore."

His hazel eyes are filled with sincerity when he says, "And I'm going to wait for you for however long it takes. You're it for me, baby."

I bite my lip, feeling the familiar swell of emotions rise up in my chest. If only there was a way to peek into the future and see if that's true or not.

Just as I come about as close to saying yes as ever, my phone starts to buzz in my pocket. I flinch, startled by the sudden intrusion. The sound seems deafening in the silence between us. I pull my phone out, glancing at the screen.

Spencer's aunt, Justine.

Of all the times for her to call me, I didn't expect it on a Saturday. Maybe she's heard something about the job. Her boss may have made her decision.

I can feel Christian's eyes on me, sharp and questioning. The phone keeps ringing, and I just… freeze. I can't bring myself to answer it yet, but I also can't ignore it. Am I ready to find out what fate has in mind for the future?

Christian doesn't say anything, but I can sense his unease, the way his body tenses beside me. He waits, eyes narrowing slightly as the phone continues to vibrate in my hand. I should answer it or at least tell Christian who it is, but my words are stuck in my throat. I don't know what to say.

The silence stretches on as the phone finally stops buzzing, the call going to voicemail. Christian's expression is a mixture of concern and what I think is disappointment.

"Why didn't you answer?" he asks, his voice almost too calm. "It was about the job at the retirement home, wasn't it?"

"I told myself that if I didn't get the job, I would have more of an incentive to move…"

"Did you get it?" he asks.

The phone buzzes again with a voicemail notification, vibrating against my palm like an urgent reminder of every-thing I've been avoiding. Christian lets out a deep breath, rubbing the back of his neck, his eyes closing for a brief second.

"Well? The suspense is killing me," Christian says, his voice harsher now, but sounding resigned.

"I'll… I'll be right back," I say quietly, getting to my feet and stepping away from Christian and Finley, avoiding his gaze as I walk a few paces to listen to the voicemail. I feel the weight of Christian's eyes on me as I put the phone to my ear, my stomach twisting into knots.

"Hi, Maya. It's Justine Williams from Abbotswood Retirement Community. Vivian wanted me to apologize for not getting back to you sooner. She's had to work the night shift this week, so she asked me to call you. We would love to officially offer you the activity director position. My nephew has been hounding me to convince her to hire you, but even if Spencer hadn't recommended you, I think Viv still would've picked you. Anyway, if you're still interested, please give us a call to schedule a time to come in next week to go over all the details. Thanks, and have a great weekend!"

I got the job.

My first job ever. My first attempt at being independent.

I close my eyes, leaning against a nearby tree, the bark rough against my back. My mind is a mess of emotions, guilt swirling in my chest.

Even though I'm excited, no, elated by this opportunity, a part of me wants to refuse the position to move to North Carolina.

But depending on Preston to pay my way for nearly six years is too long.

Christian admitted that finding out he was a father helped him grow up.

Well, it's time for me to do the same, to become independent for the first time in my life.

"Are you okay?" Christian's voice causes my eyes to pop open.

"Finley!" I exclaim, but I see him playing keep away with Preston and Elle in the middle of the fountain.

"I know better than to leave him unattended this close to roads," Christian mutters.

"Sorry. I just…I got lost in my own head for a minute."

There's a long pause before he finally says, "So? Did you get the job?"

I nod. "Yes."

He flashes me a sad smile. "Congratulations, baby." A second later, his strong arms are around me, pulling me to him in a tight hug.

My stupid eyes water with regret, but I blink the tears away and swallow past the burning in my throat. This is what I wanted. It's fate.

"Thank you," I reply.

When Christian pulls back, he keeps his palms on my waist and stares down at me. "We're going to make this work, okay? Not just for Finley, but for us. I'll sign up for a reality show and have cameras follow me around twenty-four hours a day, if that's what you need to trust me."

I laugh at his offer. "Thanks, but that would be so wrong. I just need time."

"I just need you," he says, pressing a kiss to my lips, then resting his forehead against mine. "I should've told you that years ago, but I think I was scared."

"You were scared, huh?" I ask.

"Scared of loving you, needing you. I…I lost the only other woman I ever loved."

A stab of jealousy nearly brings me to my knees. "Who…" I start to ask, unsure if I want to know her name.

"My mom," he says softly.

"Your mom?" I ask sadly.

"She was in a bad car accident when I was thirteen. I sat by her bed every day for weeks while she was in a coma, hoping she would get better before my dad…" Christian clears his throat. "She was an organ donor, so he eventually made the call to save people who had a real chance of making it."

"I'm so sorry," I tell him as I cup the side of his face. "I had no idea. Preston never mentioned it…"

"Preston doesn't know. Nobody does. Hockey was my escape, my distraction for the next several years. It still is, I guess. But I've never been fast enough to out skate the memories completely."

"You never stop missing her, do you?" I ask. While it's not the same thing, my mother is still alive, and I'm just dead to her.

He shakes his head. "She was an amazing mom like you. She came to every single one of my games and supported my dream of going pro. She never had any doubt, even when my father thought I should give hockey up because I was failing in school…"

"I wish I could've met her," I tell him.

"Me too."

"Her accident is why I'm still a nervous wreck driving…"

"You-you get nervous driving?" I ask him in concern. "And you still drove five hours to visit us?"

"Well, yeah. I would do anything for you and Finley. I would drive across the country every single day if I had to," he says with a grin.

And I don't doubt his assertion for a second. He would do anything for us.

Learning all this about Christian's past, how he lost his mom so unexpectedly as a teenager and hates driving, well, it feels like the universe is trying to give me another reason why I should give in and move to North Carolina.

But I can't upend my and Finley's life to move after a few happy weeks with Christian. Once hockey season starts, it won't matter if we're three hundred or three miles away, he's going to be too busy for us.

Christian

I don't know why I told Maya about my mom. Or why I hadn't told her before now.

I guess, since we're starting over, I just wanted her to understand how messed up I still was when we were younger. The pain of losing someone you love makes it damn hard to want to do it all over again.

But I would've tried my damnedest for Maya years ago if she had given me another chance. Because I knew, even then, that I was already in love with her when I left her to go pro.

34

Maya

Monday morning, when I wake up in my own bed back in Maryland, there's a gnawing ache in my chest that I can't shake. My skin is still tingling from the memory of Christian's touch, the way his lips felt against mine. And I can't help but smile, remembering how much fun Finley had visiting him and Preston.

God, I miss them both.

I sit up and scrub my palms over my face, trying to clear the fog from my mind. But no matter how hard I try, the thoughts keep circling back to Christian.

He cares about me, about Finley, about *us* so much.

And...I don't know what to do with that.

I care about him and want him too. I think I even still love him. But it's not that simple. It's never been that simple with

273

Christian. There's too much at risk if it ends badly, which it probably will once the season starts.

I sigh and roll out of bed, pulling on a robe as I make my way to the kitchen. I pour myself a cup of coffee, but I barely taste it. I try to distract myself with the reminder that, on Thursday, I've got a meeting at the retirement home to discuss my pay and benefits. I should be more excited about starting my first job, finding an actual purpose for myself, and being able to support me and Finley on my own.

I'm just not as giddy about the job as I was a few weeks ago.

The ringing phone interrupts my warring thoughts, and it's not my cell phone. I take my time reaching for the cordless landline tucked in the corner of the kitchen counter because I'm certain it's some sort of scam recording.

"Hello?" I answer with a heavy sigh.

"Maya?"

The woman's voice on the other side is the last one I expected to hear—my mother's.

I pull the phone away from my ear to check the caller ID. Sure enough, it's a phone number with the area code of Peachtree City, Georgia, where Preston and I grew up. Where our parents still live.

"Maya?" she calls my name again, the first time I've spoken to the woman since I told her and my father that I was pregnant, and they threw me out of the house.

"Yes?" I reply curtly.

"Maya, it's me. It's mom," she says as if I've forgotten my own mother's voice.

"Yes?" I repeat again, since I'm at a loss for what else to say. I've waited years for our mother to call and say she had left our father and wanted to be a part of our lives again, that she wanted to finally meet her grandson.

"This was the only phone number I could find for Preston," she explains in a rush.

Of course, she's calling for my brother and not for me.

"He doesn't live here anymore. I can give you his cell number," I offer. Then, because I'm still hurt by her audacity, I add, "But I can't guarantee he'll want to talk to you either."

"I know. I'm sorry. I just…I wanted to let you both know that your father has passed away."

"What?"

"Yesterday…he didn't wake up…" she trails off as if unable to explain further or like there's nothing that can be done about it.

When I don't say anything else, she adds, "I just…I thought you would want to know so you could come say goodbye."

"I'll let Preston know," I tell her.

"It would be nice to see you and the baby, too."

"He's not a baby anymore. He's five now."

"Right, well, it would be nice to finally see him…"

I want to yell at her, to tell her that she had years to see him, to be a part of my son's life, but she refused. She refused because my father put his foot down and forbade her from having any contact with me. Our mother called Preston on all his birthdays and sent him Christmas cards, but not me.

"I'll call Preston now to let him know," I tell her. "It'll be better if he hears the news from me." Mostly, I just want to end this awkward conversation and talk to my brother. He's the only one who will understand the shock and disbelief I feel from her phone call.

"Okay. I hope you can come home. The funeral is going to be Friday at eleven."

"I'll tell him," I say, refusing to commit to anything.

"Goodbye," she eventually says through sniffles.

"Bye, Mama," I reply, using her name for the first time in years.

As soon as the call ends, I dial up Preston on my cell phone while pacing around the kitchen, chewing on my thumbnail.

"Hey, sis," he answers right away, like I knew he would. "I'm about to head into training. Is Finley okay?"

"Finley's great," I assure him. "Well, other than missing everyone. And I'm sorry to bother you, but, um, you'll never believe who just called the house or what she said."

"Who? What?"

"Mama."

"*Our* mother?" he asks, his voice raised in disbelief.

"Yes, our mother called to tell *you* that our father died."

"Damn. That's…the last thing I expected you to say."

"Right? I was so caught off-guard by her calling the house phone that I could barely speak a word. She wants us to come home for the funeral. It's Friday at eleven. And she said she wants to finally meet Finley."

"Jesus."

"What do you think? Are you going to go?"

"I don't know, Maya. This is a lot to spring on me."

"Sorry. I feel the same way," I tell him.

"Let me…I've got to talk to Elle before I make a decision," he says, making my heart slump. I'm not jealous of her or their relationship. I just wish I had someone I could turn to in times like these other than my brother. My brother who has his own life in another city now. In a way, I guess it feels like

Preston abandoned me too, even if that's silly. Everyone I've ever loved has up and left me or thrown me out.

"Okay. Just call me later," I tell him before ending the call.

Staring at the phone in my hand, my next thought is that I want to call Christian. I don't even know why, though. He enjoys fooling around with me, but probably doesn't want to deal with the heavy stuff. It's not like he knew my father or will understand how badly I'm reeling right now after talking to my mom for the first time in years.

And how in the world am I going to explain all of this to Finley?

He just found out he has a father. Telling him he also had a grandfather until yesterday as well as a grandmother, but that neither of them wanted anything to do with him because Christian and I weren't married, well, that's a conversation I never want to have with him.

As I recall my father's last words to me, I have to pull out a chair at the table to sit down.

You're both a disgrace to this family.

Your brother can help you raise the bastard, because your mother and I don't want anything to do with it.

The last words my father spoke were to call my beautiful son a bastard and to say Preston and I were a disgrace to the family.

He meant those words. Even on his death bed, if he had one, he wouldn't have taken them back.

At least now that he's gone, I'll never have to hear another horrible word from his mouth.

I'm not surprised when Elle calls my cell phone before Preston calls me back, while I'm still sitting in shock at the kitchen table.

"Hey, Elle," I answer.

"Hey. I'm so, so sorry about your dad. How are you holding up?"

"It's, um, unexpected, but I haven't spoken to him in years. I guess I'm just…numb," I tell her. "How's Preston?"

"I've never seen him so…lost. He decided to go to training, even though I tried to convince him to stay home."

"Yeah, I know how he's feeling. Our father was an asshole, but he was still our father and now he's dead and gone. I spoke to my mother for the first time in nearly six years today. What they did to me still hurts like hell," I explain in a rush.

"I know it does. And his death doesn't forgive him for being so cruel to you," Elle says. "Do you think you'll go to the funeral? Preston seems torn but leaning toward going."

"Really?" I say in surprise.

"I think he wants to try to make amends with your mom, you know, before it's too late to see her. He says she mostly just followed your dad's orders."

"She didn't have to follow his orders! She could've left him."

"I know. And she should have done that rather than abandon you and Preston. Going to the funeral doesn't absolve her of anything either, though. I wouldn't blame you if you skipped it."

Sighing, I tell her, "If Preston wants to go, then I'm going too. I won't let him face that shit alone after all the times he's been there for me. He's *always* been there for me because they weren't."

"Then I would say you might want to start packing and thinking about travel arrangements. I guess we'll be driving down Thursday."

"Us too, I suppose. God, I don't even know how to explain to Finley where we're going or why," I huff as I cover my face with my free hand.

"It won't be easy, having to explain death to him. But it is a part of life. One he'll have to face, eventually."

"I know. I would have preferred us to start with a goldfish before jumping to people. Especially people who pushed us out of their lives."

"We're here if you need anything," Elle says.

"I appreciate you calling. Make sure Preston reaches out when he makes a final decision?"

"I will. Take care and good luck."

"Thanks," I reply.

Christian

While Preston and I haven't been teammates for years, I still know it's unusual for him to miss conditioning. Even in the off-season, his world revolves around hockey.

During one of my breaks from the treadmill, I towel off my sweaty face and call him up to make sure he's feeling okay.

"Yeah?" he answers. Just that one word and I know he sounds even gruffer than usual.

"Hey, is everything okay? I noticed you weren't at training."

"No, everything is not fucking okay," he grumbles.

"Finley? Maya?" I blurt out in concern.

"They're fine. She didn't tell you?"

"Tell me what?" I ask.

Now that he mentions it, for the past few nights, she's ended our phone calls abruptly after Finley's tucked into bed.

I figured she was having doubts about us now that she's in Maryland again and I'm still in North Carolina. I hate it, but I didn't want to get into an argument with her.

But now…what if it was something else going on that she kept from me?

"Elle and I are getting ready to head out. We're going to meet Maya and Finley in Georgia for my father's fucking funeral," Preston finally explains.

"Oh, shit. I'm so sorry, man," I tell him. "How are you doing? How's Maya? Was it unexpected?"

"I honestly don't know how I am. We haven't seen the man in over five years."

"Since Maya found out she was pregnant?" I guess.

"Yep. Not a peep from my father. Mama would call on my birthday, but that's about it. She hasn't spoken to Maya at all until she called her Monday and told her that he was dead."

"Jeez. That's… that must be tough. How is Maya handling it?"

Maya's known since Monday that her father passed away and she didn't tell me? Preston came to training like normal and never said a word about either. He was a little grumpier than usual, so everyone just left him alone. I guess it's a topic neither of them wanted to talk about, at least not with me.

Which fucking hurts.

I want to be the one Maya talks to about everything, good or bad.

"Maya's not great. She didn't really want to go back home, or explain it all to Finley, but when I told her I was going, she decided they would drive down and meet us there. She's missing her meeting about the new job today for this shit."

"You're headed back to Peachtree City?" I ask, remembering Preston telling me that's where he's from.

"Yeah."

"When's the funeral?"

"Tomorrow at eleven."

"Shit," I mutter.

"I know, right?"

"No, I just mean, I want to come too. If that's okay?" I ask him. "I'll drive myself, so I'm not a third wheel with you and Elle."

"Ah, yeah, of course it's okay. But you don't have to drive separately. Or go at all. I don't want to go, but I feel like I need to be there for my mom."

"I want to be there too," I tell him. For Maya and for Finley. "Maya might need me to watch Finley during the funeral, right?"

"Yeah, I guess so. I'm not sure if she wants to take him to the cemetery and shit."

"Could you send me the address or a link to the obituary when you have a minute? I'll go home to pack a bag and get on the road."

"Sure, man. Thanks, Christian."

I don't even consider whether I'll be excused from practice or if I'll be benched during our first preseason game. None of those things matter. I need to be with my family right now, screw everything else.

Maya

. . .

Our family home looks exactly like I remembered it, as if nothing has changed, even though it has. The two-story brick structure could definitely use a new roof. The home sweet home flag hanging on the porch is only a slightly different version of the previous ones. Everything else is the same.

"Mommy, I need to go potty!" Finley whines from the backseat of the car.

"I know, sweetie. Let's…let's go inside." I get out of the car and open his door for him. Finley's been a trooper since we left the house at seven this morning and have been on the road ever since. We stopped for lunch, then dinner, and had a few bathroom breaks. He's been happy enough playing games on his iPad and napping most of the way.

"Where are we?" he asks as he unbuckles his seatbelt.

"Well, ah, this…this is where Uncle Preston and I grew up." For the past three days, I've tried and failed to figure out how to have this conversation with him. Now, I guess I'm just going to play it by ear.

"You lived here?" he asks.

"I did. For eighteen years." Until I was tossed out with all my things on the curb like garbage.

Taking his hand, mostly because I need the comfort, I trudge up the four steps leading to the front door where a white wreath hangs.

The door opens before I can reach and press the doorbell, as if she was watching the driveway from the living room window.

Then, I'm staring right at the woman who gave birth to me, who took care of me as a child. She was a wonderful mother, one I thought loved me unconditionally, before that notion was proven wrong.

Mama now has a few more lines around her eyes and smiling lips, and her once thick, dark brown hair is more of a thin, sandy color thanks to the gray in it.

"Aww, my goodness," she exclaims, slapping her hand over her mouth. Her brown eyes glisten as she stares down at her grandson for the very first time. "Aren't you the most beautiful boy I've even seen?"

Finley glances up at me with a frown, either from the odd greeting from this woman he's never met before or with indignation for being called beautiful.

"Finley, this is…my…your…"

"I'm your Grandma Lawrence," my mother tells him as she crouches down to see him better, arms spread wide. "Can I have a big hug?"

He nods and doesn't seek my approval before he lets go of my hand to step into her open arms without any hesitation.

After a short embrace, Finley pulls away and she cups his face in her hands that look like they've spent too much time in dishwater. "You look just like Preston!"

I want to roll my eyes because Preston was always her favorite, but then Finley says, "I look like my dad, too."

I wince in preparation for whatever lecture or insult she may say in response to that comment.

Instead, she tells him, "Then you must have a very handsome father."

Finley nods. "This is his jersey!" he says, pulling on the long sleeve Bobcats sweater that's way too warm for Georgia in summer but was a non-negotiable for leaving the house this morning. "He plays hockey for the Bobcats just like Uncle Preston!"

My mom slowly stands to her full height as if her joints are stiffer, eyeing my navy, sleeveless cotton dress and yellow sandals with disapproval. "I thought Preston played for the D.C. Warhawks."

Of course she keeps up with her son's hockey career. I bet her and dad watch every game. *Watched* every game.

"He did, until the end of the season, when he signed with the Bobcats and moved to Greensboro."

"Well, you learn something new every day, don't you," she says. "Now, come on in and let's find you both something to eat."

"Okay, but I really need to use your potty," Finley tells her, making her laugh as she guides him inside. She certainly seems in good spirits dealing with our father's unexpected death.

When they're both inside, I text Preston, ***I'm here. Where are you and Elle?***

His response comes back a moment later. ***About thirty minutes away.***

Hurry up and save me from this nightmare.

Is she already giving you shit?

No, not yet. But I still need backup.

With a heavy sigh, I pull open the screen door and step inside my first home. The smell of warm apple pie is so familiar, my stomach growls in anticipation.

My mom's cooking is the best, even if it's made with harsh judgements.

She offers me and Finley an array of covered dishes prepared by friends and neighbors, but I decline, excusing myself to go to the restroom while Finley digs into some chicken and dumplings at the dining table.

Since there's no point in texting Preston again, I wander up the steps to see what became of my old room.

I flip on the lights, finding the space empty of my personal touch since I packed all my things up. There's a thin layer of dust on the heavy wooden furniture. My queen bed has been made up with a light blue comforter that has orange blossoms embroidered on it. And a small gift box sits on the nightstand next to the bed.

Curious, I walk over to look at it closer, finding my name on the tag. I lift the lid, finding a stack of letters tied with a pink ribbon inside. Letters all addressed to me…from Christian.

Holy shit.

I remove the first letter from the stack with a shaky hand, noticing that the postmark is from years ago, addressed to my dorm room. But I had dropped out by the date it was stamped in order to get my spring tuition refunded, moving into Preston's apartment nearby instead.

There's a neatly sliced slit at the top of the envelope, as if someone, my mother or father, opened it with their ancient letter knife and read it.

I pull out the piece of paper inside, finding a handwritten letter from Christian on lined notebook paper.

Maya,

I decided to write to you since you blocked my phone number before I could really apologize for being so careless with you. I'm sorry I put you in such a difficult position. I just want you to know that whatever you decide, I want to be there for you. I sent you all the money I had to try to help with doctor appointments or anything you need.

Just because I moved a few hours away doesn't mean we can't find a way to make this work. Please give me another chance.

Love,

Christian

He actually wrote me a sincere, sweet letter.

I sit down on the side of the bed, unable to resist opening the next letter and the next. They all say similar things, apologizing, telling me he misses me, that he loves me even though we haven't been dating very long.

One of the letters near the bottom gets significantly more interesting.

Maya,

Since you haven't responded to any of my letters, I'm guessing you've given up on me. But I don't want to give up on you. I'm not sure if it's even possible to do. I miss you so damn much. I miss my best friend too, but I know Preston will never forgive me for the pain I've caused you. I would give anything for you to come to Greensboro, either to visit or to stay with me for good. Please don't give up on us.

Love,

Christian

.   .   .

And the final letter, well, reading it makes the room tilt so badly that I almost need to lie down after reading it.

Maya,

I'm not surprised that you don't want to up and move for me after everything. I ruined your first time, then I burdened you with a pregnancy you didn't want. I'll do whatever it takes to try to make it up to you, to prove to you that you're it for me.

Being drafted, playing for the pros, none of it makes me happy like I thought it would, not when I can't share it with you.

I know you probably won't move here without being sure you can trust me again. There's only one way I can think of to prove that I'm in love with you and want to spend the rest of my life making up for my mistakes. I want to have a family with you. One day. When you're ready and have finished school. I can see us having kids together, even if the thought of being a father scares the shit out of me. Still, I've been thinking about it since the day you told me you were pregnant. I want to share a life, babies, everything with you. I may not know anything about kids, but you would be such an amazing mother that I know you would teach me what I need to know.

We belong together, Maya. I knew it from the first time I saw you in the arena cheering on Preston. You were so gorgeous you took my breath away. I could never deserve you, but that doesn't mean I'm going to give up on you.

So, will you marry me?

Hell, will you please just call me? I would give anything to hear your voice.

Love,

Christian

. . .

Oh my god. He proposed in a handwritten letter? Why didn't Christian tell me? Unless he changed his mind and was relieved that I didn't get his letters.

There's a commotion downstairs, which means Preston must finally be here. I'm sure my mom is over the moon excited to see him. But I'm still too stunned to move, to let go of Christian's last letter. He apparently gave up after he asked me to marry him since it's the last letter. He offered to spend the rest of his life with me and must have thought I ignored him.

Heavy footsteps on the stairs sound like they're headed this way. Most likely my brother coming to check on me.

Standing up, I brush my knuckles over my cheeks to wipe away the tears. Gathering the letters and envelopes, I return all but the last one, tossing them back into the gift box.

"Mommy, mommy! Dad's here!" Finley says from behind me. When I spin around, Christian is standing in the doorway, holding our son on his hip. Christian, not Preston.

"Wh-what are you doing here?" I ask in shock. I didn't even tell him my father died, or that we were coming to Georgia.

"When Preston missed training this morning, I called him and he told me you were both headed this way," he says simply. "I wanted to be here for you. You know, in case you needed anything. I can watch Finley during the service."

"That's...thank you." I hadn't even considered needing someone to babysit Finley. He's too young to see my father's casket being lowered into the ground. I want to keep my little boy happy and innocent from that darkness, at least for a few more years.

"It's nothing," Christian says, which causes me to shake my head as my eyes sting with more tears filling them.

"It's everything."

"Who wants some apple pie and ice cream?" my mother calls out.

"I do! I do!" Finley immediately squirms down from Christian's grip at the offer of his favorite dessert. He takes off running as soon as his feet hit the floor.

Christian smiles as he watches him disappear, then turns back to me. "How are you holding up, baby?"

"I'm…fine."

"You're not fine, Maya."

"I hadn't spoken to my mother or father in years, so being back here…it's…strange." I wave the letter still in my hand around, gesturing to my empty childhood room.

"What's that?" he asks.

"One of your letters. Your last letter apparently," I reply. "They were all in this box. I'm not even sure how in the world they got here. I guess…the school must have forwarded them here, to my last known address."

"Oh. Right." Christian's cheeks flush as he studies the box, no doubt trying to recall what he said in them.

"You asked me to marry you?"

"Uh, yeah." Reaching up, he rubs the back of his reddening neck. "I thought you should know that I was serious. I bought a ring right after I mailed the letter, you know, in case you said yes."

"You bought me an engagement ring?" I whisper.

"Yep. It's still in the little box in my kitchen junk drawer.

You know, the one where everything that doesn't have a place goes?"

He just referred to a diamond engagement ring as junk.

"Why didn't you return it or sell it?" I ask him.

"Because that would've been giving up on you changing your mind, and that's not something I'm capable of doing," he says casually as he shoves his hands into his jean pockets. "You didn't give up on me either or you would've dated and moved on by now."

"I-I guess that's true. Although, you obviously dated and moved on. More times than you can probably count."

"Not because I stopped loving you! And I told you that wasn't me moving on. It was me trying to ease the ache, even if it was only for a few minutes. Nothing more than temporary distractions that I fucking regret. Distractions that I can't even remember because they weren't you."

For the first time, I actually believe him, that he loves me.

Maybe it's because the old letters prove that he didn't think we were just some whim he quickly moved on and forgot about. He loved me then and wanted to spend the rest of his life with me. He even said he wanted to be there for me during the pregnancy, and I shut him out.

I was just so scared and hurt by my parents that I think I took it out on Christian. Pushing him away meant avoiding more heartbreak.

Except, it didn't work. I couldn't stop thinking about him or loving him no matter how much time went by.

And I don't want to waste another second of my life without him.

Tossing the letter onto the bed, I cross the space between

us and grab the back of his neck, pulling his mouth down to mine.

If Christian is surprised by my sudden kiss, he doesn't show it. His arms immediately wind around my waist, pulling me closer while his tongue eagerly meets mine.

"I need you…to finish what you started years ago," I whisper against his lips.

"Here? Right now?" Pulling back enough to see my face, his blond eyebrows are raised.

"Yes," I answer. "Right here. Right now. I'm tired of waiting."

"Fuck yes," Christian agrees.

Reaching behind him, he closes the door and fumbles around for the lock while still holding me, as if he's afraid I'll leave or change my mind.

36

———

Christian

As soon as the lock to Maya's old bedroom turns, my fingers reach for the hem of her dress. Before I lift it, though, I ask her one last time. "Baby, are you sure you're ready for this?"

She arches a brow, giving me a look that says, *"Are you ready?"* since I'm the one who messed up the first time. There's a small smile on her lips that tells me I'm not completely off base.

"I've been ready for this moment for years," she says lightly, though there's a seriousness in her tone that makes it clear this is more than a joke.

"Me too," I agree.

I'm not going to question her further about whether she's ready or ask if she's just looking for a distraction from her grief. I know it's none of those things.

This is Maya looking at me like she loves me, like she trusts and believes me.

I've waited too long for her to look at me this way and can't fathom allowing even an inch between us.

For now, it feels like the past is forgotten, or at least forgiven.

So, I lift her dress up and off. When she's standing before me in her matching black bra and panties, a blush colors her cheeks.

"God, you're so damn beautiful. And you're mine," I tell her as I step forward and take her hands into mine. "I know I wasn't the man you needed, that you deserved years ago, but I am now. I've had a lot of time to think about how stupid I was, how immature and insecure. I know how badly I hurt you, because I've felt that hurt, too. For years."

"I know you have," she says softly. "Let's stop hurting."

In a moment that feels like it's been years in the making, she leans in. This kiss is different from all the others, ones rushed or in the heat of the moment when we pretended that they didn't mean anything.

I press my lips against hers, letting the kiss say what I can't articulate into words. Everything else falls away. The tension, the fear, the doubts—all of it vanishes with this kiss.

It feels like finally coming home to a home I've been needing my entire life.

Maya's hands move to my chest, then she's tugging my shirt up and over my head. I pull her closer, deepening the kiss and pouring everything I feel for her into it. I want her to know how serious I am. How much I love her.

God, I love the way her hands feel on me as her palms smooth over my bare chest, down to my stomach. She undoes my jeans and shoves them down. Our kiss breaks apart for me to get rid of my clothes. While I work on removing every article, Maya stretches out on the bed, waiting for me and putting on a show. I watch, mesmerized, when she unhooks her bra and tosses it aside. And when she shimmies her panties down her legs, I have to remind my dick to calm down. I am *not* going to ruin this for her a second time.

No, this time, we're going to do it right, starting with me licking her until she's soaking wet. I grab the condom from the wallet in my discarded pants to keep it close. I don't want to risk getting Maya pregnant again until she's ready for us to have another son or daughter. God, I would love that. But until then, I'll be safe with her.

Crawling up the foot of the bed, I kiss my way along her inner thighs, taking my time. I don't give a shit if anyone downstairs realizes what we're up to. I'm not going to get in a rush.

Maya slides down the bed as if in a hurry for me to kiss another part of her body. I don't keep her waiting any longer as I spread her legs apart. I bury my face between them while sliding a finger deep inside her.

"Mmm, Christian," she moans before shoving her fist into her mouth to keep quiet. One of these days, I'm going to take her someplace where she can scream as loud as she wants. I've learned exactly what sets her off during our time together this summer, so my fingers and tongue make her back arch and her entire body tremble with a release within moments.

When her body finally relaxes, I kneel between her legs and roll on the condom before I even consider getting an inch closer to her heaven.

"Hurry up, I need you," she whispers. I'm glad I put on

protection early, because hearing those words from her lips, I can't resist crawling up her body and lining myself up as I claim her mouth. Our tongues meet, and all thoughts of going slow are thrown out the window. We both frantically grab at each other, unable to get close enough.

Like the first time, her legs wrap around my waist, urging me forward so I slide inside her wet heat. We both gasp into each other's mouths as I fill her for the very first time.

"Are you okay?" I ask against her lips.

"God, yes," Maya agrees before her stroking tongue silences mine.

I try to pull out and ease back in slowly a few times to give her time to adjust to the intrusion, but Maya's fingernails dig into my ass, urging me to go deeper, faster with each thrust. I'm so turned on I couldn't hold back any longer if I wanted to. I slam inside her again and again.

"Fuck, you feel good," I tell her as I kiss down her neck, trying to keep from finishing too soon. I want Maya to come again for me. Just when I'm about to reach between us to try to get her there, she cries out, then silences the sound by biting down on my shoulder. Her inner walls clench around me, her body shuddering with pleasure underneath mine.

God, it's everything I've ever needed, as I let go, my face pressed to her neck. "I love you so much, baby. So much. Now you're mine and I'm never letting you go again."

I feel too amazing to even be embarrassed by my blurted-out declaration. Not that Maya seems to mind. Her arms wind around my neck, holding me tightly to hers long after our bodies go still. "I love you too. I've always been yours."

37

Maya

Last night with Christian was…perfect.

My perfect first time.

Finally.

I fight against the persistent smile on my face since it's inappropriate for a graveside service. But I can't find it in me to care.

My father may have been an asshole, but he had a ton of friends at the local church who showed up to say goodbye to him.

I'm just ready for the service to be over with so I can get out of the heat and back to the house. Christian stayed with Finley, even though I wish he could've been in both places at once. Nobody said a word about how we spent about two hours in bed together last night before joining them downstairs, either.

After apple pie and ice cream, my mom gave Finley a superhero Lego set with dinosaurs, as if she knew exactly what he would love before she ever met him, so he certainly didn't notice our long absence. Only Elle couldn't keep a straight face at the sight of us with ruffled hair and faces flushed.

Finley wanted to stay at the house with Elle and Preston, but Christian and I left for the nearby hotel for some alone time. I'm surprised nobody called security on us for being too loud. I have no doubt our laughter and other sounds could be heard up and down the hallway all night.

"So, I guess you're all leaving this afternoon," my mother says as soon as the funeral home's limo drops us back off in front of the house. The woman didn't shed a single tear during the funeral. In fact, while there may have been dozens of people who showed up, nobody cried for the loss of my father.

"Yes, we'll take our *sin* and be out of your hair soon," I reply as I start up the porch steps.

"What she said," Preston agrees from where he and Elle are following behind me.

"Well, if sin is what made my beautiful grandson, then… you should do more of it."

That has my feet freezing for a second before I turn to face her. "You don't get to call him that. He's not your grandson. You're not his grandmother. You're a stranger he didn't even know existed until yesterday," I remind her quietly, because my throat is a little sore from the cries of pleasure last night and I don't want Finley to overhear from inside.

My mother doesn't even flinch at my harsh words. "I hate

what your father did to you, Maya. But what choice did I have? You know he never let me work a day in my life, and I don't have a brother or anyone else who would've taken me in!"

I'm not sure what to say to that. I guess, in a way, my mom's options have always been just as limited as my own. "You could've come and lived with me and Preston."

"Could I? I wasn't sure if you two would ever speak to me again!"

"If you had left dad, then we would've welcomed you into our home with open arms," Preston tells her as he steps up beside me. "But you loved him more."

"What he said," I agree rather than admit that I missed her, that I would've loved to have her in my life during the pregnancy and raising Finley.

"Yes, I loved him, even when he was a judgmental jackass," our mother declares. "But I loved my kids more." Sighing heavily, she says, "I hope it's a decision you never have to make, choosing between your children and your husband or wife."

"Let's grab Finley and then hit the road. I want you two to get home before it gets late," Preston says to me rather than continue a pointless argument with her.

"Please…please let me see him again," Mama begs from behind us.

Preston glances at me, then tells her, "You want to see him again, but not us."

"I want to see all five of you, but Finley's the only one who doesn't hate me!" she declares.

"Five?" I ask in confusion.

"Preston, you, Elle, Christian, and my grandson," Mama says simply. "Elle, you're a nice girl, but I know you're angry at me on Preston's behalf. And Christian, well, I can't imagine how much he despises me since I never sent you his letters." She wrings her hands and adds, "Your father told me to throw them out, but I hid them in one of my shoe boxes. I know I shouldn't have read them. I didn't until he died. I just wanted to know if they were worth giving to you after all these years. If I had known the boy wanted to marry you, then I would've sent them on…"

"Wait, what?" Preston jumps in and asks. "Christian wanted to marry you?"

I nod. "He asked me in a letter that I just read *yesterday*." I glare at our mother in silent accusal. "He even bought me a ring, one that's still sitting in his junk drawer."

Elle gasps. "That's why he got so mad when I opened the drawer one time looking for a fork!"

"I'm sorry!" Mama exclaims. "I wish I could go back and make it all right, but I can't. Now that your father is gone, I just hope I can try to fix what he broke."

"That decision is up to Maya," Preston says. "You destroyed her. I wouldn't blame her for never forgiving you."

She looks to me…waiting for my verdict.

"You never called me," I whisper. "You never sent me and Finley a Christmas card like you sent Preston. Daddy wouldn't have known if you had reached out, so why did you pretend like my son and I didn't exist?"

"I…well, I couldn't risk him finding out."

That excuse makes me scoff.

"You don't know how he was after you two turned your

backs on us!" she exclaims. "I-I yelled at him, told him he needed to apologize to you, or I was going to leave him, and he hit me so hard I woke up on the floor." She reaches up and rubs the side of her face absently. "I missed church for two weeks to hide the bruises. After that, I kept my mouth shut. And I thought…I thought maybe you two would be better off without him in your life."

Aw, crap.

Hearing what she went through as a mother myself now, what she was willing to put up with to protect us, I can't help but forgive her a tiny bit. I even do something I never thought I would do again. I throw my arms around her shoulders to hug her.

"I'm glad he's dead," I tell her.

"Me too," Preston agrees as he grabs us both in a bear hug.

"Me three," Mama says, making me smile through the tears. Eventually, we break apart. While we're all three swiping at the dampness on our cheeks, our mother says, "Please consider inviting me to the wedding."

"What wedding?" Preston and I ask at the same time.

"Yours!" she exclaims. "It's only a matter of time for you and Elle, right?" she asks my brother, who shares a look with Elle. "And you and Christian…well, it seems like you're back together."

"I guess we are," I admit. "And I'm not ashamed of anything."

Mama nods, then says the last thing I expected. "You have to admit…Christian is an ironic name for the man who got you pregnant out of wedlock."

"Mama!" I huff, shaking my head at her even though

there's a smile on my lips. "Technically, I was a virgin the day Finley was born."

"*What?*" our mother and Preston both asks with similar brows furrowed.

"You know what? Forget I said anything," I tell them with a dismissive wave of my hand as I hurry inside to see my guys.

38

Christian

I only feel a smidge guilty about watching out the window, witnessing Maya, Preston, and their mom's argument in the front yard while Elle stands by watching uncomfortably. I mean, if they wanted to keep it all private, they should've come inside first.

Mostly, I just wanted to make sure Maya was okay. After all, it's my fault she became estranged from her parents.

It's a relief seeing them all embrace. That's the whole reason I think Maya and Preston came for the funeral—not to say goodbye to their father but to try to reunite with their mother.

Returning to my seat on the floor where Finley and I are helping Spider-Man save the dinosaurs from extinction, I tell him, "Your mom and Uncle Preston are back. Are you ready to head back home?"

"I wish I was going home with you," he says, lip pouting.

"I wish you were too, buddy. But I have to get back to training. I'll still see you on the phone, though."

"It's not the same," he mutters as his action figure knocks over a triceratops.

"No, it's not," I agree.

I had my agent ask the team about releasing me to the Warhawks so I could move to D.C., but it was a lost cause. The Bobcats wouldn't agree to give up their best player to the team that just whooped their asses in the playoffs.

"Maybe we can grab some lunch together before we leave town," I offer, hoping Maya won't object.

After last night, I think I know a few ways to convince her.

And fuck, I wish I could hold her again tonight, along with every other night…

The family makes their way inside, and I give Maya a smile when I see her glistening eyes. She joins us on the floor, pulling Finley into a hug. "You two have fun while we were gone?"

"We did," I agree. "We're just a little sad about having to leave soon."

"Me too," she replies. "If we leave now, we can make it home before midnight."

I cringe at the thought of her and Finley driving so late. "You sure you don't want to go halfway today and the rest of the drive tomorrow?"

"No, we have to get back. I've got my meeting tomorrow at the retirement center. I already feel bad for postponing it yesterday."

"Oh, right. Then I guess we don't have time to get lunch together?"

Maya shakes her head. "No. Sorry."

"Let me know when you get home?" I ask her. "No matter how late?"

"Sure."

"Thanks. I'm thinking about maybe going to see my dad and crashing with him tonight."

"He lives in Tennessee?" she asks, somehow remembering that from the one time I mentioned it.

"Yeah, near Knoxville."

"Be safe. Let me know when you get there?" Maya asks with a smile.

"Absolutely. And maybe you two can come with me next time." Seeing Maya and her mother making amends, I want to do the same for my father once and for all. Oh, and tell him he's a grandfather.

"Definitely. But for now, Finley, let's go say goodbye to… Grandma Lawrence."

"Everything good there?" I ask her.

"As good as it can be," she replies before she leans over and kisses me on the lips, right in front of our son. "Thank you for coming down here."

"Anytime, baby," I tell her, even though having to tell her and Finley goodbye is getting a little harder each time.

39

Christian

"Dad?" The name is heavier than it used to be when I walk into my father's one-level house built into the side of the Blue Ridge Mountains, the place where I grew up. The only changes are probably the solar panels on the roof to make it even more eco-friendly. The entire front of the house is made of windows, letting natural sunlight into the minimalistic interior that's all about function over style. "Are you home?" I call out.

A moment later, he strides out of the library, one of the only rooms in the place without sunlight so as to not risk ruining the precious tomes inside. One of which is still in his hand. He looks…less intimidating now that I'm a few inches taller and wider than his lean frame. His once blond hair is now more white, but his eyes are still shrewd as they narrow at me.

"Christian? This is a surprise."

"Sorry I didn't give you a heads up. I wasn't even sure whether I was actually coming by or not until I got on 23 North."

"It's fine. If you had told me you were coming, I would've cooked up something." As usual, my dad has a way of turning everything into a complaint.

"You don't have to cook for me. I'm not even sure how long I'm staying." I had considered staying tonight, but that depends on how the conversation goes. If he's in too foul of a mood, I'll just drive back to Greensboro.

"Well, come have a seat at least," he says, leading the way to the living room. He gestures for me to sit in one of the red plaid chairs facing the sliding glass doors leading to the back-yard. There's still no television to be found in this part of the house. "So, what brings you by?" my father asks when he sits in the identical chair on the other side of a wooden side table. "You haven't come home to visit in…over a year."

"I know. I'm sorry. I didn't want to bother you."

"But you decided to bother me today?" he asks with a single bushy white eyebrow arched.

"I, um, I guess I just wanted to tell you this in person instead of on the phone."

"Okay?"

Gripping both chair arms as if bracing myself, I tell him the reason I'm here. "I have a son."

"*You* have a son?"

"Yes. His name is Finley, and he just turned five." Releasing my grip on the chair arms, I reach into my jean pocket to remove my phone. I then pull up one of the many photos in my camera roll to show my father.

"Wow," he says. After slipping on the reading glasses hanging around his neck, he takes the phone from my hand for a closer look. "Well, I can certainly see the resemblance."

"Yeah, I guess he looks a lot like me, but I mostly just see his mom in his dark hair and eyes."

Handing the phone back, he glares at me over the top of his glasses. "And who is his mother?"

"Maya. Maya Lawrence. Do you remember my friend Preston from the minor leagues? She's his sister."

"Why did you wait five years to man up and be the kid's father?" he grumbles.

"Because I didn't know about him until a few months ago!"

"Oh. Well, did she need money? Why wait so long to tell you that you have a son, that I have a grandson?"

"It's…complicated. But no, she doesn't want my money. I was angry at her when I first found out, for missing out on so much. But we didn't end on great terms. There was a misunderstanding when she told me I got her pregnant. I didn't think she was going to have him…"

"Well, it sounds like you've got your hands full."

"I do. At least Preston and I are good now. He's just been signed to play for the Bobcats. I've spent the summer up around D.C. to get to know Finley better. We threw him a birthday party at the Warhawks arena. It was great."

"I bet it was, and yet you didn't think to invite me."

"Really, Dad? I can't picture you at a five-year-old's party in a hockey arena, especially one out of state when you hate leaving town."

"He's not just any five-year-old, though, is he? He's my grandson."

"Well, I'm sorry I didn't invite you. We're not exactly

broadcasting to the world that he's my son yet." Again, I find myself apologizing to the prickly man because nothing I ever do is good enough for him. He thinks I'm still the same teenage fuck up who barely graduated high school because I spent all my time on the ice or with girls instead of studying. Nothing could be a bigger embarrassment for Dr. Michael Riley, the renowned philosophy professor.

"Why not tell the world? Are you ashamed of knocking up some poor girl and walking away from her?"

"Ashamed? No. I regret the time Maya and I have been apart. I wish I had known about Finley so that I could have helped her raise him. Maybe then she wouldn't have had to give up on getting her degree and pursuing a career instead of being a single mom. At least Preston was there to help her. Her parents threw her out when she refused to marry me."

"Marrying her is what you should've done as soon as you found out she was pregnant."

Laughing even though his criticism is anything but funny, I stab my fingers through my hair, tugging on it as I tell him, "I would've married her in a heartbeat, but it's not easy to get someone who doesn't want you down the aisle. Maya broke up with me. She ended things, then I got signed with the Bobcats and moved…"

"I'm sure you gave her plenty of reasons for calling it quits. If you had been more mature and less selfish back then, maybe things would've been different with this girl."

"Why do you do that? Why is everything my fault? Did I make a mistake in giving up too easily? Hell yes. But the rest was all her. I asked her to come live with me in Greensboro. I told her I would be there for her if she changed her mind. I even asked her to marry me. Unfortunately, she didn't get those letters until the other day since they were forwarded to her parent's house after she dropped out of college."

"Letters? Son, you know you shouldn't have trusted the postal service with something so important."

"Well, since she wouldn't take my call, return a text or voicemail, and didn't want to see me face-to-face, the only other option I guess I could've tried was a sky writer."

"Don't be a smartass."

Throwing my hands up in the air, I get to my feet and tell my father, "I give up. I don't know what you want from me. I've tried to make you proud for twenty-six years and I'm just over it."

"What are you talking about? Why wouldn't I be proud of you?"

Pacing away with my hands on my hips, I say, "Oh, I don't know, because you bitch about everything I do. I'm sorry hockey is the only thing I've ever been good at, that I'm not a genius like you."

"You could've done better than risking your neck, literally, in hockey…"

Turning back to face him, I remind him, "I'm making millions of dollars a year doing what I love! I nearly won the championship this past season and am one of the best forwards in the goddamn league. I know that it's not the career you would've picked for me, but tough shit. It's what *I* chose. And you can bet your ass that I'm going to let my son choose what he wants to do with his life and not make him ever feel less than me for a second."

"You got into hockey for the wrong reasons, for the fame, the parties, the endless revolving door of women. All I wanted is for you to do more, to realize that there's more to life than a fucking sport that could cripple you."

"Trust me, I'm well aware that there's more to life than hockey, now more than ever, when it feels like I'm being split down the middle, choosing that fucking sport over my family."

"Then walk away."

"I can't! If I walk away, then there goes my big fat payday. How can I support them if I'm unemployed?"

"You haven't been saving most of the millions you earn?"

"Yes, Dad. I put fifty percent into those accounts with high interest rates or whatever, but it's not enough to last forever."

"You just don't want to give up the spotlight."

"I would give it up for them, but she isn't ready to commit to me!" Yes, Maya finally slept with me. I thought it meant we were a couple again, but she didn't magically agree to move to Greensboro after our night together, so who knows?

"It sounds like she doesn't want her and her son to come second to a fucking sport."

"Fine. Maybe you're right and I'm about to screw this all up again. God, I don't even know why I came here. I should've just sent you a text, 'Congrats, you're a grandfather. Not that it matters though, because I don't want you near my son'."

"You don't want me near your son?" he asks, with the heaviness in his eyes that looks like genuine hurt as he gets to his feet.

"I'm not going to let you treat him the way you treated me. I won't let you belittle him or make him feel like he's not good enough to be your grandson."

"He's five-years-old, how could he not be good enough?"

"I wasn't when I was five!"

"Bullshit," he huffs.

"When I was in kindergarten, I remember you telling me that I was reading at an infant's level and needed to catch up to the rest of the kids in my class."

"I don't remember saying that."

"Well, I remember. I remember all the times you made me feel like an idiot, so I will not let you near my son if you're just going to tear down his confidence. He's smart and funny, and yes, he's already great at hockey, but I didn't have anything to do with that. And you know what?I If he told me he wanted to be a circus juggler when he grows up, then I would spend time with him every goddamn day helping him be the best damn juggler he can be."

My chest is rising and falling like I've played an entire period without a break from the growing anger.

"Are you finished?" my father asks.

"For now."

"Do you feel better getting all that off your chest?"

"A little." I shrug and cross my arms over my chest as I turn toward the mountain view.

"I don't know what you want me to say, Christian. Do you want me to beg you to let me see my grandson?" my father asks from behind me.

"No. I just need you to promise not to be a condescending asshole when you see him. That's what I need."

He slaps his palm over my shoulder. "Fatherhood looks good on you, son. I'm proud of you."

When I spin around to face him, his hand falls away. "You're proud of me for knocking up a woman over five years ago?"

"Not particularly, but I'm proud of the man you are now;

taking responsibility, protecting your son, for finally realizing that there's more to life than a popular sport with puck bunnies."

I wait for more insults to come, but I guess he's finished when he asks, "Are you hungry?"

For the life of me, I don't know why the hell I say, "Yes," but I do.

And so, I sit at the wooden table facing the kitchen and watch while my dad makes Teriyaki chicken, feeling like a weight has been lifted from my shoulders.

Despite how much I usually hate his opinions, hearing him tell me that he's proud of the father I've become means the world to me.

It makes me think that I'm actually capable of filling the role.

40

Maya

While I only got about six hours of sleep last night, once we got home and unpacked, Finley got plenty of sleep during the ride.

He was up bright and early, and I had to do the same since my orientation meeting is this morning. Bree, one of the high school girls from down the street, should be here any minute to stay with Finley.

I'm sitting on the steps of the porch on a blanket, wearing my navy pantsuit and freshly pressed, bright yellow top, watching Finley hit around the plastic ball with his hockey stick unenthusiastically.

He looks like I feel.

"Are you okay, buddy?"

He shrugs, giving me a sad little smile. "I miss… everybody."

I nod in understanding. "I miss everybody, too."

The house, the yard, the whole city feels like it's emptier than it's ever been before.

Standing up, I go grab one of the sticks propped up against the side of the house.

"I'll play goalie until Bree gets here," I offer.

"You're not going to be any good at it."

Scoffing, I get in position in front of the goal and tell him, "Try me. We're going to take turns, see who can make the most shots out of five," I tell him, causing his face to light up.

Getting a running start, Finley takes his first shot, sending the ball flying right between my legs.

He jumps up and down in celebration.

And while I love these moments alone with my son, we both know someone, two someones, are missing.

I'm so sick of missing them, especially Christian.

"Mommy, you're wearing the Bobcats colors!"

I glance down, noticing the navy blue and yellow are the Greensboro team's colors for the first time.

And the dress I chose to wear to Georgia was the same dark blue with yellow wedge sandals…It's like I've been subconsciously dressing for Bobcat home games.

I really want to be in North Carolina for every single game.

Is this job, my independence, worth being apart from the man I love?

Is anything worth being apart?

It's possible I could find a similar activities director's job in Greensboro. I think I've always known that and was just being stubborn, too afraid to take the chance. Being so close to Christian without being with him would be so damn hard. But living without him is even harder.

I wanted this move to be my decision alone. God knows getting kicked out of my parent's house wasn't my choice, nor was it my choice where Preston had to move to play hockey.

The only big decision I've made in six years was to have my son. The rest I conceded for him, for us.

But now, well, I'm ready to pack up and move. I'm ready to take that chance with Christian, to try to be a family.

Life is short. I don't want to get a call anytime soon, losing someone I love and have any regrets.

Grabbing the ball, I toss it back to Finley who chases after it. While he's bringing it back toward the goal using his stick, I ask him, "Do you think it would be worth it to leave this house, this yard, and your friends to go live in the same city as Christian and Uncle Preston?"

Finley's head lifts, the ball forgotten. "I wish we could take this house and everything else with us."

"Everything inside would come along," I explain. "Just not the house."

"We could find another house near them, right? So that we could see them every day?"

"We would definitely find a place to live near them, and you would probably see them most days."

"Could we go to all the Bobcats' home games like we did the Warhawks?"

"Absolutely."

"Then I want to go!" He finally takes a shot at the ball, but I stop this one with my stick and shoot it back to him.

"You would have to go to a new school and make new friends," I tell him.

Flashing a confident smile that looks identical to Christian's, he says, "I like making new friends. It's not like it's hard."

"Okay. Well, we would have to move soon too, before school starts." He takes another shot that slips by me on the left.

"Yay!"

"Nice one!" I remark in honest admiration. "Do you think you could help me start packing up all your toys and games?"

"And hockey sticks and pads?"

"Of course, those too," I assure him. "I'm sure they have hockey leagues for your age in North Carolina, too."

"When do we leave?" he asks.

"Ah, I don't know yet. As soon as everything is packed up?"

Tossing his stick down, Finley runs to the porch. "Then let's go, Mommy!"

Laughing, I pick up his stick and carry it with mine to the collection. "First, we're going to need lots of boxes. I bet we could find some today. I just need to make a few phone calls..."

One to the retirement home and one to Bree first and foremost.

I hate turning down the job offer, but I'm doing what's best for me now. Me and Finley.

We're moving to North Carolina.

Oh, the list of things we need to do is going to be so long, starting with finding movers for the furniture, then choosing a school in Greensboro that is still accepting admission, finding a house or an apartment...

But there's no longer any tightness in my chest. No fear or hesitation at the thought of doing those things. My only concern was how Finley would handle giving up our life here.

Since he only seems excited about the change, I'm feeling confident about this decision.

In fact, I'm certain that everything is going to work out just fine for us.

~

Christian

Tonight is an exhibition game at home, the first of the season. The veterans play against the rookies, including the local minor league team. While it's mostly for fans, and a way for the coach to fill any last roster spots, it's also a way to raise money for the local children's hospital. It feels good to help a worthy cause. The entire team has been buzzing with excitement all week, ready to get back on the ice.

While I love playing in front of the home crowd, I'm missing my two favorite fans. Not seeing them every day after getting back from Georgia has been agonizing. At least I'll see them in the morning. Since tomorrow is Finley's first day of school in Bethesda, I'm driving up after the game to be there so I can walk him in with Maya.

Still, I wish they were both here tonight. And that I hadn't missed school shopping.

"You look like shit," Preston remarks as he skates up to me when we take the ice for warmups.

"Thanks, asshole."

Laughing, he says, "I guess that means you haven't seen their sign yet."

"What sign?"

Oh god. The last time there was a notable sign in the stadium, it was Elle's, comparing the size of "my stick" to Preston's and underperforming. Now what embarrassing shit has she written in glitter?

Preston points a finger over to the seats at the glass where Elle is standing. A giant blue and yellow posterboard sign takes up at least three seats and says, *My Dad is our MVP!*

Dad.

"Is that…"

"Maya and Finley," Preston answers. "Who else would it be?" Scowling, he adds, "You better not have any other baby mamas."

"I don't, I swear!" I tell him as I skate over to the glass. The sign lowers to the ground, revealing my two favorite people in the world. Both of them are wearing my jersey, making my heart swell. I press my gloved palm to the glass. "You're here!"

Reading my lips over the crowd noise, Maya replies, "We're here!"

"Hey, Dad!" Finley says as he jumps up to high five me through the glass. "Did you see our sign?"

"I did! I love it!" I shout loud enough for him and the rest of the arena to hear. To Maya, I say, "I'm so glad you're here, but doesn't school start tomorrow morning?"

Maya shakes her head. "Here. Next week." She points a finger to the ground, meaning…here, in town?

"You're moving?"

She nods. "The movers brought everything down to a little house in the suburbs we're renting earlier today," she says. "Surprise!"

"Holy shit," I mutter, wondering if I'm misunderstanding

or dreaming. When Maya frowns at me with her brows raised in chastisement, I know it's real. "I meant, holy crap!"

"Riley, we've got to get warmed up!" Preston calls out to me.

"Coming!" I shout over my shoulder. Then to my family, I say to them, "I love you both so freaking much. Thank you, baby!"

"We love you too," Maya calls back. She blows me a kiss, which Finley copies, and I blow them one back.

EPILOGUE

Christian

Two years later...

"Mom, Dad, can we go out on the ice now?" Finley asks.

I glance over at Maya, raising an eyebrow. "What do you think? Is it time?"

She nods, her smile widening. "Everyone's here, so let's do it!"

"Just...please be careful, baby," I say as I take her left hand, the one where her wedding band and diamond ring shimmer underneath the arena lights. I help her step down onto the ice in her sneakers, since skates would be even more dangerous.

Finley skates laps around us while Maya and I slowly make our way to center ice, where our friends and family are gathered around. Maya and I decided to invite our parents, even though we didn't think they would show. But both are here, waiting expectantly with Preston, Elle, Audrey, Luke, Jason, and the rest of our teammates.

"I'm so excited," Maya whispers, her voice barely audible over the sound of happy chatter.

"Me too," I reply, squeezing her hand.

She smiles up at me, her eyes shining with unshed tears. "You really don't have a preference?"

"I don't," I assure her. "As long as he or she is healthy, right?"

"Right."

We've been through so much the past two years, but we've made it to the other side. And now, we're a real family. One that's about to become a little bigger.

It's sort of funny how Maya and I got pregnant with Finley after one time together, or half of a time, but it took us months trying before we managed to do it the second time.

Not that I minded the practice. Besides, I knew we had the rest of our lives to grow our family.

Maya

The crisp, cool air from the ice bites at my cheeks as Christian leads me to the waiting crowd. There's something almost magical about how empty the arena is other than our little group.

With a kiss to my cheek, Christian takes two hockey sticks

from my brother, then skates off closer to the goal where Finley is waiting.

"Ready to find out?" Elle asks as she holds up the two pucks.

I glance over to see if my guys are ready, and I can't help but smile brighter. Seeing them together like this, bonding in their special way, makes my heart swell. It feels surreal, like the kind of life I used to dream about but never truly believed I'd have. Yet here we are, my family—complete and whole. Or it will be soon.

"Ready?" I call out to them.

"I am!" Christian ruffles Finley's hair with a grin. "You ready, buddy?"

Finley skates backward then forward, excitement radiating off him in waves. "I've been ready to find out for weeks!"

Preston takes the pucks and skates over, placing one in front of both guys, then backs away.

"On the count of three," Christian says as he lines up his shot and Finley does the same. "One...two...three!"

They both hit their pucks at the same time, sending them shooting toward the goal...and leaving a burst of pink powder behind.

"It's a girl!" I exclaim.

"I'm having a sister!" Finley cheers with his stick raised in the air.

"Great job, buddy!" Christian tells him, giving him a hug before skating over to me, wrapping me in his arms, making me feel like the luckiest person in the world. "We're having a baby girl!" His laughter echoes through the arena, filling the space with pure joy.

"Did you ever imagine we would end up here?" Christian asks quietly, his voice soft and full of awe.

I shake my head, smiling. "Not like this. But it was fate."

Not long after Finley and I got settled in our house down here, I found my perfect job at a retirement center a block away from Finley's school. During winter break, Christian and I were married by a magistrate at the courthouse. He moved in with us, and we had our first family Christmas together.

Two years ago, I never could have imagined having this life—never could have believed we'd be here with so much love between us.

But Christian and I built something strong, something real. We've fought for each other, for Finley, for the life we have now with a little one on the way.

It hasn't always been easy, but it's been worth every moment of doubt, every hard decision, every step it took to get right where we belong—together.

The End

AFTERWORD

Thank you so much for reading Pucking Fate!

Sign up for my newsletter to receive updates on new releases
and discounts!
bit.ly/438eTar

Until the next release, pick up a collection of free books from
my author store: https://bit.ly/3ZmCzFt

ABOUT THE AUTHOR

L.A. Hart is the alter ego of New York Times and USA Today bestselling author Lane Hart. Under this pen name she writes new adult and sports romance.

Most of Lane's steamy stories take place in her home state of North Carolina where she lives with her husband, fellow author D.B. West, and their two beautiful children.

Connect with Lane:

Newsletter Sign-up: https://8d74dec5662811e9930706b4694bee2a.eo.page/cg1j3

Instagram: https://www.instagram.com/authorlahart/

Facebook: https://www.facebook.com/SportsRomanceAuthorLAHart/

Bookbub: https://www.bookbub.com/authors/l-a-hart

Goodreads: https://www.goodreads.com/author/show/52249255.L_A_Hart

Website: https://authorlahart.com

Email: authorlahart@outlook.com

www.ingramcontent.com/pod-product-compliance
Lightning Source LLC
Chambersburg PA
CBHW071755110726
47908CB00006B/1810